Other Books

The White Wolf Prophecy – Mating – Book 1
The White Wolf Prophecy – Hall of Records – Book 2
The White Wolf Prophecy – Scroll of Time – Book 3

The Anaerris Code – Part 1 – The Gemma

WOLF CANYON MEMORY

LK Kelley

Wolf's Moon, an Imprint of DragonEye Publishing

Publisher info. Contact
DragonEye Publishing
753A Linden Pl.
Elmira, New York, 14901

For Questions Phone: 1-(607)-333-5256

For information about our books, and for special discounts for single / bulk purchases, please contact DragonEye Publishing Ordering Dept. at:
Website: DragonEyePublishers.com
Email: Orders@DragonEyePublishers.com

To request one of our authors for speaking engagements or book signings, please contact DragonEye Publishing Publicity Dept. at:
Directors@DragonEyePublishers.com

Published by
Wolf's Moon, an Imprint of DragonEye Publishing

ISBN 13: 978-1-61500-201-6   (Mass Market Paperback)
ISBN 13: 978-1-61500-202-3   (EBook)

Library of Congress Control Number: 2018931425

DragonEye Publishing First Edition: January 29, 2018
First Printing: January 29, 2018

10 9 8 7 6 5 4 3 2 1

Manufactured in the United States of America

Reviews

I love this book! The action is thrilling and nonstop from the first page to the last page, making it difficult to put down. It's filled with love, romance, friendships, and bravery. I learned so much about wolves, and found their world fascinating. The adventures of Kassie and Jakob are enthralling, and nobody should miss out on the excitement their story brings.

Georgia Trosper

~~~

This is a most extraordinary book written by LK Kelley! I have read her other books and I have to say that this one is her best one yet! It is about the intermingling of humans, wolfs, werewolves, and the supernatural - expanding all areas of folklore about them and bringing to life the characters in a most modern and ancient way. Jakob is the Alpha wolf male of his clan in Colorado who meets his human soul mate Kassie and growing their family, ultimately uniting and keeping it strong. A phenomenal must read that is so good it will have you hooked all the way through it. The story culminates to a plot that will have you curiously reading at light speed to get to the answer! It is incorporated with great detail, comedy, love, feelings, and towards the end it was emotional, tearing one up with joy, including beautifully written sensualism in a most powerful way!

Author Anita Meyer
~~~

Dedication

I want to thank God, for my ideas and places, where these ideas come to fruition.

I also want to thank my husband, Wesley, whose very patience is the inspiration for my heroes. I also want to thank my awesome daughter, Laura, and her friends, who inspire the dialogue in my books.

I also want to thank my great friends for their help: Anita Meyer, Georgia Trosper, KJ Simmill, and so many others for all their help!

I love you all!

LK Kelley

WOLF CANYON MEMORY

~ Prologue ~
Is dying supposed to hurt this much?

Geez! Her head was splitting open, and to boot, she felt like she was going to puke! A metallic sound caught her ears, and she was being drug out of something? The metal sound was a door opening. A truck? Car? Next thing she knew, her bottom had hit the ground, and her head struck something relatively sharp. At least, from her point of view, it was sharp.

"Ow!"

Someone struck her face very hard, making her head hurt even worse. A sticky substance was starting to run down her face from the vicinity of her nose. Blood. It had to be. The girl passed out, then awoke, hearing voices. Were they having an argument?

Barely gurgling, she mumbled, "Who...," before she was struck once more.

"Shut the fuck up, bitch!" a female voice said. Then, "What the hell are we going to do with her?"

Well, dang! If they didn't want her to speak, a simple, "shut up," would suffice!

A male voice answered.

"Throw her off the bluff?"

There was no answer, and that made her think that she had agreed with a silent nod. Everything about her hurt so badly, all she wanted was to pass out just to escape the pain! But, someone dragged her across the ground over sharp rocks, and with each painful move, rocks scraped her back. Her brain sent a *"struggle and get away as fast as possible"* signal, but she, quite literally, could not move. She felt as if her body had beaten to a pulp!

1

"Well? Pick her up! I can't very well be expected to drag her down the bluff's trail by myself!" the woman said.

Laughter followed from the man.

"You have to be kidding! With your strength?

Hell! You can carry her better than I can, so shut up, and just do it!" he ordered.

She heard a huffing sound, and the next thing she knew, she was hanging over someone's shoulder. A sharp object dug under her left arm.

"*Well, that's going to leave a mark!*" she almost giggled aloud at the inappropriate hysterics, bubbling just underneath her pain-wracked body.

Now, with her head hanging over someone's shoulder, she was bouncing up and down with every step the woman made! Each movement just sharpened her body with agony, and even though she tried to shriek, no sound exited her mouth. Who were these two? She was having a hard time concentrating.

After what seemed a lifetime, that someone pulled her from the shoulder, and slammed her onto something that was either concrete or stone. Her head hit something on the way down, and it just made her crave the darkness of death. But, for whatever reason, she wasn't going to die – at least not just yet. Something inside her kept her conscience. She didn't want to be awake! She wanted to die now, because she already knew that she was dying anyway. Why couldn't she just give up the ghost?

"OK. No one's around. Just do it, and let's get the hell out of here, before someone sees us!" the man growled.

The girl felt a plop, as she was placed upright, leaning against something obviously metal that was scorching hot! Her body jerked forward, only to be thrust back once more.

"What the hell are you waiting on, bitch?" That was a masculine voice.

"Oh, hold your fucking horses," the woman demanded. "Let's kill her, and then I'll fuck your brains out!"

"Whatever! Just do it!" he growled, once more.

While she puzzled over the fact that she knew that voice, her body was jerked toward someone, and whoever it was, whispered into her ear.

"You are dead, you cunt! I've wanted to do this for a long time! I want nothing more than to see your broken and bloody body in front of me. But, since I can't do that without revealing, who we are, and what we are, well…have a good trip - to HELL!"

She felt another very, very sharp stab on her left side as she was shoved backward, over the top railing, and began the long plunge to her death. Her body wouldn't respond, so she didn't wave her arms to grab something, nor did she kick her legs. She sure wasn't wind milling it all the way down, and probably resembled more of a human "dummy" as her body was slammed against rock after rock on her way down the mountain. Seconds later, she blacked out, and that was probably a good thing, since her body stopped barreling downward, as with one final hit on the rocks below, her body was bashed several more times, against something very sharp. And, then, she landed, head first, into a roaring, icy cold river. Immediately, rapids carted her quickly down the river, drowning her head in and out where she caught a breath here and there as her head poked above the water. She couldn't struggle too much, but the ice cold of the water had revived her a bit, and covered her body like a wonderful, cold cloak, numbing her injuries… into the cold of darkness and death…until she awoke!

Struggling to hold onto consciousness, she just had to ask the question that everyone does in situations like this.

"Am I dead?" she questioned the cosmos.

As usually, of course, there was no answer, but at least she tried. But, she decided to answer her own question aloud.

Well, actually, she had two questions…

"One, what happened; two, well, it's obvious that I am not dead – right? At least, not, yet!"

...but *damn*...she sure as hell wished that she were...

WOLF CANYON MEMORY

~ 1 ~

**I wish I were dead! I wish I were dead!
So, why am I not dead?**

Dizzy, and with a terrible headache that would not go away, the girl stumbled across loose, river rocks, wondering one, where she was, and two, WHO she was. In addition, why was her body so hot and her head so cold? It was at this point that she realized that she really was laying half in and half out of a river. She hadn't wanted to wake up – ever, because the pain all over her body was excruciating! But, something in her pushed her to stand anyway. Wobbling a bit, she looked around her, but there was no one to be seen, and she certainly didn't recognize her surroundings. Wherever she was, it was deserted. Not one person was anywhere around her!

Her eyes blurred a bit, but she blinked several times, trying to get some moisture in them so she could see. Close to her left was that rushing river where she awoke. Huge rock faces enclosed the river all around, reaching into the sky above her, and where she stood, rocks were everywhere with a little brush scattered here and there. As she grabbed her head, she realized that just about every part of her body had cuts, scrapes, and blood was everywhere on her clothing and body. She reached to the crown of her head to try to stop it from hurting, and when she brought her hands away, she notice that they were coated with a sticky substance. Bringing her hand away, she saw that it was blood. A lot of blood. Even though it was obviously crusting somewhat, a few of the cuts were still bleeding. One cut in particular was really bothering her. She lifted what used to be a white tank top, that now, resembled nothing but a destroyed piece

"Well, what do you know? It actually works!" she muttered in surprise. She scooped another handful of mud, and repeated the process, rinsing, again. Now, her hair really was clean! She reached back up to feel the place where blood had been, and brought her hand away. No blood for the moment! That was good, right? The icy water had sealed the cut – temporarily, at least.

Next, she used mud to clean her arms and legs of the dried blood. She looked down at herself, noticing that her clothes were also covered with blood, so she did the best she could to rinse them as well. The white tank wasn't so much white any more, because of the blood and red clay stains, and because, her shorts were black, trimmed in teal blue, which didn't show stains or dirt. She looked as if she had come directly from a gym, except for her flip-flops, which she had placed on a large rock. Picking them up, the girl rinsed them well, still wondering not just why she was here, but where she was. Slipping on her shoes, she began walking, only to stumble on the rocks, and fall, succeeding in causing more cuts to her hands and knees!

"Damnit!" she complained, and walked to the water, rinsing the cuts off quickly.

Finally, she managed to walk, without stumbling, and followed the river's direction. The sun dried her clothing quickly, but a slight dampness still remained, as sweat poured down her. Looking into the sky, she could see that the sun was about to disappear from the rim above her. That meant that dusk was quickly descending, and the heat of the day would also dissipate. Somewhere, she remembered that it was a peculiarity in a canyon. Night came fast once the sun disappeared, behind the horizon at the top of a canyon, and the temperature would drop like a rock. While grateful on one hand by not having the blazing sun bearing down on her, on the other hand, she knew she wouldn't survive the night. Her shorts and sleeveless top would not be enough to keep the cold out, and her head was hurting, once again. Raking her hands through her hair, she brought them down to see they were covered in blood. She was very thirsty, despite the drinks she had taken, but hungry? Even just the thought of food made her sick. But, another drink might help her a little. Worse, now, she was extremely dizzy. In her mind, she registered the simple fact that she was dying, yet she still tried to keep going. She knew that with a head injury, she shouldn't sleep. But, it was getting so hard to not just lie down, and let her eyes close – if for only a minute's rest!

She continued to walk, pushing against the pain and the dizziness. Well, perhaps the better description was she staggered down the side of the river. Finally, the canyon widened a bit, and she saw some greenery near the base of the canyon wall. First, she drank some water, and then headed for the patch of green. If she was going to die, then, by golly, she would make sure that she did so, well, as close as possible to comfort. Darkness began to fall fast, and just before night began to descend, she finally reached that green patch – and…she, finally, collapsed onto her hands and knees. She turned around, and sat. The girl wasn't stupid. She would most probably be dead by morning. She looked around the dusky light, and even though she could feel the coolness of the day beginning, she realized that she was still burning up and sweating heavily. She clawed at her top. She wanted to remove it, because her body was so damn hot! But, her hands were far too weak to do anything, and she lay back on the grass. The sweating and fever combined with the cold, and caused her to shiver violently. With what little reasoning she had left, it most likely was from infection and exposure, along with slight sunburn as well, but that was the least of her problems. A decision had to be made. Either she would keep going to nowhere, or she would just let death take her.

"Well, that wasn't a hard decision," she said into the darkness.

Slowly, she stretched her limbs, straightening them out, and her arms she placed on her chest. She would not to fight it. If she didn't fight, death would come faster, and she had heard, it would be much easier. If an animal killed her, she couldn't complain, either. Her pain was too bad for her to care. Life had become too hard for her. Death would be a sweet release.

Distant howls from animals could be heard along with the night's insects as they replaced their singing with the singing of the birds of the day. It was with regret that she was going to die without knowing who she was. No matter how she tried, thinking was getting far too difficult, so instead, she listened to the noises of the night, and yet, her mind still wandered. It should be really easy. All she had to do was to close her eyes, and let death take her. Her head was killing her, and even though the blood had stopped, her head felt full. And, except for the sharp, painful cut in her left side that just didn't seem to go away, her legs and arms hurt too badly to move. As long as she didn't move them, the pain didn't seem as bad.

Her eyes had not been focusing well. Probably because of her head aching from that cut, but they settled down a bit, now that her head was still. Her eyes rose to the Great Creator's sky as it darkened, and stars appeared, piercing the black velvet with their brilliant light! As it continued to darken, she was amazed how clear they were – and so many of them! Away from the lights of the cities and towns, they were so much brighter, even if she didn't understand that particular reasoning. The cold was finally making its way through her body, but she didn't care. It couldn't be much longer, before she would die, and looking on the stars above was a wonderful way to go. Perhaps she would be joining them very soon? That seemed like an awesome place for her soul to be. She gave a gentle sigh. If only she could pass from this life, remembering who she was, and what had happened to her, but, thinking was much too hard for her, now. She believed that it would be best to let her mind go numb and her eyes began to droop. Death would be a welcome friend. Her eyes closed, and she started to drift, her pain becoming less and less. The girl's breathing began to slow, her heart ceased its hard beating, and she knew her soul was ready to depart from this world, when suddenly, her human ears heard a growl. A very, *loud* growl. Her soul plopped back into her body, and her eyes opened. Above her body, a wolf the size of a truck with coal black fur and ice blue eyes stood above her. Her voice, garbled and weak, but understandable, she spoke to the wolf, and strangely enough, she wasn't scared. Maybe she should be, but she wasn't.

"Hi, wolfy! Gee, are you here to help me into the next world? It's OK. You can eat me." She saw him cock his head as if he thought she had horns growing out of her butt! She giggled. "I would appreciate it, though, if you could wait until I'm unconscious, so I won't feel it? But, after all, that's your decision, isn't it? I'm just a human, and can't fight back."

A low growl came from the throat of the wolf as its ears twitched. It cocked its head the other way, as if it could understand her. And, for whatever reason, she could have sworn its eyes registered shock at her words.

"I can see you are definitely a boy wolf."

She could easily see how large he was by looking underneath him. Whoa! It was huge! Why it was extended, she didn't know. Maybe he had just had an encounter with his female. Wolves mated for life. That's something she did know. So, where was its mate?

She followed her eyes, looking at his hindquarters, and then turned back to her, giving her what seemed, for all the world, just like a deliberate smirk. She blinked. Surely, he didn't understand her? That would be too weird! She must be delirious.

"I hope you found your mate, wolfy. It's obvious you were having a good time!" she giggled, then started to cough…hard.

The wolf came closer to her, and leaned down, sniffing her. His nose tickled her face, and she giggled again, only to be interrupted by another coughing spasm.

"You're tickling me!" she laughed. Tentatively, she reached out her hand and petted his head. Strangely, the wolf allowed it. "You are so soft, Wolfy! Such soft fur! It's OK. I'm going to go to sleep, now. I won't wake back up. You can have my body to eat. I won't have any use for it again. I'm so…t-tired…so…sl-sleepy…I welcome death…" Her voice trailed away, and her eyes began to close for the final time.

The wolf nudged her to see if she moved. She groaned silently at the movement. He nudged her again. This time harder. Her eyes flew open, and she was not one bit happy!

"Stop it! I want to die! Please!" she begged, "just let me die!"

Her eyes started to close, again, when suddenly, she was picked up in strong, secure arms. She had to be dreaming. But, those arms were warm, and she buried her head into a strong bare chest. She sighed in happiness. It was as if she were home, and gratefully, let the darkness take her.

The girl woke up, because she felt herself being bounced gently. And, she felt speed. Great speed. It was enough to make her sick to her stomach, anyway. Opening her eyes, she looked upward, and saw she was in the arms of a man. A very big, hunk of a man! His chest was broad, but she could barely make out his face.

"Just my freakin' luck! I just had to die, now, with this gorgeous, sexy man holding me!"

The moonless night of stars refused to show it. His hair was long to his shoulders, and then, she felt herself bounce a bit harder, and her head and her body were overwhelmed with pain. She screamed, and knew nothing more.

Sounds were coming through her ears. Was that talking? Yes. Someone was talking. She felt something wiping on her body, and screamed when whatever it was touched her wounds. It burned! Badly. OH, GOD! Why wouldn't they just leave her alone, and let her die!

"STOP! OH, PLEASE, STOP! LET ME DIE!" she heard, only realizing it was her own voice doing the screaming.

She tried to push the hand that was hurting her away, but it gently, but firmly, pushed back. She didn't have the strength to do it again. Her head was lifted, and she was forced to drink something horrible tasting. It was bitter, and caused her to want to throw it up, but after a minute. And, of course, she passed out once more.

She drifted into a deep sleep to dream of a black wolf standing by her, nudging her, and not leaving her alone. It refused to eat her, and kept trying to keep her awake. She finally screamed at it that she wanted to die, but it wouldn't let her.

Finally, she slowly woke up, feeling more focused, hearing voices. It took all her concentration just to keep her eyes closed, and to be quiet, so she could hear what was going on around her. It wouldn't do for her to let them know that she was awake, until she knew what was happening. Something she had learned as a teenager. Keeping quiet, you learned a lot more than demanding answers. Wait! That was a memory, right? No. It wasn't a memory. It was more like deductive reasoning.

"If you hadn't found her, Jakob, she would be dead by now. As it is, she is hovering between this life and the next." The man turned to address another. "And, in answer to your question, Venus, she is bad. Very, very bad. I still don't know if I can save her. I may be a doctor, but humans aren't in my practice, you know."

Huh? Did he say humans? What did he mean, humans? Perhaps he might be a vet. She kept quiet, and continued to listen. She needed to know more about her condition.

"Well, it looks as if she had a hard fall from a very great height. How in the hell she lived through it, though, is completely beyond my comprehension."

"Fever is high?"

"Yes. She definitely has infection due to her injuries and exposure to the elements."

"How long was she out there do you think?" asked the girl. Venus. Wasn't that her name? How pretty!

"If I had to guess? Probably twenty-four to forty-eight hours," Tyrone answered. "From her injuries, it looks as if she may have fallen from a great height. But, to have no broken bones? That is something that I cannot fathom. Human's normal temperature is about 98.6 degrees. Hers is upwards to almost 105 degrees. A human brain cannot survive long with so high a temp."

She felt a hand stroke her brow gently. It was so soothing. Why didn't they just let her die if she had fever that high? She was obviously causing them problems.

"She needs a human hospital, Venus."

"Will she make it?" the woman asked. "I mean, wouldn't it just be a lot easier and kinder to let her die? If she makes it, we are the ones who are in danger! She cannot be here! She is too much of a risk. Let her die!"

"Let me die! What the hell? Did I really hear here say that?"

Those around her were stunned into silence. She could just imagine everyone's mouth drop, because she had a hard time not dropping her own in shock at this Venus's words! Then, a deep, bass voice answered.

"That's enough. Tyrone, you will do the best you can for her. We cannot allow her to go to a hospital. She's already seen far too much, whether or not she is conscious!" There was a pause. "Venus, why don't you go home to Devon. You aren't helping anyone."

"No, Jakob? I won't! She's HUMAN for God's sake! She can't stay here, and you know it! She's a danger to our kind! She has to die! I'll do it if you can't!"

The girl frowned to herself. Ignoring the fact that a woman was admitting she wanted to kill her, what the hell did that mean? Their kind? What was she saying? She felt the gentle touch of those fingers again, and relaxed.

"Venus, do I have to order you to leave?" she heard Jakob demand.

Funny. She didn't have a problem remembering the name of the man who belonged to that deep voice! Jakob. She didn't hear anything except a slight close of a door. Venus must have left. Good. She was annoying the hell out of her!

"Tyrone?"

"Jakob, if I can't get her temperature down, her brain will shut down, and she will die. The only way to do this is with ice. And, you know it's something we just don't use out here in the desert heat!"

The words were becoming muffled, and she realized she was dizzy, once again, and very tired. It was getting too hard to listen. Probably the fever, so she let herself slip over the edge of darkness.

~ 2 ~

Death is kind of Peaceful, unless someone is nudging you!

Brrrrrr! What the hell? She was really cold! She knew she had goose bumps all over her body, but the odd thing was that even though she was cold, she also felt warmth! Realizing that she felt as if she were almost floating, she also knew that she didn't feel as hot as she had. Was her temp down?

A wonderfully relaxing sound came to her ears. Water. Water falling gently? Wonder where she was? Was this heaven? Didn't matter. It sounded so good! She realized that the cold was water swirling around her body, cooling it down. She sighed in relief. Her wounds were being soothed, too. She felt the icy water being drizzled over her head wound. It all felt so wonderful! Because she was so calm, a memory hit her. She loved to swim! Being in the water was the next best place to be, because she was able to swim like a fish! Well, at least that's what her friend had always told her. Kassie had always been open to swimming. Wait! Her friends called her Kassie! Kasseiopia! That was her name! Sighing, she was thrilled to remember her name, even if it was only part of it, but try as she might, nothing else came to her. She knew pushing it would not make her memory come faster. Lowering her temperature with icy water must have caused her brain to work a lot better. Probably she had been on the verge of delusion. Well, duh! Of course! The black wolf! There wasn't one! How silly could she be?

Something very hard pushed against the outside of her right thigh. It wasn't really painful, but it was making her stir with something she didn't understand right now. A hand swept a gentle path across her cheek.

"Wake up, my love. Please, wake. Can you hear my voice?"

That wonderful voice!

"Jakob!" she sighed.

That beautiful voice belonged to Jakob! His name broke through her confused mind.

"Hmmmm?" she managed to get out, still without opening her eyes.

"Yes. It's Jakob, your mate. Wake up!" he ordered.

Lifting her hand weakly, she tried to push his hand away. She didn't want to wake up!

"Mmmmnnoo." was all she could say.

"You *will* wake up, now! Do you understand me?"

This time she felt a pull to do exactly what he said, and she sure didn't like it! No one ordered her to do a damn thing! But, still, the compulsion she felt caused her eyes to open anyway. Blinking a couple of times, her eyes widened as she beheld what had to be an angel!! OMG! The man's eyes were gorgeously icy blue – the color of Elsa's blue ice gown in Frozen. His hair was coal black, and his face looked as if it belonged to an archangel! It was strong with a slightly off-center nose that must have been broken, once upon a time, and he was the most handsome man she had ever seen in her life. She could easily see his broad, dark, bare chest that had been tanned by the sun. His arms were larger than her waist, and muscles rippled throughout as he moved them. His lips were slightly thin, but kissable, and….just why would an angel be snickering at her?

He was looking at her with his left eyebrow up, and a slight smirk.

"Feel a bit better?" that gorgeous, deep voice asked her.

"Uh…well…cooler, I guess." She was a bit hesitant at answering him. Then, "Am I dead?"

He laughed out loud.

"No. I think I can safely say that you are not quite dead…yet!" He grinned down at her.

"Oh."

Why was she was kind of disappointed? That would mean this man was not an angel.

"What? You want to be dead??" he asked her in horror.

"No. No, of course not. Well, not really, I guess. It's just…I was in such pain, I wanted to die so badly." She looked up at him. "You going to tell me who you are?"

"I'm Jakob Derrick Allan Lane."

The girl frowned. "Why do you have four names? No one has four names!" she complained.

"Well, I do. It's a…well, royal thing, I guess you could say."

Seeing her eyebrows raise, and the question that was about to come from her lips, he rushed to explain.

"My Mom has always been fascinated by royals, especially their long line of names. She thought she would be funny, and do the same, but Dad stopped at four, and wouldn't let her continue," he grinned at her.

"Uh huh. Right," she answered in a skeptical tone.

"No. Really. That's how my names came to be, but I only use two of them…Jakob Lane."

"Well, I guess I'll let that go for the moment," she said.

"So, my dear. What is your name?" the dark angel asked her.

"My name? Oh, well, I-I can't really remember all of it. But, I did finally remember my first name. It is

Kasseiopia. My friends call me Kassie. I can't remember anything else, though," she told him, sounding disappointed.

"Hmmmm. Sounds like you might be suffering with temporary amnesia."

"Temporary? Is that what it is? Whatever. It's really frustrating, now that I can think again."

He nodded. Damn! She started to wiggle, trying to find a more comfortable position. That hardness was jabbing her right thigh! When she couldn't find one, she tried to get him to let her go. Instead, he only tightened his arms around her.

She was lying in his arms, feeling the water swirling around her.

"Ouch! What the hell am I lying on, because it's just hard? It's hard!"

Hearing a muted sound, her face darted to his, seeing the left side of her mouth lift. Did he just snicker at her? The smirk on his face just solidified her belief. She turned her head a little sideways as if it was completely normal.

"What?" she asked, looking around. She wondered where she was…well…wherever it was, she was.

"Where am I? Just how the hell did I get here?" she asked. She didn't want him to know that she had been awake for a short time.

"Well, how you got here is kind of hard to explain, really. But, where you are is an area within Wolf Canyon."

"Wolf Canyon? Where is that? Is that where I am?" She shook her head. "Never heard of it."

"Sort of. As I said. Hard to explain."

"Sort of? How does one just 'sort of' get to the Wolf Canyon?"

He shook his head. .

"OK. So, *where* am I right now?" she demanded. Why was he hesitating?

"It's a pool that is close to my, uh, home."

Evasive enough?

"Can I sit up a bit? That hard thing is bugging me, and it has to be uncomfortable for you."

"Actually, I find it quite nice. You are very light, Kassie."

His look at her suddenly made her blush, and she had no idea why.

"Please? I'm feeling a bit cramped," she begged. "Am I hearing a waterfall?"

He looked at her for a moment.

"Yes, you are. It's right over there," he told her, pointing behind her. She turned to look at it.

"Oh! It's so beautiful!"

She turned her head in all directions, and realized that they were in a cave-like structure, but it had a couple of large, arched openings on two sides – one behind him, and one to her right. And, it's amazing features were its pool and waterfall. Jakob's next words brought her back to him.

"Kassie, there is only one reason we are here right now. Your fever shot up far above 105 degrees. You were dying. This is the only place I could think of to bring it down. Tyrone, our doctor, told me ice was the only thing that would work. However, we usually don't have that here. We depend on refrigeration. However, this pool is naturally cold, and makes a great substitute for ice." He looked into her eyes. "We've been in here for a couple of hours, now."

"Oh, I'm so sorry! You must be freezing!" she exclaimed.

"Not at all. I happen to love it here. It's my own private space."

She shifted to sit straight, and felt air hit her breasts. She gasped, and looked down. She was naked? Her eyes darted to him, and he was looking at her in amusement, even while his eyes dropped down to her chest. Her nipples were hard and pointed from the coolness of the pool, and she ducked right back down under the water in horrible embarrassment.

"Nothing to be embarrassed about, Kassie. It's not like I haven't seen a woman's breasts before, you know," he laughed at her.

"Are you serious?" she asked. "Oh, shit! Am I naked?"

"Of course, you are," her shock showed on her face. "What? Did you think I'd drop you in here with clothing on? Your body was burning up, Kassie. Tyrone said you had to be immersed without your clothing."

"And, you just HAD to get in with me? Why didn't you just put me in here, and leave? And, while we are at it, just what kind of place has no ice?"

"We don't have ice, because we have refrigeration, and when we do need it, like tonight, and, no, I couldn't have left you. You would have drowned if I had not held your head above the water."

"What kind of a place doesn't have ice," Kassie muttered. Then, suddenly, she had another wild, if embarrassing, thought.

"And, you? You're not, uh, naked are you?"

"Are you a prude, Kassie? Does nudity bother you that much?"

"You're telling me you are naked, and I'm on your l-lap?" she squeaked.

"Yes," he said simply.

OMG! Now, what was she going to do? She remembered her name, she was in a pool, naked with the most gorgeous man she had ever met, and he was naked, too? And, he called her a prude?

"Of course I'm not a prude, but for goodness sakes! It's a bit unconventional for a man and woman, who don't know each other, to be nude, and one sitting on the other one! Don't you think?" she said, making an effort to cover herself.

"Not at all. In fact, don't be embarrassed. Your body is completely beautiful, you know."

Her face grew redder than a tomato. She pushed against his chest a bit, and he let her go, but kept his eye on her. She looked down. The pool they were in was totally clear. You could see everything. Her eyes came up in shock as she looked at Jakob. He was sitting on a rock, his chest, and abs above the water. His chest was broad and she could see his abs were hard as the rock on which he was sitting! His arms were built like a body builder, but stronger. And, then she couldn't help herself. She looked down under the water. His legs were bigger than her entire body, and then, she saw what had been stabbing her thigh! His manhood was long and hard! He made no attempt to cover himself, but he seemed to be enjoying the fact that she saw him. Her eyes came up to his. Oh, no! No, no, no! She had seen naked men before, but this man? Oh, GOD! He was beautiful! There wasn't a woman on Earth who wouldn't have let him take her to his bed – or hers, without a second thought!

His eyes and mouth were grinning at her.

"Seen enough? Or, do you need a bit more time? I mean, if you need more time to look, I am very happy to accommodate," he laughed.

"Oh, uh, I-I, uh. Oh, hell!" Kassie grouched.

Jakob laughed outright.

"I think, if you are ready, we can start back, but I will carry you. You were in very bad shape, and you are too weak to walk far."

He proceeded to stand up, and Kassie watched the water slough down his body. His hardness was very apparent – probably caused by the cold, because the cold made her nipples hard. Yeah. Right. Keep thinking that, Kassie! As he turned his back to her, she saw his naked profile. He was hard, and she tried desperately not to notice how it stood out and up from his groin. Ok. So. She *was* a red-blooded female, and what female could resist starting at a naked man, especially one as sexy as the one standing before her! Wetness pooled between her thighs in that moment. He was totally unashamed of his body. His head turned back, and Jakob grinned at her in a challenge to stand.

Kassie crossed her arms in a valiant, but defiant, attempt at modesty. Well, she would not stand until he turned his back! But, exhaustion was the thing that betrayed her. If she had been well, she probably would not have backed down. And, then again, Jakob had already seen and held her naked body next to his to save her life. She sighed, because she was still weak, and really had no fight left in her. So, she stood slowly. Surprise grabbed her when she realized that the rock at the bottom of the pool had been smoothed, and it felt soft under her feet. Kassie began to tilt sideways, and began to fall. She wasn't ready to stand by herself. Before, she could fall, Jakob caught her.

"I knew you were too weak. I will be carrying you back," he admonished softly.

Picking her up, Jakob carried her over to the bank, and sat her down. Quickly, he pulled on his jeans, then turned back to Kassie. He had seen her nude body several times, since he had brought her back from the river. It had stirred him to harden while in his wolf form the moment he found her almost dead. She even noticed it, causing his wolf to be happy that she noticed. Then, Kassie had thought he'd had a fling with a female wolf! As if, he would have another female, after having laid eyes on her. When he had stared into her dull and lifeless green eyes, even though she was bloody and filthy, he had been thrown into the flames of a desire neither he nor his wolf had ever felt. Now, that desire stirred him, again, as he boldly looked at her. Kassie was beautiful, when she blushed, and he unabashedly ran his eyes up and down her slender form, watching the pink stain her fair skin. Her long, blonde hair framed her beautiful round face, and was long enough that it brushed against her luscious, and buxom breasts tipped with rose. Jakob made no apologies as he scanned down Kassie's body to the blonde curls hiding her sex. She was, by far, the most beautiful woman he had ever seen in his life. He wouldn't tell her why he was hard, because she was already embarrassed, but Jakob had no problem letting her see it. In fact, it caused him great pleasure to show her his manhood. Their kind had no problem with nudity in front of their mate. Shock registered through him as he realized what word he had just used! Kassie was his mate! He still wanted to scream to think that he had found her only to almost lose her! But, he was still confused, because no werewolf that he had ever known, in his eight hundred years of life, had chosen a human mate. So why did Jakob's wolf choose Kassie? He just didn't have an answer.

He turned, and picked up the pair of jeans that he had left lying on the rock, pulled them on, and then walked over to her with her clothing. He handed them to her. She looked at the gray, over-sized sweats, looked up at him with a smirk, then tried to dress, but Kassie just didn't have the strength.

Sighing, Jakob helped Kassie dress, remembering how his sister had canvassed the clan to find some warm clothing for her. Being in the desert, there just weren't a lot of women who actually had warm clothes in the clan. Those were all back in Denver, Colorado. All the women were very kind when they heard about the plight of the young, human girl. Unlike a couple of other women in the clan, Venus to name one of them, none of them had any prejudice against her, and were eager to help as much as they could. After a while, the only warm clothing that they could find that might fit her was an older pair of clean sweats, but they couldn't find a bra at all that would fit Kassie. Most were not as well endowed as the young girl their Alpha had brought into their midst. Women in their clan didn't even wear them, anyway, and many believed that human females always needed to wear them. But, for werewolves, it was not necessary, and the men preferred their mates not to wear one so they could get to their mate's breasts easier. All of the women had bras, though, because they worked in the human world when they weren't on the Retreat. Jakob was OK with this particular need of the males, especially, now, he had found his own mate. And Jakob would never let his mate wear one, again.

He sat Kassie on his lap, picked up her feet, and slid a pair of plain, white cotton panties onto her legs, helping her hold on to him, as he lifted her hips. Then, he helped her slide the sweat pants on by using the same motions. Next, he helped her pull the sweat top over her head, pulling gently to cover her modesty. She refused to meet his eyes as he dressed her, but he noticed a furious blush on her cheeks. That only made him grin. Night would be falling very soon, and

Kassie would know really fast what it was like to be really cold. He doubted that she remembered from the previous night. Even though dressed, he had scented her arousal for him as she had stepped from the water, and it smelled wonderful! He knew she was his. She would know it soon enough that she was, but he wondered how long they could keep the truth of what they were from her. Well, not too long, of course. Being a human mate to an Alpha werewolf would definitely have its ups and downs, and Kassie would need to be a very strong human to become the Alpha female to his clan – human or not did not matter. It was what it was.

The entire time he was dressing her, she had averted her eyes. She knew Jakob had looked at her, while she in and out of consciousness, more than once, and he made no bones about his frank assessment. But, since she was awake, it was so different. Almost dead, it hadn't really mattered. She was still a bit embarrassed that she was still wet between her thighs just from looking at this hunk of a man, but her exhaustion kept her from making any more, despite the vision of his most perfect body. Setting Kassie on her feet, she was barely standing and really tired and sleepy. Her eyes closed, Jakob caught her when she fell.

Normally, as before, Jakob would have run with her, but her body was finally cool, her fever gone, and he wanted to make sure that he was careful. Letting her get chilled was not an option. Besides, he wasn't overly anxious to get back soon. He relished his mate in his arms, and held her to his chest with a tenderness he never knew he had. In seconds, Kassie had fallen asleep in his arms.

It took him a bit of time to walk back to the retreat, but all too soon, they reached the clinic, where Jakob placed her in the hospital bed, followed by Tyrone. Kassie didn't move a muscle. She had checked out of the time zone.

Tyrone nodded, but said nothing. Gently covering her with a blanket, he turned to Jakob, whose glowing eyes glared at him with concern, and motioned to his office. Jakob sat down while Tyrone sat down opposite his desk, tenting his fingers in thought.

"Well, it worked. She's going to be OK. You got her there just barely in time. When her fever suddenly shot to 108, I knew there was little to no time left. You kept her in the cool for at least three hours?"

"Actually, it was more like four. She didn't wake until the fourth hour. And, she remembered her first name. Kasseiopia, but she says her 'friends' call her Kassie."

Tyrone nodded, and smiled.

"That's good! It means her memory isn't completely affected. How else did she appear?"

Jakob smiled.

"Well, she was a bit shocked at the fact we were naked!"

Tyrone's hearty and boisterous laugh made Jakob grin like a teenager!

"That's a real thing with humans. They really are prudes, aren't they?"

"Indeed they are! But, she did notice that I was hard. That was very difficult for me to hide, but then, again? I wasn't trying to hide it from her."

Tyrone nodded.

"Then, she must be your mate, isn't she?" he shook his head at Jakob's sharp nod. "A human mate. I've never heard of such a thing in my life!"

"I know. Neither have I. I don't understand it either. Do you have any idea why?"

"Not a one! Oh, well. Have you thought about asking your parents? Perhaps they saw a similar case, before you were born. Why don't you sit with Kassie for a while, Jakob. She sleeps and rests better when you are there, because you are her mate. She just doesn't know it. But, I have to say I do not envy you. How *are* you going to handle this situation?"

Jakob shook his head as he opened the door. He stood, and dropped his head.

"I have no idea, Tyrone. See what you can find for me, will you? And, your idea is a good one. I'll e-mail my parents."

He looked at the doctor who nodded, and Jakob shut the door to go to his mate. Tyrone released a nervous sigh, not realizing how wound up he truly was over this. He was worried. Really worried. He wasn't yet ready to tell his Alpha his suspicions about the girl, so he sat in his office, hand stroking his short, black beard, his eyebrows were drawn down into a frown that only someone with a great burden would sport. Anyone entering his office would see an African American male, whose skin was almost bordering on true black. His black eyes matched his blue-black hair that was barely sprinkled with a little bit of white just forming at his temples. Just being a werewolf doctor was hard enough, but although his face and body were the epitome of a twenty-seven year-old man, his slumped shoulders, and his frown made him look far older. Of course, he *was* fourteen-hundred years old, but he had not changed, except for that bit of white. His body was similar to Jakob's in that it was strong, with broad shoulders and chest slimming down to hips that filled out his jeans. It was a safe bet that most women would say he was as much a sex on a stick as all other werewolf males. Approximately six-foot four, just an inch shorter than

Jakob, he was the epitome of a woman's dream male. He had been mated to a beautiful young woman, who was his life long ago. Sadly enough, Tala wasn't his true mate, but she was sweet, lovely, caring, and eternally happy. It had been almost a thousand years, now, and he missed here every bit as much today as when she passed to the next world, thanks to an ancient battle, they had deemed the "Vampire Wars". She was tiny compared to him, and a medicine woman who held great power. She was far more than human. Today, she would be called Native American, having long, black, glistening hair, small nose, luscious lips, and surprising blue eyes, she had given him his first, and only child, Ronick, and then, died in childbirth – one of the single, few ways a werewolf could die. Tyrone had raised Ronick as best he could, but the truth was, he was a bit of a disappointment. Inheriting his Mother's looks, they could have almost been twins. Ronick was on the other side of the world, having joined another clan, and apparently had straightened his life out, but Venus? Well, his bat shit, crazy sister was a real problem! Actually, she was his stepsister. As beautiful as she was, he wasn't naïve enough to know that she was born without a heart. A lot of problems within the clan could be traced right back to her. And, that was a whole other story! He still didn't understand how in the hell his Mother could possibly have married her Father, because he was exactly like Venus! They were both selfish and mean! He just hoped that she had not seen him put the blood vials in his pocket as he left the office. She had an uncanny knack of observation, and it didn't take a rocket scientist to see how she despised Kassie. Tyrone was still puzzling why she hated her so much, but the truth was? He had no clue. Each werewolf was given a special gift.

His special gift was medicine, while Venus's was observation. Nothing got by her. As for himself, Tyrone just looked at an injury or illness, he not only knew what it was, but he knew how to treat it. While the werewolf community rarely had health issues, they did crop up now and then. With Kassie, though, a human, all of that flew out the window, and he had been sent scouring his medical books and online on how to treat an injured human. It had truly taxed his limits.

Putting aside Venus, for the time being, he pulled his hand from his chin, stood, and walked to the window putting his palms on the sill. Unknown to anyone, he had taken several blood samples from the girl – well, Kassie. May as well use her name, since she did remember that much. He hoped that she would be able to remember more as her brain healed. In the meantime, hoping that his suspicion would not be validated by their lab, he pulled out a vial of her blood from his pocket. The obvious fall she had taken should have killed a human being immediately. Not telling Jakob his burgeoning suspicion, Tyrone estimated that she had fallen from the top of the canyon, which alone, should have killed her. He only said she had fallen from a great height, but not how high. However, Kassie gave every indication that she had also been hit on the head with a very heavy, sharp object. He guessed it might have been the blunt edge of an axe, or even a lug wrench. Either, or other things, would be a possibility. Someone was intent on killing her, but why? It also didn't take a genius to figure out that she was pushed over the canyon wall, after being slammed in the head. But, aside from that, there had been a mark under her left arm. A scratch? Maybe, but he had another idea, and it was not a good one if it proved true. He really hoped it was not what he thought it was, but he had to know. The cuts were so tiny, he really hadn't thought about it at that time, but now he wondered, and needed to be sure. If it turned out that it was, the implications within the clan – within their entire world – would be enormous. Could Jakob handle this? And, honestly, could any Alpha handle it? A case hadn't been found like this in almost eight hundred years, since it had been banned among their kind. And, if it proved to be true, then for the first time in forever, their laws had been violated. And, that particular law was punishable by death. There was no reprieve for this act.

"Billie?" Tyrone asked, walking into the outer office. "I have to leave. Keep me informed on Kassie."

She looked up from her work.

"What? Oh, yes, Doctor?" Billie asked, always formal in the office when addressing him. "Oh, right! You have been teaching a class. I almost forgot!"

"I have to get to Denver. I'm already late by a couple of hours. Oh, and it appears that Kasseiopia – that's her name, by the way – is finally out of danger, or I wouldn't contemplate leaving. Call my cell if I'm needed."

Billie nodded, and went back to her work. Billie was their Beta's mate, and Jakob's sister. Hunter Levenson was one of the best Beta's in the business, and Jakob had declared, numerous times, he couldn't run the clan without him! Just like his Beta, Tyrone considered Billie his own "Beta". Billie Levenson was, also, incredible at her work as his nurse. She had been studying under him, since she was in her teens, and by rights, she should be a doctor, by now, and his partner. He had been trying to get her to finish her internship, before graduation, but had become pregnant. That's when she decided that she would come back to the clan, and decided to wait until she had her baby to decide if she would finish or not. After she had her son, she stayed on as his nurse, and despite his pushing her, she still wasn't ready to finish. She knew almost as much as he did, so he felt safe to leave her in charge of his rare cases of illness. Trying to doctor a human, though, was a challenge for both of them. Kassie was proving to be a very strong female. Truth was that as far as Tyrone was concerned, that was a true mark of an Alpha female. He doubted that any of the other females in the clan could hold a candle to this human female. Only time would tell, though – and the lab work. Billie was such a little thing, but her small stature of five-foot five was quite deceiving to those who met her. Her hazel eyes belied her intelligence, and her light brown, chin length hair curled around her face, and contributed to the pixie look that was so much like her Mother. Her medium toned skin covered a form of a slender female with small breasts and a gentle, curvy ass. Mated or not, just because he was older by a lot of years, that didn't mean he couldn't appreciate a female of beauty. Besides, age in their world meant nothing at all. One could find a mate at five or five hundred. But, he never would have suspected that it could happen with a human – until now.

Puzzling this question, he went back to his house, packed, and took off running across the desert floor, until he reached his car that was parked in their Southern office, so he could drive into university. He was going to ask his oldest friend, and fellow clan member, Dr. George Mason, to help him look at Kassie's blood later in the week. George was like them, and even though he was still part of the clan, he preferred to live in the human world, and act like them. Even though he had never found his true mate, Tyrone wondered just how he would react if George ever did find his mate? Like, George, and most of the rest of them as well, Jakob, lived in the human world most of the time, but he also could run the entire corporation from right here at the retreat as well as his clan. Jakob's parents were living in Italy, but still, Jakob sought out their counsel when needed.

Jumping into his black SUV, Tyrone backed out of his designated parking space in their Clan's lot, and took off to Denver, Colorado for his teaching "gig", and verify that his findings were correct, through George. He really hoped that what he thought might be true, wasn't, but he'd been in this business long enough to tell when his gut instincts were fact or fiction. This one, he was absolutely certain, was fact.

"Damn!" he muttered, as he turned onto I25 North.

~ 3 ~

Stop and listen in secret. You'll find out a great deal of information, even if you don't understand it.

Kassie slept soundly for the first time in ages. The bed she had been using at the clinic was even comfortable, even though it was quite obviously a hospital bed. She had no idea how long she had been here, but she wasn't going to argue about sleeping. Every so often, she would wake up, and every time, Jakob was sitting by her bedside. He would be reading, or working on a computer. On occasions, she would catch him napping. But, still, he was there. She would fall asleep, again, and dream of them at the pool together. Her dreams were of the erotic variety – the two of them having sex. Maybe it was because she had seen him naked, and he had seen her, but she would wake with wetness between her legs every time. And, it was almost constant. She couldn't seem to help it, though. Kassie was drawn to Jakob.

When she would wake, Jakob would turn and smile at her, giving her something to eat and drink. His smile was devastating. But, the real reason he smiled was her arousing scent. Of course, she didn't know that he could smell her arousal for him, but it truly gave him happiness to know that she found him as desirous of him as he was for her. And, it would be even more so when he could act upon that scent! Since George was in Denver, he trusted Billie with his mate's care. And, according to Billie, Kassie did seem to be healing quite quickly for a human, and that gave him a bit of excitement that they would get to act on their attraction to each other, soon.

Finally, she woke for good. And, man! Did she feel great! This time, though, looking around her,

Jakob was not there, and she felt bereft of him. In the meantime, Kassie decided to see if she could sit upright. She wiggled her way to a sitting position, and sat for a minute. She cocked her head. Well, so far, so good. Hmmm. Just a little bit wobbly, when she decided to stand, but she could do it. She felt much stronger. In fact, she more than felt stronger. She really, really felt fantastic! Slowly, she started walking toward the door. Putting her hand on the door jam, Kassie continued to walk out of the room she had occupied for almost two months. The first thing she saw was a young woman with light brown hair, brilliant hazel eyes, and medium colored skin sitting at the desk.

"Hi?" Kassie said.

The girl looked up, smiled, and immediately jumped up and ran around her desk to grab Kassie's hand.

"Hey, yourself, sleepyhead! I'm Billie Levenson. I'm Jakob's sister, and Tyrone's nurse."

Kassie took the hand held out to her.

"Jakob's sister?" Kassie was shocked. How could they even be brother and sister, when they look nothing alike?

"Yep. I know. I know. We don't look alike, but we really are brother and sister! He is almost the exact image of our Dad, and me? Well, I am more like my Mom,"

"That's rather cool. Wish I could remember things. So...how long have I been here? Well, out of it, anyway?"

"Well, technically? Oh...about two months or so."

Kassie's mouth dropped. Two months? She scratched her head. Had she been that bad?

As if to answer her thought, Billie said, "Yep. Kassie. I mean, you were almost dead, hon! It was really touch and go for a while, and honestly, we really didn't think you would make it for a bit."

Kassie's eyes almost popped out of their socket at this information!

"That's just almost impossible to believe, but if you say it's true, it must be! It's just so weird, thinking I've been out of it that long!"

"Well, it's not all that unusual with the severe injuries and concussion that you suffered," Billie told her. "Doc kept you knocked out for a while, while he treated your injuries. He said that you would be in a lot of pain with all he had to do, so keeping you sedated was the best course to keep you away from the pain."

"I was injured that badly? And, a concussion? Did I really hit my head that hard?" she asked in surprise.

"Yeah. Apparently, you had a huge gash on the back of your head. I stitched it up, of course, but it was pretty wide." Watching Kassie put her hand up to the back of her head, she continued. "Hey. Don't worry. I'm really good at it, and I didn't need to have to shave part of your scalp to do it."

Breathing a sigh of relief, Kassie grinned. Billie bit her tongue to keep from telling her that she had healed very fast. For whatever reason, she felt sure that Tyrone wouldn't want her to reveal that piece of information. She was also sure that he suspected the reason for it, and so did she. But, voicing her own suspicion would be stupid unless she actually had so me proof. And, to her knowledge, neither of them had any proof. Billie was certain that Tyrone was on the case. She really, really, really hoped that her suspicions didn't pan out, however her particular gift, as it were, was she just knew things. Jakob had always laughed at her ability, but the fact still remained, she was an empath.

"Is there some place that I could clean up a bit?" she asked. "I mean, I haven't had a shower in ages! Two months?"

Well, except for the water bath she took naked with an equally naked Jakob. The visual only made her face red in embarrassment, even though they did nothing at all.

"Of course! Look, it's quitting time, and you are my only patient. Are you up to following me back to my house, Kassie?" At her emphatic nod, Billie continued. "Trust me! I'm sure something better than those sweats, OK?" She shook her head, as she looked at how Kassie was dressed. "What was my brother thinking! I mean, sweats? And, they don't eve fit you!"

Looking down at herself, Kassie's nose wrinkled at how much weight she had lost during the last month, and the baggy clothes that she wore. She looked up with a frown and a smirk.

"OK. Guess I've probably looked a bit better!"

Both girls looked at each other in horror – then, laughed. Kassie knew that she would be glad to have a new friend.

As the two girls walked to Billie's house, they made small talk that people do when they are getting to know one another. Suddenly, Kassie remembered something else. A bit reluctant to say what was bothering her, she took the plunge, hoping that Billie wouldn't think she was a bit off her nut.

"You know, while I was in and out as I lay dying...you know...I mean before I was found, I thought that I saw a huge black wolf just before I totally blacked out."

OK. That just sounded as if a crazy was messing around somewhere in her gene pool!

"I mean is it even possible? Are there wolves around here?" Kassie asked.

"A wolf? Really? That's kind of odd." Billie put on what was her perfect "surprised and disbelieving face. She also deliberately seemed a bit vague. "I honestly have never seen one. But, I didn't know there were any around here."

"Well, maybe I didn't see one. I was just probably hallucinating. I'm sure I had a high fever. That would cause someone to see things that aren't there, right?"

"Well, you did have an abnormally high temperature, and hallucinations can happen."

Billie was trying to make sure that she didn't spill everything to her.

Kassie was still in awe of the little she had already seen, as she and Billie had traipsed down the dirt road that ran through a small settlement of houses and a general store. No cars were to be seen anywhere, either. That was just weird. This whole place was a little bit odd. A place that had technology, but no vehicles. Well, there were bicycles some people were riding, but that was about it. Children were happily playing on the side of the road, and one group seemed to be playing football between two houses! Billie noticed her confusion.

"I know. Weird, huh? We are a group of people who love our tech, but we also love nature. We have an entire community here, but no cars are allowed. Besides, they couldn't make it around, anyway."

"Well, I have to admit. This is a bit weird. But, oddly enough? I kind of like it. It's so nice and quiet here. Relaxing."

Billie nodded her agreement.

"I know. The land is owned by Jakob and me, of course. We have owned it forever and a day, thanks to our parents. No one knows how far our cla – uh, I mean, line goes back, but we love it. And, the peace it gives to us all is what we all crave."

Kassie turned in surprise.

"Does that mean that you guys live here all the time? You don't live anywhere else?"

"Oh, make no mistake, Kassie. We live in Denver. Most all of us do. Our business is there, but he comes here – we all do – to get away from all of it, several times a year."

Confusion gripped her. A company that lets its employees off to come to a retreat several times a year? Was there any company that actually did it? But, more than that, how could they afford to do so?

"Oh, I see. It's like a retreat, right? Wait! You do this for everyone? Your employees, too?"

"I guess you could call it that, yes."

Nodding, Billie led the way into a small, two-story house that was literally a stone's throw from the clinic. Billie stood aside, and let Kassie enter a small, but spotless kitchen. The moment she entered, she got a whiff of something grilling, and did it ever smell heavenly. She could feel her mouth watering for whatever it was.

"What a charming place, Billie!"

And, it was! It was designed as a house should be – wood everywhere. Stranger, was that these massive houses looked completely out of place in this desert-type area. She shrugged, and promptly forgot about it. The kitchen and breakfast nook contained a bar, and a rather large table with six chairs. An antique stove that Billie used as a sideboard, stood opposite the chairs, while the three stoves and two refrigerators that were state of the art technology, even with a wifi screen set right into the door! Above average and contemporary and all in stainless steel, there was also a large island in the center of the room with a bar sink, and a bar that had about six chairs around it. A few pictures lined the walls. Pictures of wolves. Billie saw the connection. She also realized that Kassie was about to utter questions, and jumped in to stop Kassie from asking why there are wolf photos everywhere if they never saw a wolf in the area.

"My ma – uh – hubby and I are having a cook out for the cl – uh – neighborhood tonight. Are you feeling up to coming?" she asked.

"Is that what smells so wonderful? Food! Real food? Oh, man, does that ever sound great!" Kassie laughed. "You know, I feel really good, Billie! Better than good! So, what's for dinner?"

"Let's ask. Hunter?" Billie yelled from the kitchen.

"Out here, Babe!" a deep voice called.

"Come meet Hunter, and then I'll take you upstairs to meet our little boy. He's barely 4, and a total terror!"

Before they could move, a deep voice interrupted.

"If I know Hunter, he's barbecuing ribs. We all love those, right Billie?"

"You mean steaks," Billie answered.

"No. I mean ribs."

"Steaks!"

"Ribs!"

Jakob glared at Billie, and Kassie thought she would be witness to a family argument – until he and Billie broke into laughter. That's when he leaned toward her, giving her a grin.

"Wanna be my date, Kassie?"

Billie started toward the bar, only Jakob waved her down.

"Date? Well, uh, yes. I guess so?" she blushed. *Damn! Just looking at him set her body afire with lust*!

Billie almost laughed out loud at her shyness, as her brother strolled out the kitchen door. She and Kassie followed him outside, where Jakob was already watching the grill with hunger. It always made her giggle when the wolves drooled over food over their own mates!

"Good. You'll have real food tonight, my ma-uh-Date. Glad that's settled." Well, that was great! If he kept this up, he'd be having to explain himself before he was totally ready!

While Billie secretly rolled her eyes at her brother, they stopped just outside the door, and Kassie's mouth gaped when she saw Hunter.

"Hunter, this is Kassie. Kassie, my hubby, Hunter."

She was stunned into silence as she looked into his eyes. Holy shit! Another gorgeous man? He was glorious, Kassie thought. Billie was as beautiful as her husband was gorgeous! Not less than six-feet four, his tanned skin was a rich dark brownish gold. His eyes were as black as night, and his hair an amazing honey blonde – a stark contrast to his wife. Dressed in jeans and a tight, black t-shirt, he completed the title of "GQ" to Kassie. In contrast, Kassie was a bit petite compared to Billie, and that was really saying something. Billie's face was heart shaped, and her lips were full. She had little in the way of a neck, but her bust was small and her waist tiny.

"Well, how dee do, Kassie!" he said, reaching out his hand. His sexy smile belied the fact that he was more like a huge teddy bear, as she shook his hand. But, his southern drawl was just downright cute!

"Hi, Hunter. It's nice to meet you, too."

"So, do ya like ribs?"

"Ribs, huh?"

"Yep!" he drawled.

She laughed, and felt her mouth water.

"Geez! Real food? That'll be a change for me!"

Hunter threw back his head, and laughed loudly.

"Or, wouldja prefer one of those delicious steaks a-sittin' over there waiting' to be grilled?"

While Kassie really liked ribs, she wanted something with real meat.

"Steak, please?"

"You got it! So, how do ya like yours?" he asked, as he pointed to one of the sizeable cut sirloins to his left.

"Well, if you don't mind, I kind of like mine medium rare to medium?"

He smiled in approval.

"Excellent! Now, Billie, here, loves hers medium well. I keep tellin' her that she's missin' out on the real taste of steaks, but she doesn't seem to care! The meat is always tough that-a way. Medium rare to medium it will be!"

Billie stuck her tongue out at him. But, Kassie saw their eyes as they stared at each other. There was nothing but love mixed with a bit of lust in them. Kassie wondered if anyone would ever look at her that way.

"Watch it, woman! That tongue of yours is way wicked!" he growled.

"And, you wouldn't want it any other way, hunkalicious!" she smirked back at him.

Then, she turned to Kassie. "OK, now that that is settled – Hunkalicious, I want ribs! Now, I'm going to take Kassie upstairs. She just has nothing to wear, obviously."

"Well, you watch out for my Billie, Kassie! She may be a nurse, but she's also a woman who loves to do makeovers!"

Kassie laughed, and looked down at herself. The dull, gray sweats were already showing wear. But, they were comfy wearing them to bed – or after a dip in an icy cold pool with a gorgeous man! She laughed at herself, then turned her eyes to meet Billie.

"Well, maybe I do need a makeover at that!"

The three of them laughed, and she noticed Jakob just licked his lips, as he stared at Kassie like she was a "steak with legs". She gulped deep, while Billie grabbed the blushing Kassie, pulling her into the house.

"Yeah, yeah, come on!" She turned to Kassie as they walked into the house. "I just hate it when Hunter is right! I'm always looking for a new project! And, you'll do just fine!"

Hunter just shook his head, giving Kassie a look of pity, then turned back to his grill after Jakob tapped him on the shoulder, and pointed to a steak, indicating that it was the one he wanted.

As the girls left, he turned back around to watch the woman, who had captured his Alpha's heart.

"Kassie, huh? A human? Jakob, are you just tryin' to get yourself in trouble?" he asked, and his eyebrows rose.

Nodding, "Yeah. I guess I am."

"Oh, shit! Nothing is worse than having a female in your life. Your thoughts, and life, will never be yours again to control!" Jakob frowned at Hunter when he shrugged and tossed a towel at Jakob. "Hey! Don't ya come gripin' to me! I know when to keep my place, A! So, here, Lover boy! Time for you to get a-learnin' about domesticity! Get to work!"

Hunter couldn't help, but think that when his Billie got through with Kassie, Jakob's heart would be totally gone. Still, he was worried. How would a human mate fit in with an all werewolf community? Already, the entire clan knew of Jakob's feelings for her, and most of them thought it was terribly exciting. However, a human had never been mate to a werewolf before, and he was afraid for his brother-in-law and Alpha. He turned back to the grill. Poor Kassie had no idea what she had stepped into, and Hunter just hoped it would work out for the two of them.

Billie saw Kassie look after Jakob, as she pulled her new friend who was laughing into her house. Her Alpha brother sure had it bad, and one look at Kassie told her that she did, too. But, no wolf had ever found a human mate. This whole thing was just so strange. Billie just couldn't help but think about this constantly. But, regardless, there was just something about Kassie that she really, really liked. That, in itself, was strange, because when she studied to be a doctor, she could count only a handful of humans she even liked, and even those, she never wanted to be around very much. But, truth be known, Kassie was an enigma, and Billie just couldn't explain why. There was no doubt in her mind that her brother had been scared to death when Tyrone had told him that Kassie was dying. He was scared, and the sadness he exhibited had been completely off the wall. Only mates would do this. And, therein lay the problem. How could she be her brother's mate when she was human? Oh, it wasn't completely unheard of, but it was certainly unusual in today's world, and had not happened in contemporary knowledge. When her fever spiked to 108 degrees, Jakob almost lost it – and Kassie. Thank God, he thought of his personal pool at the last second! Jakob was extremely private, and no one was allowed at it, except for Hunter and Billie, who were allowed to use it for their honeymoon. She had no idea what would have happened to her brother if he found his mate, only to lose her hours later. Their kind always followed their mates to the next life, but she wasn't sure how that would work with a human mate. No one knew!

Kassie followed Billie across the kitchen, through the large living area, and up the stairs. Billie was rather petite. Even after her baby, Kassie knew that any man would think she was a sexy lady. At the moment, her hips swayed back and forth, as she climbed the stairs. She wore very short jean shorts and a tight royal blue t-shirt – with no bra. That was obvious, especially when she had seen Hunter openly gaze at them lustfully. Yep! Billie would definitely be getting some tonight, Kassie thought. She suddenly felt like a washed out female next to her. She wasn't all that beautiful, and she knew it. Especially at the moment!

Kassie looked around the house as Billie led her through it and upstairs. Billie's house was not as small as she had thought from the outside, but that could be that it was backed up against a cliff, and she discovered that it actually was built into the side of it! It was deliriously cool, too! The furniture didn't match, and it seemed Billie and Hunter liked casual everything. Eclectic. That was the word for it. Where nothing matched, but it all went together just right. She loved that, because she knew she was like them. Wait! That was a memory, right? She could sort of remember an apartment. Well almost. She did know that she didn't like knick-knacks. Her place had nothing, which matched, either. Then, her memory hit a brick wall. OK. Well, maybe not exactly a memory. But, it was, at least something, right?

Billie led her into a bedroom, where her little son, Jimmy was playing. The room was done in various shades and pastels of blue. She stopped for a moment. That was called…! Yes! Monochromatic! Around the top of the wall was a border that also had wolves on it, romping through the woods in pairs. She decided to let it go for now, and concentrate of the little boy whose eyes were staring at her in wonder! He was so adorable that Kassie wanted to just pick him up and hold him. He epitomized all the wonder a child always seemed to have. About four, maybe five, he had his Mom's brown hair, and his Father's darker skin. When he turned to look at them, she gasped. She found his Mother's eyes staring back at her! Oh, man! He was going to be every bit as gorgeous as the rest of the family! She felt a bit depressed. What she had noticed was that everyone here was beautiful. From Jakob to Tyrone to Venus to Billie to Hunter, all she saw was hunks and beauties all around her. She'd be willing to bet that the rest of the town was every bit as gorgeous. And, that just convinced Kassie, more than ever, that she didn't belong here. Well, of course she didn't! She belonged wherever she should be. For a second, there was a niggling in her brain, and she got a momentary feeling that something bad had happened to her? No. Not her. Someone else, but then, it was gone as fast as it appeared, and she turned to watch the little boy running toward Billie.

"Jimmy?"

"Mommy!" he squealed, and launched himself into his Mother's arms.

After a big hug from his Mom, she turned to Kassie.

"Jimmy. I want you to meet a new friend to us. This is Kassie," she said, and put him on the ground.

Jimmy's blue eyes looked at Kassie shyly.

"Hello, Jimmy. It's very nice to meet you," Kassie said, stooping down to his height, and holding out her hand.

He looked up at his Mother for a second, then took Kassie's hand. But, shyness was obviously not his normal personality, as he became frank with her almost immediately.

"Hi! Do you like to play jacks, Kassie?" he asked.

"Well, I haven't played in a while, but I do, Jimmy!"

"Wanna play with me?" Kassie looked at Billie for approval.

"You sure you want to play with him? He can be a real handful!" she laughed.

"I'd love to, Billie. Do we have time?" she asked Billie.

"Weeeelll, I don't know...," she teased, looking serious, while rubbing her chin as if deep in thought.

"Come on, Mommy! Puhlease?" he begged, blinking the most beautiful brown eyes at her.

Billie laughed. Her son was going to be a heart breaker, and was just like his Daddy – getting his way far too much for his own good! For the first time, she was a bit sad, that she didn't have a little girl...unless...? Well, the two of them had been trying for a while, now. She was late, and been having morning sickness for the last couple of days.

"I guess about 10-15 minutes would work. Then, Jimmy, I'm stealing your playmate, who will need to get ready for the cookout."

He just nodded while grabbing Kassie's hand, and dragging her into the center of the room, where Kassie plopped down on the floor with Jimmy, and the two started giggling like old friends. Billie watched Kassie for a minute with her son. In that second, Billie knew that Kassie would be a wonderful Alpha for the women, even if she were only human. She seemed to care about everything, and everyone, and for a grown woman to sit in the floor playing with a five year-old, well, that just endeared her that much more to Billie. She cocked her head studying Kassie. Then, with a sly grin, she went to prepare the vegetables for the cook out, and fifteen minutes passed before Kassie knew it.

Billie returned quietly, and for a few minutes, watched Kassie play with her son. She had once been an awesome hairdresser, and she perused the small girl in the floor. Billie saw that she was about five foot one. She should have noticed it before, but Kassie had been so sick, Billie hadn't been able to judge her true size, while in the hospital bed. Her hair, though, had obviously lost its blonde luster, while she had been so ill. At the moment, it was a dirty blonde color, dull, and stringy. She hadn't been able to wash it thoroughly, due to the cut on her head. Kassie had also lost considerable weight in the month she had been infirm, and her skin was extremely pale, due to the lack of being in the sun. But, her face was round, her nose small, lips full, and her eyes were still a rich, Kelly green, which sparkled when she smiled. Her figure was similar to Billie's, now, except Kassie was even more endowed in her chest. Her waist was slim, and in truth, probably just a bit larger than Billie's. Her hips, though, were rounded and in perfect proportion to the rest of her body. Grinning, Billie sneaked back out, and let them play a while longer.

~ 4 ~

How do you eat when your stomach is filled with butterflies that have nothing to do with food?

"Oh, Jiiiimmy! It's time for your baaaath!" Billie called in a singsong tone, about thirty minutes later. She stuck her head in his door.

"Ah, Mom! Aunt Kassie and me were just starting to play!"

"Aunt Kassie and I, Jimmy," Billie corrected her son.

"OK, OK. Aunt Kassie and I! We just started playing!" Jimmy whined.

"Yeah, Mom! What he said!" Kassie mimicked, holding out the jacks and ball, her eyes twinkling. She had been having so much fun with Jimmy, time just seemed to have flown out the window.

Billie whipped her son up in her arms with him giggling, as she tickled his tummy.

"So, it's Aunt Kassie, huh? OK. Go get your bath."

"Yes! She's my official new Aunt!" ignoring the word 'bath'.

His mother just cocked her left eyebrow at him. He knew that look.

"Oh, alright!" he griped.

"If you're good, Jimmy, maybe I'll tuck you in later, after the cookout!" Kassie offered.

He grinned. God, this little boy was going to be a heartbreaker, Kassie thought.

"Really?" With the promise of getting to play with Kassie, again, he said, "OK, Aunt Kassie! I'll go and get my bath!"

And, that was all it took as Jimmy happily skipped off to the bathroom, after his Mom put him down. And, that's when Jimmy was full speed ahead.

Billie motioned for Kassie to follow her into her room.

"Well, he'll be in the bath forever, thanks to you! I can't get him to take a bath that easily! And, I can't believe how good you are with children, Kassie! You must have known them to be so patient and, well, patient!" she laughed. "It's always a battle royale to get him into the bathtub! OK. Now, it's time to concentrate on you."

She put her hands together and rubbed them quickly, then took one hand, and stroked an imaginary moustache, as she looked Kassie up and down. Kassie just giggled at her new friend and her antics.

"I think we can do a lot better than those silly sweats you're wearing, don't you? I wonder what my brother was thinking dressing you in those things! Let's rummage around in my closet, then we will take care of the rest of you."

The two girls laughed and giggled as they dug in her closet, because Billie was finding things she had forgotten about, and were old. Kassie laughed as she listened to Billie's constant diatribe as she pulled clothes and shoes out of the closet to give away to Goodwill.

"OMG! That thing is just ancient! No way! Did I really wore these things? I will never, I repeat never put that on again!"

But, finally, she emerged with a couple of pairs of very short jean shorts, and a bright red fitted tank top. "Yes. I think these will do? What is your bra size?"

"Oh, it's a 38C. But, the shorts? Really Billie?"

"I figured, and I'm so jealous! My bust is so much smaller than yours," she said, then stopped to look at her. "Did you just say that you wore a 38C?"

"Yes, why?"

Kassie realized that she had remembered another fact!

"Holy shit!"

"You did remember something!" exclaimed Billie.

"I did! But, why would I remember my bra size, before anything else?"

"Well, could be that is because my brother was ogling your boobs!" Seeing Kassie blush, she said, "I'm right, aren't I? Men! They are all so damned predictable!"

"Maybe, but I noticed that your husband doesn't seem to mind you bouncing all over the place!" Kassie grinned at her. Billie looked over at her new friend, surprised at her wit. There was a lot more to this woman than they knew.

She laughed.

"You're right about that! I have to admit that I'm always hot for him!"

Both girls giggled hard.

"Are all the men here like that? I mean, horny all the time?" Kassie gasped, trying to stop laughing.

That only made Billie laugh even harder. Kassie joined in, again. It took them both a while to calm down, because every time they did, one of them said something that just set them off howling with laughter once more. Finally, calming down, the girls got busy.

"We tend to wear shorter shorts, because of the heat," Billie pointed to her own, but she had no intention of telling Kassie that they wore the shorts for their mates' sakes. It was about as revealing as they could get away with, without wearing a swimsuit, or being naked. Truth be known, most of the women in the Clan wouldn't have a problem going au naturale! Once, Billie innocently suggested it at their weekly meetings, causing the females to laugh at the expressions and reactions of the males. And, the males promptly vetoed that idea. Werewolves needed constant visuals and touch with their mates, she had argued, but they still said no to the howls of the females' laughter. She almost giggled. She had every intention of making sure her brother and his mate were together, alone, for a night of love. And, this was just the ticket! She knew her brother, and knew how to push his buttons. He would never be able to resist Kassie dressed in the :barely decent" shorts, and the thin, red tank top that would hug her figure tightly. OK. They weren't really even decent, since her ass would easily seen.

"Uh, Billie? These are – uh – well not really – uh – decent. I mean…they'll show my ass!" Kassie whined.

Aloud, she said, "OH! Well, I guess they were made a bit shorter than the others?" she said, pulling out another pair of shorts that she knew were just as short, then measured them against the shiny assed ones.

"Yep! See? These are even shorter than the ones you just put on."

Kassie sighed, and Billie did everything she could to keep from laughing aloud at her friend's face.

Aloud, Billie said, "Hope you don't mind not wearing a bra?" Kassie shook her head. "Are you sure? Because, I'll check tomorrow to see if I can find anyone who had that size bra for you.

Again, Kassie shook her head.

"And, uh, you're not all that modest about your breasts bouncing some, are you? Most of us don't usually wear them around here due to the heat. I really hate the things!"

This time she was telling the truth. Bras bind and stick to a woman in the heat, making them miserable.

Kassie smiled. She hated them as much as Billie did. Well, the truth be known, she didn't know one woman who wouldn't be happy to get rid of them! Unless she was working out, that is. She needed her sport bras to keep her breasts from bouncing and flopping all over the place. That made exercising very uncomfortable.

"I hate them, too. But, you can't let them bounce around forever, because they sag as you age."

Well, Kassie was only partially right. Werewolf female's breasts never sagged with age. They were highly fertile as well – most becoming pregnant the first time they mated. That's why bras weren't needed. Billie just nodded. The pair of sparkly, assed short shorts and the brilliant red and very tight, tank top were thrown at her.

Taking off the horrible looking sweats, and throwing them aside, Kassie put the shorts on, first, then the very tight red tank top. She looked in the mirror. Wow! She knew she had lost weight over the two months she had been out of it, but now, her figure was much slimmer than before! Her bust was front and center, and even larger if that were possible! Yet, the entire outfit left little to nothing to the imagination! That had her blushing a bit. Turning to look at Billie, she noticed, for the first time, that even her breasts were in her very tight fitting royal blue tank top, and like hers, also left nothing to the imagination. Trying her best to ignore her tight fitting clothing, Kassie was truly grateful.

"Thank you so much, Billie. You have been so kind to me," she said, as she hugged her.

"I'm being kind to myself."

She stood back, and looked at Kassie – and frowned.

"What?" Kassie said.

"OK. Makeover! Come on, let's do something about that hair! It's a bit shaggy, you know. I'll cut, and style your hair, and then, you can take a proper shower. Then, after that's all completed, you can get dressed!"

"You sure you don't mind?" she asked.

Kassie did know how terrible her hair really was, so she took off her outfit, and replaced it with the ugly sweats, again, while Billie did her hair.

Kassie was a bit leery, because Hunter had told her the same thing.

"Yep. Trust me. Before I became a nurse, I actually cut hair for a living!"

Before her hair was cut, Billie had decided she needed to give it some shine and color. She mixed up a platinum color, and quickly applied it to her scalp and hair. If she had more time, she would have foiled, but she didn't. Billie gave her a magazine to read for the next thirty minutes.

"When the dryer goes off, go ahead, and get into the shower, and wash the color from your hair. Use this silver shampoo a couple of times a week. It'll keep your hair from turning brassy."

"What?" Kassie asked.

Billie giggled, and leaned down to yell at her. Kassie nodded, and closed her eyes while she tried to relax.

Leaving Kassie, she ran to the kitchen to slice vegetables, sprinkling them with her own special spices, which took her longer than she had planned. She rolled them in foil, handed them to Hunter to place on the grill, and then ran back to the guest room to finish Kassie's hair.

Behind her closed eyes, Kassie let her mind wander. The bad thing was that depression settled in, because no matter how she did try to relax, all she could do was push herself to remember something – anything at all! But, no matter how hard she tried, it was as if someone had placed a door over her memory, and only opening it a crack at a time, letting some things trickle into her memory. And, all that while only allowing a memory here, and a memory there pass through the door! What was she? Buckingham Palace?

Following Billie's instructions on time, Kassie lifted and turned off the dryer. Stripping and leaving her clothing across the bed in the other room, she jumped into the shower, and used the shampoo that Billie had given to her while she was coloring her hair. She was just finishing and toweling it dry, when a flustered Billie ran into the bathroom.

"Whew! Well, I couldn't have timed that better if I had tried!" Seeing Kassie's confusion, she laughed. "Oh! While you were 'cooking', I went to fix some vegetables for the grill. I make a mean grilled vegetable skewer with my own special seasonings, roll them up in foil, and give them to Hunter to slow cook on the grill."

"Yummy!" Kassie told her. "I am a lover of veggies! I can't wait to taste them!"

She paused in surprise. That was a memory! At least, she thought she like vegetables? She searched her brain. Yes, she did! Noting that Billie was busy pulling out scissors, hair dryer, hot plates for curling, Kassie sank into the chair in front of the mirror.

Billie quickly cut, dried, and styled Kassie's hair. Kassie was putting the finishing touches onto her face with some makeup Billie had loaned her, when they heard voices chattering outside, as they began to show up for the big shindig. She stepped back. Billie had thought she needed a shorter style, and she had been right.

Gasping, "Is that really me?"

Kassie was thrilled with the new bob she was now sporting! Longer in the front than the back, it was almost shoulder length. Cocking her head, Kassie, somehow, knew her hair had always been long. Her clean, shiny, platinum blonde hair curved around her face, framing it with bangs, and they looked exactly right! After she dressed in the sparkly, jean short-shorts and the red tank top, she looked, and felt, amazingly human again! She still wasn't too sure about showing off this much of her skin, let alone her breasts that were jutting out in her tank, showing her hard nipples, but when in Rome, as people said. She really wasn't quite as self-conscious about it, since none of the other women wore bras. She'd just be one in the crowd. And, there was only one man she wanted to see with her girls out in points! She grinned.

"Wow! Billie, you are amazing!" she said, turning to face her. "Why did you stop being a stylist?"

"Well, as I said before, Tyrone asked me to help him out in his clinic a couple of days a week, and we discovered that I had a really great aptitude for medicine. So, I went to school to become a nurse, passed, and have been working for him ever since. Then, Tyrone decided I should become a doctor, so I began studying. That was when I met Hunter, and as they say, the rest is history!"

"But, you are going back to school?" Kassie asked. "Aren't you?"

"Well, I'd like to, but I wanted to wait until Jimmy is just a bit older."

"I guess I can understand. He's such a sweet little boy!"

"He is, but he can be a real handful, too!" Billie laughed.

Together, they went to Jimmy's room, where an excited, naked little boy launched himself into her arms as he had done earlier in the day with his Mom.

"Aunt Kassie!" he squealed.

Pretending to be stern, Billie asked her son with an accusatory glare, "And just why aren't you dressed young man?

"Uh, because I like being naked, and everyone else gets nak…," he started to say.

Billie interrupted his answer, while grabbing his clothes out of the drawers, and motioning Kassie to set him down. Just as she started to dress him, and had barely pulled his underwear on, she heard Hunter calling.

"Oh, great! Kassie, can you finish helping him?"

At Kassie's nod, she darted out the door, and down the stairs. Jimmy had apparently been allowed to take a longer shower than normal, and he'd made the most of playing in the tub, while his Mom made Kassie into a new woman! She stooped down to hug him tightly. This tiny boy had already worked his way into her heart in, well, a heartbeat. She held him tightly, and felt like she had always been around him.

"Aunt Kassie?" he asked as Kassie sat him down, helping him to put his legs in his little jean shorts.

"Yep, urchin?" Kassie kissed his little head, helping him dress.

"I wuvs you!" he said, throwing his arms around her neck.

Kassie's heart melted forever. She would always love this little boy, whether or not her memory ever did return.

"Well, I love you, too," she grinned with a tiny tear making its way from her right eye.

He gave her a gentle and shy kiss on her cheek, as she sat him on the bed so she could put his sandals on his feet. She had no idea that Jakob entered the room behind her, and was watching her every single move. His face was almost unreadable as he watched his mate with his nephew. Jakob's breath caught, when he saw his nephew kiss his mate's cheek, followed by Kassie, hugging the little boy, then putting him on the bed, and strapping on his sandals.

"Aunt Kassie?" Jimmy asked.

"What, Jimmy?"

"Are youse married?" he asked her.

Kassie stopped a moment, and her face became blank. That was a question she couldn't answer at all, and it had not occurred to her until he had asked. Was she? No. She wasn't…was she? She let her eyes drift around for a moment. Then, no. No, she wasn't. She was certain of it…or was she? She honestly had no answer.

When Jimmy asked her if Kassie was married, Jakob had frozen. He had not even thought about the fact she might be married. His stomach tensed. What if she was married? The thought of another man in bed with her made his wolf angry. He had to stop his wolf from taking over at the thought, and chastised his wolf's anger. His wolf flopped back down, pouting with glowing eyes.

"*She is ours!*" the wolf growled.

"*No she isn't!*" *Then, seeing the wolf's eyes, he made an offering.* "*At least not yet. She will be, though. Just take a chill pill, and back down. She doesn't know a thing about us yet, and I don't need you to come out to show her, before I can make her fall for both of us!*"

With a tight growl from his wolf, and his head on his paw, he glared at his human through his glowing, blue eyes.

"*When?*" he whined.

"Soon. Do not worry, buddy. She will be ours, soon, and once she is, we will never let her go!"

Finally, his wolf settled down just a bit, but still the man and wolf were restless.

"No. No I'm not, Jimmy."

Kassie sure hoped she wasn't lying, so she dug down deep in her soul. After a moment, she was absolutely positive she was not married, but did that constitute an actual memory, or was it all just wishful thinking.

"OK. You are not married, Kassie. You've never been married, so drop it," she admonished herself, and she finally sighed with relief.

"Goodie! ' Cause when I'se grows up, I'se gonnas marry you!"

Kassie laughed, ruffling his little dark hair, so like his Mom's hair.

"Well, then, I'll just have to wait for you, won't I? But, I don't know…"

"What, Aunt Kassie? What?" Jimmy demanded.

"Well, you are going to be a real heartbreaker! You will find your perfect match, so I bet you can't wait for me," she told him.

"Why?" he asked innocently.

"Because, one day, that perfect girl will come into the picture, and whisk you away!"

"Ewww! A girl? Nope! Not gonna happen!" Jimmie said, screwing his little face up in distaste at even the thought of girls. "I'se waiting for you!"

Suddenly, a deep voice answered behind them. Both of them turned to look at the tall figure standing in the doorway. Kassie gulped, and was very sure that she was looking at Jakob far differently than Jimmy! Jakob looked absolutely yummy! He had changed his clothes and combed his hair, which was now tightly tied back on the nape of his neck, and he looked delicious enough to eat! He wore jean shorts and a tight charcoal-gray t-shirt similar to the black one Hunter was wearing. It hugged all his tightly coiled muscles, and he wore flip-flops on his feet. Slowly he walked toward the two of them, until he stopped in front of Jimmy. Kassie had a deja view moment that reminded her of the night she had first seen the wolf. Jakob's eyes looked like it. The wolf was a predator who would seek out his prey, and right now, Jakob's eyes were locked on hers as if she was the prey, and her heart started beating in overdrive!

"I'm not sure about that, Jimmy. You do know that Kassie is a girl?" he said, giving Kassie a heart-wrenching and devastating wink.

Surprised, Jimmy looked back at Kassie, then answered his question.

"Weeelll, yeah. I guess she is," he said, then hurriedly added, "But, she's better than a girl! She's a buddy!"

Jakob heard Kassie snicker at his nephew's response. But, his little nephew would just have to wait for his mate, because Kassie was his. His mind caught in surprise as he realized just how territorial he was around her. How could he possibly be jealous of a child? His own nephew?

"*We don't share with anyone!*" the wolf growled. Jakob rolled his eyes.

"*Will you stop that? He's our nephew. She is our mate. His mate will come at the appointed time.*" Jakob stared into her amused eyes.

"That may be true, little buddy, but perhaps Kassie might meet someone in the meantime," he told Jimmy.

~ **5** ~

This memory thing is getting a bit tricky!

It was at that point that Jimmy looked at the glances between his uncle and Kassie. He stuck his lip out in a pout. He knew that look. It was the same look his Mom and Dad always got when they made googly eyes at each other. He huffed, and realized that Kassie was out of his league. His uncle was one of the oldest of the werewolves, and had been waiting a long time for his mate. In the exuberance of youth, as well as his own tiny little wolf, he realized a lost cause when he saw one. So, she would just be his aunt, and that would be alright. Kassie was cool!

Kassie's mouth opened as her heart picked up, and her breath came short and fast. What was it about this place that was so special? There was something about it that she just knew was different. She had loved to read paranormal books, and this just seemed a lot like a plot in one of them. She stopped. Kassie loved the paranormal, but she never thought for a second the books were real!

"No, that is just ludicrous!" she told herself.

Her mind was taking off into all kinds of areas of "are you a crazy person". But with Jakob's body standing right I front of him with hard muscles straining at the material of his "one size too small" t-shirt, she realized that is what the heroine of the book always said! Another thing she wondered about was why are all these people in such skimpy and revealing clothes? Very little seemed to be left to the imagination, and yet Billie and Hunter had eyes only for each other. And, then, there was Jakob's face and eyes. Those eyes were really, what drew her to him, though. His eyes were bright blue as they stared at her

– kind of shiny. It almost made her a bit wary. His eyes sure looked like the wolf's eyes, who stared at her while she lay on the rocky grass in the canyon, knowing she was about to die. While she stared, she saw his head morph into said black wolf, and she had to shake her head of the vision. OK, Kassie! That's enough of that type of thinking! There are no such things as those types of creatures! What had she been thinking? This was just so stupid!

Jakob looked at his mate, realizing that his sister had completely worked her magic. Kassie was gorgeous! He thought she was beautiful before, but now? Oh, crap! He was getting hard just staring at her! How would he ever be comfortable again if he didn't make her his soon? Somehow, though, he doubted that mating her would take care of that problem. With his luck, he'd always be hard for the rest of their existence! The jean shorts she had borrowed glittered on her tight little ass, and the ribbed red tank top clung to her body, showing the clear outline of her breasts as it stretched tightly over them. He could tell she wore no bra, but then, most of the women in the clan wore none due to the heat. And, to his delight, and erection which he seemed to constantly have around her, Kassie's hard nipples were prominently displayed, and seemed to be hardening as he stared at them. He wasn't sure he liked that other males would see them, but as he said. The women in the clan sported their nipples all the time. He had never noticed theirs. Hopefully, no other male would notice Kassie's either. She was his; they were his.

Jimmy stretched his arms for his uncle, who scooped him up, throwing him into the air, while he giggled. It was their favorite game.

"Nap time, Uncle Jakob!" Jimmy gave his uncle a big hug, as he walked over to the bed, and sat him down. For a few minutes, Kassie watched their interactions complete with tickles, giggles, and rough housing. Her throat was tight as she saw how much he loved his nephew. A little sadness crept into her at that moment. Would she ever have a little one herself one day – even if she couldn't even remember who she was? Would that be wrong? Was it wrong to think of having a baby in these circumstances? Fair? Her hand automatically went to her belly as she felt an empty womb. Her thoughts were ripped away when she heard Jimmy squeal, so she turned her attention back to Jakob and Jimmy

"Well, are you not hungry?"

"Hungry?" Jimmy asked, seeming a bit puzzled.

"The cookout?" Jakob reminded him. "You know…you are going to get to stay up later than you normally do, and no nap!"

Jimmy started bouncing on his bed.

"I forgot! Yummy for my tummy!" Jimmy squealed.

Jakob gave Jimmy a kiss on the top of his head.

Scrutinizing his nephew's attire, he shook his head, and walked over to one of the dressers.

"Those clothes will just not do! I think it's time the big boy wore something a bit older for him. What do you think?" he asked Jimmy, whose head was nodding a mile a second.

Jakob pulled out a black t-shirt like his Dad's, and turned to march back to the bed. Jimmy had already removed his striped t-shirt.

"How do I look, Aunt Kassie?" Jimmy asked for her approval.

"Aunt Kassie?" he asked Jimmy, a little surprised.

"Yep! She's my new Auntie!" Seeing the possessive gleam in his Uncle's eye, although not understanding it, the tiny little wolf and boy warned, "Uh-uh! I love her, Uncle Jakob! No poaching!"

"Well, not sure I can do that," he told his nephew. "Now, let's get you dressed for dinner!"

Strangely, Kassie had noted that Jimmy's speech had suddenly changed from a child's words into a more mature way of speaking. Did kids change their speech patterns that fast? She really had no idea.

"I'll just wait out in the hallway until you are dressed," she laughed, as her eyes met Jakob.

Jimmy just glared until she stepped out and shut the door.

"Now, Jimmy. Let's get you dressed."

It didn't take a long time, because Jimmy was as hungry as Jakob – only Jakob's reason was vastly different. For the first time in his existence, Jakob wanted children, and it surprised him that he did. In his long life, never once had he been interested in kids. Not until he met Kassie, that is. While helping Jimmy, he had a sudden vision of her swollen with his child. Her body was perfect for it. Carrying his child. Oh, yes. He had every intention of having a child with this woman! Very, very soon. Maybe tonight he would mate her, and fill her full of his seed – more than once! He conveniently "ignored" the niggling in his mind, that he had to tell her what they were, first. It was actually a law that he had established long ago – one law he had established long ago that allowed a human to join a clan, and become one of them. It was to keep as many humans as possible out of their world. However, he did have to allow for some, and thus the reason for his law. In order to bring a human into their world, first, she had to be told what they were, and if she could accept it, then she had to agree to become one of them. The change wasn't easy, but he had allowed for that as well, by ruling that only a mate was allowed to turn their human mate. It was so rare, that in known memory, it had never happened. And, that was hundreds of years ago. The last one he even knew of that happened was his own Father who had been turned by his Mother. He had already been an aristocrat in England – a Duke. But, when he had met his Mother, he had fallen for her big time. He had not even thought twice about becoming one of them, and not five months later, Jakob was born. His sister was born some one hundred and thirty-five years later. And, they had built an empire in the oil industry. Rich didn't even begin to describe them, yet neither he nor Billie ever thought anything about it. They were both as down to Earth as their parents, who treated their employees with great respect and reverence. The few humans who were allowed to work with the weres, knew who, and what, they were, but they were loyal to their core. These were those who had accidentally stumbled into their world over the years. At the time, he thought it prudent to not kill them, but offer them a job in their companies as long as they kept silent on the existence of werewolves, and if any ever wanted to join the clans, they would be allowed to do so. They were paid extremely well. Because of the fair and kindness of the werewolf community, not only did any human tell anyone about them, but a vast majority did decide to join them. There were also those who had spouses and children, but decided not to join. Then, again, there were others who found themselves mated to a werewolf, and while the established law pertained to those who found themselves in the presence of werewolves, if they found themselves mated to a werewolf, the mate was only allowed to turn his or her mate. He was very happy he had made that law, because he had found Kassie.

"OK, little man! You're ready!" Jimmy jumped down from the bed, and sped to open the door.

Jerking it open, he grabbed Kassie's hand, and tugged it to make her follow him. The three of them walked down the stairs together. Everyone else was already outside. Jakob and Jimmy both grabbed Kassie's hand, and pulled her with them into the kitchen, where Jimmy saw his Daddy outside grilling. He squealed, and dashed out the door to see if he could help, leaving Kassie alone with Jakob. Reaching for her hands, he pulled her toward him, their eyes locked. The shared tenderness with his nephew had weakened Kassie's heart, and she didn't resist him. She didn't want to resist. There was a definite magnetic draw from both of them, and they felt it. Kassie didn't understand it, but she wanted him to kiss her so badly, she could taste it! And, then, she wanted him to take her to his bed to make love to her! As if he knew what she was thinking, his mouth lowered to hers. Kassie closed her eyes as his mouth touched hers. His tongue licked her lips, and she opened her mouth to him. He plunged his tongue into hers, lightly licking the inside of her mouth. Her tongue met his, and they tangled together as they kissed.

"Well, well, well. I see Jakob's finally got a piece!" a sneering voice came from behind them.

Jakob growled as his lips left Kassie, and he growled, before he turned to face Venus.

Kassie was stunned to hear the pure, unadulterated hatred in the woman's voice, who stood behind Jakob. What had she done to her to make her hate her so much? If looks could kill, Kassie would already be dead, and buried six-feet under the ground! Jakob cleared his throat, before he made the introductions.

"Kassie, this is Venus Mars."

Kassie's eyes widened. *That* was Venus? She was so beautiful, she would rival the goddess for which she was named. The goddess of love. Tall, tanned skin, brown hair, long and sleek, she was tall. About five foot eight? Her dark brown eyes were blazing with hatred and malice. That place that goes six-feet under, or lower? That's where her heart sank. Not only did she not even acknowledge Kassie, but she actually growled at her, before she broke eye contact! What the hell was that all about?

"Venus," Jakob said.

"Yes, Alp.. uh.. Jakob?" she crooned with a syrupy grin to him.

"Don't you have somewhere else to be right now?"

"Why, Jakie! I'm supposed to be right here with you!" she gushed, reaching for his arm. Her eyes flinched, when she saw Jakob's eyes glow at her, and her arm jerked back as if she had been burned! She knew she'd pushed too hard. She reluctantly stopped, because she had too much to lose.

"Oh! You are right! I do. Devon is waiting for me!" she turned to Kassie. "Nice to meet you." Venus sneered.

"Yeah, sure you are," Kassie muttered.

Kassie was not a bit fooled by Venus's demeanor. That woman hated her guts. Why, she didn't know. She had known it when she first heard her talking to Jakob, when she was pretending to be unconscious. Well, Kassie wasn't going to let that bother her on her first time out in ages.

"Are you sure you don't want to go with her? I mean. It's OK with me," Kassie said with a low voice.

"No!" he startled her with his vehemence, and she jumped. "Sorry. Didn't mean to scare you. But, trust me. There is nothing at all anything between us. There never has been. It's important that you know this, Kassie."

Kassie believed him without a doubt hearing his tone. In fact, if she didn't know better, she could swear he hated Venus's guts! She was suddenly very happy about that, but she knew there was more. She didn't say anything. Just waited. If he wanted to say more, he would.

"Maybe, but she thinks there is, Jakob," she said, not really intending to say anything.

She slapped her hand over her mouth. Jakob only laughed.

"She is taken." Jakob told her, while Kassie wondered what that meant.

Kassie stared at him, waiting for an explanation, but Jakob said nothing at all. So, she shrugged, and filed it away for later.

"Come on. Let's go eat! I'm hungry. You?" he asked, ignoring what she had just said.

Kassie decided to err on the side of caution, and she nodded. She was really hungry - for real food! And, if she were honest with herself, she was hungry for something quite large, hard, and wet deep inside of her. She pushed that out of her mind, otherwise, she, too, would be wet all night from want and need.

Jakob led her out the door, and into the huge back yard. Tables were set up everywhere with traditional red gingham checked tablecloths, that were loaded with all kinds of condiments, chips, pork and beans, baked beans, green beans, and bean-beans. The tables were also stocked with salt and peppershakers, steak sauces, coleslaw, salad and several kinds of dressing. There were bowls everywhere, and some of the women were putting food into them. Kassie and Jakob grabbed their plates, and before they could move, Hunter plopped two thick, juicy steaks, some ribs, a couple of baked potatoes onto said plates, and while Jakob chose corn on the cob, Kassie grabbed grilled asparagus and the roasted vegetables that were in the foil Billie had prepared. Carrying their plates carefully, Kassie and Jakob sat down at a table with several other people, who were already digging into their food, and looked around. Kassie was surprised how many people were there. At their table sat two other couples. Jakob introduced them, and high-fived the men, only earning rolled eyes from the women!

"Kassie, this is Yvonne and her husband Michael Andrews."

Yvonne was a jovial, but a *very*, pregnant woman.

"Hi, Kassie! We've all been dying to meet you. I'm so sorry about your accident!" she drawled with a very heavy Texas accent.

"Thank you, Yvonne. It's nice to meet you."

"Howdy, there, young lady!" Michael said, standing and reaching across the table to shake her hand. His wife slapped his hand.

"Mind you manners, Michael!" she admonished.

He sat back and gave her a sheepish grin.

"I'm sorry about your accident, too," she laughed.

"Thanks. It's nice to meet you both, too."

"And, this," Jakob continued, indicating a couple sitting next to Kassie, "is Jane and her husband, Brian Rosen."

Nodding and shaking hands with them, Jakob and Kassie dove into their steaks. Her mouth watered at her first bite. She groaned as she chewed slowly, then washing it down with a sip of her large glass of beer. Did she even like beer? She took a second sip. Why, yes. She did.

"Hungry much?" Yvonne asked her, laughing.

Kassie took her napkin, and wiped her mouth, looking a bit sheepish.

"After having liquid and soft food for two months? You betcha!" Kassie took another bite, and then another, until she finished her plate long before anyone else.

"Oh. I'm so sorry. Where are *my* manners? But, it was just so darned good!"

Kassie was horribly ashamed of how fast she had eaten.

"Are you kidding? I love to see a woman who enjoys her meat!" Michael remarked. "I mean, I think Yvonne beat YOU in the eating contest!"

The entire table laughed at the women, while both Kassie and Yvonne glared at him.

"Yeah? Well, I'm eating for two, and Kassie hasn't eaten real food at all. So, there!"

She stuck out her tongue, and if Kassie's eyes weren't failing her, she saw Michael look at her tongue as if he wanted to eat it! Whoa! Apparently, being pregnant didn't cool his jets at all! Judging by the hunger in his eyes, she realized that it was the same look Hunter gave Billie every time he looked at her.

After a huge bowl of strawberry shortcake, Jakob introduced her to everyone else, as they went table to table. Everyone was so friendly, and they all seemed as if they really liked her. She was having such a great time! Welcoming the girl who almost died into their midst, was the best. Well, except for Venus. And, Kassie cared nothing about her anyway. She did notice, though, that she was alone at another table with four other men. She thought about that for a minute. Was Venus doing all of them?

Kassie was immediately ashamed of her thoughts. Thank goodness, no one could hear them!

"OK! Time for dancing, and singing!" yelled Hunter. "Grab your partner, and swing her around the floor!"

Both Hunter and Michael turned out to be the DJ's. Jakob grabbed Kassie's hand, and led her to the dance floor. Making sure she didn't get too tired, he only let them dance slowly locked in each other's arms. Her head tilted back, she looked up into his eyes. In that second, she saw the same desire and lust she'd seen in both Hunter's and Michael's eyes as they looked at their wives. She sucked in her breath, as she realized it was not in her imagination! His hand rested on her hip, and she didn't even think to move it. Kassie didn't want to, because she loved it there. And, she wanted the rest of him pressed against her – preferably with no clothing!

However, at this particular moment, Kassie felt as if she could stay in his arms, and dance all night…

…Except…

"Hey, Aunt Kassie! Can I'se haves a dance?"

Her head turned to Jakob, who just shrugged, and grinned.

"I'd be honored to dance with you, Jimmy!" and, she allowed him to lead her in a dance at which, surprisingly, he was very, very good!

~ 6 ~

Dreaming about something is wonderful; but doing it is unbelievably incredible!

"OK, gang," Michael yelled. "It's time for the dance contest! All the participants on the floor! The winner will receive an all-expense paid Hawaii vacation!"

Kassie's mouth dropped. Who in the hell gives out a Hawaii vacation for free at a dance contest?

"Walk with me?" he asked her, as the music started to blare in an all out dance contest.

"What? Don't you want to win that vacation?"

"Nope. Can't. I own the company, so I'm not eligible."

"Oh. That kinda sucks," she told him.

"Depends on the way you look at it. I can take us to Hawaii at any point in time. Some of our employees, though, have families, and although we pay them some of the top salaries and hourly wages in the United States, the truth is, it's still hard to save up a for a great vacation like Hawaii. So, once a year, we hold our retreat for a couple of months, and we arrange expensive surprise prizes throughout that time. You missed the hunt two weeks ago. The winner of that were Sam and Sarah Fanton and their family of six."

"Six? *Six kids*???" Kassie squeaked. There was no way she could even imagine having that many children!

"Yep. Our employees have a tendency to have larger families than most."

"OK. That sounded a bit condescending. I'm so sorry!" she explained.

"Don't be. It's the truth," he said, and suddenly she realized he was leading them away from the others.

"Walk with me?" he asked, once again.

She nodded, and he led them away from the others grabbing a couple of beers. She followed him into the wilderness without a word. For whatever reason, following him felt normal, but there seemed to be some butterflies in her stomach! He popped the tops of the beer bottles, and reached for her hand, while putting the tops in his jean pocket. They walked hand in hand for a long time, sipping their beers, but not saying a word. It was a good, companionable silence, and Kassie was happy. Even after a good five-mile trek, Kassie felt as fresh as ever. Kassie was puzzled why, as sick as she had been, shouldn't she be exhausted? It actually made no sense at the moment. Looking up, she realized where they were. She remembered that huge cactus that had a bloom on it the size of Texas on it. Jakob was taking her to his private pool. She shook as she remembered his naked body against her. It was different, now. This time she wasn't sick. And, she really, really wanted him. Her libido kicked into overdrive, and she couldn't stop it – even if she wanted to do so, which she didn't.

Once they arrived, they ducked under the arch that led to the pool. Pulling her along with him, he walked to a soft patch of grass, and sat down, pulling her down with him. She drew up her knees, and linked her hands over her knees.

"I wanted to get away from them." He turned to her. "No. That's a lie. I wanted to be alone with you, Kassie."

"I'm glad. So did I, Jakob," she said to him.

Her eyes looked up into his trustingly. His stomach clinched, and his blood rushed to his manhood.

He took her hands, and pulled her to him.

"Do you know what those tight little shorts, and your tight top are doing to me?" he groaned.

She grinned, and answered.

"Nope! Exactly what is it doing to you?"

What was wrong with her? She was flirting – with fire – and she liked it!

"You're going to make me say it, aren't you?" she smirked.

Jacob nodded in agreement, rolled his eyes, then jerked her onto his lap in a straddle, and brought her sex tight against his erection. He left her in no doubt about how he was feeling about her. She groaned when she felt it next to her. She couldn't help but wiggle against it.

"Kassie, I want you to know that I have had dreams about you being here with me. Having your naked body against me, when you were so sick, didn't stop my desire for you. Honestly, I should be ashamed of that, but I'm not. I told you, then, that I have no problem with nudity. That's kind of a lie. I have no problem with it, as long as it is with you. When I first saw your fragile body ravaged by whatever had happened to you, I thought that I would try to find the bastard, and kill whoever had done that to you. To have your body broken and bleeding like that devastated me." He shuddered, as he remembered how she looked. Her cuts were totally healed, now. And, they had healed extraordinarily fast according to Tyrone, but he didn't know why! He tightened his hold on her.

Kassie's face blushed, but she told him the truth.

"I wasn't totally out of it, Jakob, but I'm glad you found me. By the way? I think your body is gorgeous! Your naked body was the most incredible thing I had ever seen!"

He grinned, and pulled her tighter to him. Without beating around the bush, he declared, "I want you, Kassie. I've never wanted any other woman."

She frowned at him. How could that be?

"No. It's true," he told her, growling with a look that defied description. "When I saw you, I knew you were mine, and I was yours. You feel it, too, don't you."

It was a statement, not a question.

She nodded.

"Yes. I do." She looked up at him. "The truth is, though, that I don't understand what's happening, but I know that I am yours, and you are mine."

She wanted him so much, she was already wet for him. She silently apologized to Billie, because she knew Billie would see the stains on her panties and shorts. She had no idea that he could smell her arousal. With her scent permanently ensconced on his brain, he would always be able to find her, now. He hardened as his wolf felt his mate this close. His wolf needed his mate. Now.

"Will you let me make love to you, Kassie? Here? Now? This place is very special to me, and no other has ever been here with me."

Kassie shuddered in sheer excitement. Her eyes met his. He asked her, and didn't try to take it. Somewhere, in the back of her memory, she knew that another man had tried to take it, but that she had managed to get away. She was a bit nervous, because it would be her first time. Oh, great! She was a virgin! Great time to remember that, Kassie!

"I want you, too, Jakob," she said simply.

His arms came around her, pulling her to him. She felt his hardness – even through his tight jeans – against her opening, as he ground it against her. A huge burst of wetness flowed out of her sex, and he smelled her desire for him.

"I need to feel you against me, Kassie. I need to feel your naked body against mine."

"I need to feel you inside of me, Jakob…all of you," she said, feeling her anxiousness drop to be replaced by a deep fire igniting within her womb.

Without a word, Kassie stood, stepped back, and pulled the red top over her head, revealing her full breasts and hard nipples to his gaze. He'd already seen their hardness through her shirt all evening, and he had been dying to grab her breasts and fondle them. There was no reason to be shy since they had both seen each other before this. He did the same, and pulled his shirt over his head. It was one thing to strip her when she was unconscious, but now? His chest was muscled and strong. His abs tight. A dusting of hair adorned his chest, and a little bit dipped down below his jeans. She wanted to see where that hair went, and what it hid from her eyes. She watched him stare at her breasts. They were not just full, but swollen with nipples pointed and hard. His cock expanded as he looked at her. His wolf wanted to be inside his mate just as he did.

He pulled her down to him, and she straddled him, again, without stopping. She pushed her breasts against his bare chest tightly. He moaned as he felt her hard tips press against him. His mouth grabbed hers in a full on, sexy kiss.

Kassie could feel his hardness through their jeans, and felt him pressing against her sex. She had totally ruined Billie's jeans, because of the wetness that spread through the material, and even onto his jeans. She never knew she could even get that wet! Stranger things have happened.

Jakob couldn't wait any longer.

"I can't wait any longer."

She nodded.

"I need to feel you, too, Jakob. I want to feel your hardness against me…in me!"

She stood to unzip her jeans. Jakob kneeled to help her strip off her shorts right along with her panties in one motion. Then, while his eyes raked over her nude body, he also stood, and unzipped his jeans. And, again, in one movement, ripped them off along with his briefs.

Kassie sank back down to the soft grass, and slowly stretched, presenting herself to him as if she were on a platter, served up just for him to nibble. And, Jakob lay across her, plastering his naked body against his, and lowering his mouth to hers. Kassie moaned into his mouth as she opened hers. She arched her back, and of their own accord, her legs bent, as she let them fall wide. She so wanted him to suck her nipples, and in the next instant, his tongue had flicked out to lick first one hard bud, and then the other one. Gently, he licked and tickled her nipples with his mouth and tongue. She groaned loudly as he nipped the tip, hardening it further. She grabbed his head, and pushed her breasts even tighter to his mouth.

His hand slowly slipped down to her curls as he suckled.

"Kassie," he murmured.

His fingers were as gentle as a feather as he found her clit. It caused her back to arch more, her gasp was audible, and he felt her flowing wetness. He dipped into her liquid silk, and circled her clit with his fingers, causing her to thrust her hips upward for more.

"You are so wet!" he murmured, against her breasts.

"Wet for you, but are you hard for me?" she whispered against his lips.

"Why don't you find out?" he teased, nibbling on her lower lip.

Her hand slipped down, feeling the hair just below his waist. Kassie slid her fingers through the short hair, and traced it downward, where it curled around his hard shaft. She had already seen it up close. Had it dig into her thigh. Now, she wanted to feel it. Her hand slipped around him, and she squeezed it gently. Jakob growled.

"You are wet, too," she gasped, feeling the wetness flowing from his slit.

His cock jerked at her touch, causing him to suckle her nipples even harder, while he continued to circle her clit slowly. He flinched, again, when she gently circled his tip, spreading his liquid over it, and just up under the ridge. She used the lubrication to gently stroke under the ridge, sliding up to his slit to catch more fluid, only to stroke him again and again. He knew she could feel it move in her pussy with every touch.

"I won't take that movement any more, Kassie!" he cried, and quickly, sank two of his fingers inside her wet channel. Moving them individually within her, caused Kassie to arch, and cry out his name.

Kassie had never felt anything like this. But, she couldn't tell him, since her desire kept her from talking for the moment. She was truly glad she had saved herself for this man, as yet, another memory burst through her clouded, and hazed by lust, mind. She had to use what breath she did have to feel his hands against her body. But, she also knew that she wanted him inside of her. Now.

Jakob wanted her, now. His wolf wanted his mate, now. And, they would have her now. Jakob rolled over to grab his jeans, pulling out a condom. He'd made sure he had several of them, because he needed to make sure, he did not impregnate her, yet. All wolves impregnated their mates the first time, and as much as he wanted to feel her warm wet channel engulfing his cock, he knew he couldn't. He was too far gone to open his mouth to tell her who, and what, he was. His wolf growled at him. It did not want to use one. She was his mate. It desired to impregnate her, and it was not happy as Jakob rolled it onto his hardness. His eyes glanced at Kassie whose eyes were wide with surprise at his size, and fascinated by how he put the condom on his hard cock. He turned over, and before he could even climb onto her body to spread her legs with his, she stopped him from going further. She had to tell him, first. He deserved that much.

"Jakob, wait! I-I have to tell you…"

Jakob's heart almost stopped. What could be so bad, she had to stop him from taking her?

"What is it, Kassie?" his voice was raspy.

"I-I…Jakob, I'm a virgin," she admitted, quietly.

Both he and his wolf jerked, when she told him. She was a virgin? Really? She really *WAS* his? Theirs?

"I'm glad you told me, my love. I can go easy at first, so I don't hurt you. Are you still sure about this, Kassie?" he asked her carefully. If she told him no, now, it would kill him…kill both of them.

"Yes, Jakob! I'm more than sure!" she told him, and he released the breath he never knew he was holding in anticipation of a negative answer.

"I will be gentle with you. The first time may be a bit uncomfortable. I might have hurt you if you had not told me, and I would never want to do that. I don't want you to associate your first time with pain."

"And, you deserved to know."

She looked at his hardness. It hadn't softened at all. And, dammit, she didn't like seeing the condom on it! A vision suddenly appeared in her mind's eye – as if it were really happening. She was standing with his son – their son – in her arms receiving a kiss from Jakob, while his twin sister slept in her bed. She wanted a child. She wanted *his* children inside her. Should she be feeling this at all? And, the next question, why? No answer was forthcoming. While Kassie didn't know where this feeling was coming from, she actually didn't really care. Maybe seeing Yvonne's swollen belly, and her glowing face, had something to do with it? Without thinking, she reached over, and before he could stop her, she yanked it from his cock.

He jerked.

"Kassie! What the hell are you doing?"

"I want to feel your flesh inside me. I need *all* of your cock inside of me! We are meant to be together. I feel it in here."

Her hand went to her belly, indicating to him that she felt it in her womb. He followed her hand, and placed his over hers, his excitement growing that she wanted his skin inside of her, and not some piece of plastic between them.

"Kassie…are you sure about this?" he asked her, one more time, because there was no way he would ever be able to ask, again, before he impregnated her.

"More sure than anything I have ever known, Jakob," she whispered to him.

"You do know that it can only take one time, right?"

Yet, he still didn't tell her it would happen anyway, and that in just a few minutes, he would send both his and his wolf's seed into her womb.

She nodded.

"Of course I know it. Unless...unless you don't want to be inside me without a condom?"

Kassie said it so softly, he was not even sure she said it. He looked into her eyes to see she truly meant it. Without hesitation, showing her that he did want her, he rolled on top of her, spreading her legs with his.

"I want this. I want you more than I have ever wanted anything in my entire life. I want to feel you wrapped around my bare cock. I want to feel your skin gripping me tightly, until I come inside of you! I want to send my seed into your womb, Kassie!" He closed his eyes, holding back for just a few more seconds. He opened them, and looked at her, before he admitted, "When I saw you holding Jimmy, I also saw you holding our child in your arms."

She grinned at him shyly.

"Well, I saw a bit more than that," she groaned, when she felt his mouth open, and grab her nipple.

"What?" he asked her, as he suckled her nipple at the same time as he teased her core with his cock, rubbing it against her. She was so wet, he wondered if he could even keep from coming the minute he entered her channel.

Kassie gasped, as he slowly slipped inside her.

"What did you see, my love?" he asked her, again, slowly slipping even further into her welcoming depths.

"I saw our children, Jakob," she whispered against his lips. "Both of them. A girl and a boy. Do you want this, Jakob? Most men would not want a child at this point."

"Kassie!" he groaned. A boy and a girl? "Oh, yes! I want them, but with no one but you!"

"Jakob, I only want your children!" she cried, feeling his hardness stretch and fill her deeply.

Jakob growled loudly, and his mouth came down on hers in a desperate kiss, while he continued to sink inside her wet folds as deeply as he could get. When he met with a slight resistance, he stopped, his eyes widening in shock and surprise. His eyes met hers in question, and she just nodded her head. Jakob almost pulled out of her, but she stopped him by pushing downward on his hips.

"No! Don't stop, Jakob. I am yours. All yours. A little temporary pain is nothing after all I have been through. Please, take me now!"

He raised his head, seeing that her eyes were telling him the truth, and while watching her, he pushed through the barrier, keeping him from her womb. He stopped, again when he saw Kassie grin.

"Oh!" she gasped in ecstasy, as she realized. "No pain! There is no pain, Jakob! Take me!" she cried.

In one fast, and hard thrust, Jakob literally shoved himself all the way inside her warm and welcoming body. He grew bolder, moving inside her, working his way even deeper. His wolf's cock was harder and larger than the man's, and it grew bigger the deeper Jakob pushed. Suddenly, he felt their tip meet her cervix. Only a werewolf could enter his mate's womb, and he fought the urge to plunge past her cervix to bury their cocks into her. So, instead, he began to move inside her faster and harder as she cried out his name. She held onto his back, digging her glorious nails into it, while her legs wrapped around him, opening her up to him for easy access.

Kassie was gasping in need. Her need was becoming almost an obsession as Jakob pushed still deeper into her. She needed his seed. She desired it so badly, she couldn't hold it back from him.

"Jakob. Give me your seed!" she whispered into his ear.

Jakob's whole body jerked at her words, causing him to have a great need to release their seed into their mate. Werewolf anatomy allowed him to grow very large in order to penetrate her cervix, letting their cocks into Kassie's womb to coat it with their semen. So, the wolf and man could easily deposit their seed directly into her womb. This ensured that the female would become pregnant immediately. They also didn't need to wait for ovulation upon the first mating, and that just caused his balls to fill even more, as they slapped against Kassie's ass. Now, his control was completely lost, and he allowed his wolf's cock to take over. It grew at least three inches longer into her, pushing through her cervix ever deeper. Kassie had nothing to go by, but she knew that this was not normal, and shouldn't happen. His huge, thick cock move past her cervix with every thrust deeper. But, it didn't hurt at all. In fact, it felt right to her. Her cervix was actually stretching for him, allowing him to pass through it and to enter into her womb. She arched her back as much as she could begging him with his body for even more. As he moved outward, then back, it came into her womb even deeper. It wasn't hurting her at all, and she relished it! She realized that with each thrust, it passed her cervix, and she could feel the slight tightness both at her opening, and again, at her cervix! And, it gripped his cock tightly, squeezing it hard.

"Deeper!" she begged, then cried out in extreme pleasure.

"Damn! Your pussy is so tight, Kassie!"

Surprisingly, he didn't think he could get any deeper than her womb. But Jakob didn't stop, and gave her what she cried for, penetrating her body, driving their cocks through her cervix and into her womb over and over. His balls grew much larger than he would have thought. Every second he delayed his release, caused him to be in more pain with the desire to release his seed into his mate. And, then, her channel clamped down on him hard as she came, and with one mighty thrust, he shoved deep into her womb as deep as possible, flooding his mate with his seed.

"I'm coming, Kassie!"

His hardness flexed, and shot his hot semen spurted incredibly deep into his mate's womb, coating it thoroughly. He had a lot of it, and he didn't stop until he emptied all of it into her. It shot into her, until she had milked him dry, and he finally had nothing left.

Kassie arched upward trying to take him even deeper. Then, her walls tightened around him, and she felt one mighty thrust into her womb. Her cervix expanded, and squeezed him as well, until she felt him tickle the top of her womb, followed by something hot and wet. At the same time, she felt her ovary pinch, and Kassie knew an egg had been released. She continued to squeeze his cock, forcing his semen to coat the inside of her womb completely. She cried out when she actually felt her egg drop into her tube to start the journey to meet Jakob's sperm. She had never been happier. She was going to be pregnant!

Finally, they both collapsed holding each other tightly, but he found he could not leave her body. It's where he wanted to be. Where he was supposed to be.

"Kassie! Are you alright? I'm sorry if I hurt you," he gasped, trying to catch his breath.

Kassie's arms came around his neck, while her legs continued to wrap around his waist holding him inside of her.

"You didn't hurt me, Jakob."

After a few minutes, she finally said something that surprised him. Pushing his hair out of his face, she looked into his blue, glowing eyes, and her own widened. But, Kassie took the plunge anyway. "Look, I know something strange happened just now. I've been around all of you enough to know you are not what you seem to be. For one thing, your blue eyes are glowing! And, I'm pretty damn sure that it's not a normal thing."

His eye bugged out. They were?

"Huh?"

She nodded at him.

"Yeah. Look, Jakob. I don't know what you are, or what the others are. But, I sure as hell know one thing. A normal man could never have reached my womb with your cock, and there was no doubt that it was far bigger than any human male." He started to answer her, but she put a finger over his lips. "Shhh. Let me finish. I don't care what you are. I wanted this as much as you did. I don't know why this is all happening, but I know there is a reason. I could feel the heat of your semen, and I could also feel my body release an egg. That is just as strange to me, because I shouldn't feel it! But, does it really matter, Jakob? I want *you*. Forever."

He raised his head, and his eyes were stunned. She released an egg? What did it mean, and how could she possibly know? Humans never knew when they became pregnant until a few weeks after, while werewolf women knew immediately. At just this moment, though, he didn't care, and he was honestly thrilled that he didn't need to hide from her any longer. He let her see his eyes glow even a brighter blue, showing that both of them loved her.

Her own eyes widened, and she place her hands on either side of his face, her green eyes searching his glowing ones, and then, she smiled. Kassie began a slow grin as she realized what he was. He didn't need to tell her.

"You are truly my giant black wolf with the huge cock, aren't you?" she whispered to him, licking his lips. She grinned. "So, who did you have fun with that night?"

His wolf began to grow inside her, again, but not his human cock. It was all wolf! And, he let his wolf have his mate, even though she was human. If she wanted, and knew what he was, there was no point in holding his wolf back. He decided to explain it to her as he began to move gently inside of her a second time.

"First, the only reason I was big that night, was because of you. My wolf's cock grew instantaneously, when we saw you. We knew that you were our mate."

"Mate? You mean like married?" she asked in shock.

"No. I mean mate. It is far more binding than human marriage, although we do marry to blend into the human world. It makes things a lot easier."

"Oh," she said. "So, we are mated?"

Dang! Just that word conjured up all kinds of sexy, naughty things, all over, again! But, would he want to marry her?

"Not quite yet. There's a whole other ritual for that, and we will. And, make no mistake, Kassie. We will also marry. You are my mate. And, once the bond through blood is completed, then we are bound together for eternity."

"Oh," she said again, and pushed against his pelvis. "So, what does that mean? Till death do us part?"

"Hardy!" he laughed. "No…I mean, quite literally, eternity. We have an extremely long lifespan, Kassie, and once the mate ritual is completed by blood, well, you'll live with me as long as I do. That is a 'perk', I guess you could say, and even applies to a human mated to a werewolf."

OK. That she wasn't prepared for, and how…. Her eyes bugged out.

"How long?" she asked in a little voice. "I-I mean, how old are you?"

"Why Kassie! It's not nice to ask someone how old they are!" he smirked behind a laugh. She whacked him on the arm.

"That's women, dunce! Now, come on! If I'm to mate you, and marry you, the least you can do is tell me how old you are!"

When he told her, Kassie's eyes bugged out, and she fell backwards, catching herself on her forearms.

"I am almost eight hundred years old," he said, tapping his chin as if he were contemplating something.

"You said what?" she squeaked.

"Well, of course I'm not!" he grinned wickedly.

"Oh! You were just teasing me! I mean, that's just ridiculous! Now, stop it, and tell me the truth!" she demanded.

"I guess, technically, I was actually born in Europe in the year 1063. So, that makes me about 954 years old." He scratched his head completely oblivious that Kassie had started to hyperventilate. "Well, that is if it is really the year. Mom and Dad said that was my birthday, so I guess they would know. To tell you the truth? I honestly never really thought about it since we only celebrate the day of birth, and not the year."

Kassie kept shaking her head in disbelief, while watching Jakob bite his lower lip in concentration. Finally, he looked over at her, realizing she wasn't breathing, and grabbed her.

"Kassie! Come on, Baby! Breathe!" he kept saying. Finally, Kassie gulped a deep breath, while staring at him.

"No! How is that possible?"

"Kassie, surely you know that the world of the paranormal is different than the human world. You also have to remember that long ago, even mankind lived much longer than they do today. Look at Methuselah, and no one thinks a thing about his age, right."

Well, damn! He was right! She nodded her head.

"Ok, good. And, remember, after the Great Flood, it was deemed that mankind had not earned long lives any longer, so the final tally of mankind would be 120 years."

"Hey! I remember that! But, we haven't reached that yet."

"Yes, that's true. But, humans are now, actually living even longer with each passing year. Some have made it to 107, now. It's actually just over the horizon till they reach that magical number of 120."

That made her think of something else.

"Uh…about that. Your Mom and Dad?" she asked hesitantly. Were they even still alive? She didn't have to wait long.

"Oh, yeah. My parents are living in Italy, but are taking the corporate jet to America, after I contacted them yesterday." He waggled his eyebrows at her shocked face. "I told them that I had found my mate. My Mom is jumping with joy, and can't wait to meet you."

Oh, great! Not only did she have to deal with the fact she was pregnant, but the father was a werewolf, who was eight hundred years old, and his parents were still alive, and coming to meet her!

Kassie started to hyperventilate – again. Jakob grinned, and gently stroked his knuckles over her cheeks.

"Don't panic, Kassie. By the time they are here, our mating will be completed. We can mate with a human. Our anatomy allows the combining of my wolf and my human cock, letting it grow longer, and harder than a human male. When our release comes into our mates, it will grow larger, Kassie. It lets us extend deep inside the female. Our females do not have a cervix. I'm not sure why, or how, I am able to move through yours. But, a mating between a human and a werewolf hasn't happened in hundreds of years. The process isn't completely understood. I'd tell you if I knew."

Kassie groaned, feeling his cock grow hard and large. She needed him deeper, again. Just feeling it grow larger and larger gave her an excitement she never knew she could have.

"We are also able to penetrate to the female's womb, as you already know. It's how we procreate, Kassie," he told her.

"And, exactly why do you feel bigger than before right now?" she gasped, lust rising heavily within her body. In fact, it was really a strange feeling. More than lust. It was almost an indecent feeling within her, but she grabbed onto it, because it felt so right. He was half man, half wolf with cocks for both. What did that make her? A freak who liked bestial? Ok, she was soooo not going there! That wasn't quite true, because he had not taken her in his wolf form, so technically, that was not true. She heaved a huge sigh of relief with that realization. The other was just way too gross to contemplate.

For a moment, Jakob was a bit surprised as he felt himself trying to transform. It took all his effort to keep from doing so, but then, he realized that his cock was not combining with his wolf, and that was something he didn't expect at all! This time, it was his wolf's cock, using him to drive into her deeper and deeper. How in the world could his wolf be fucking his mate without him? He remembered what she had said about his cock that night when she was about to die. Usually, the couple transformed into their wolves, and mated in that way as well, but with Kassie, he couldn't do it. So, what? Was his wolf taking over, as if she were a wolf, so that he could mate with her in some kind of weird wolf form? It was the only explanation. But, he didn't know it could be done!

"I'm not really sure," he panted. "It's my wolf, not me."

Her eyes shot to his in surprise.

"Wait!" Not missing a beat as she met his thrusts, she continued. "Are you saying I'm being fucked by a wolf?"

Jakob cried out as he penetrated her cervix, and he felt the top of his wolf's cock hit the top of her womb.

"Yes!" he growled. "My wolf is fucking you! We transform after the first mating into our wolves to mate with our females, but you are human! He's using me to fuck you all by himself!"

"Somehow that just sounds so…OH!" Kassie screamed, as she felt his wolf's cock hit the top of her womb. "Fuck me, Jakob! It's OK! Let your wolf fuck me! I need him just as much as I need you!"

"You really don't mind my wolf taking you?" he asked, a bit surprised.

"No! It's part of you, right?"

He nodded his head, feeling his wolf take complete control over his body.

"Then, I told you! I want all of you! And, if that means your wolf – and I remember how big that gorgeous cock was when you were a wolf – then, yes! I want it! I want him! I want you! I want both of you! Let you both take me however you want!" she cried.

Jakob tried to continue.

"I-it doesn't usually happen like this until the blood-bond. My wolf is taking me over, Kassie! I can't stop him!"

She stroked his face with her fingers.

"Then, don't let him. I want both of you deep in me. Please, Jakob? I told you. I want *all* of you inside me."

Jakob saw her eyes were not lying, and he finally let his wolf take him over completely. Blue eyes glowed into hers as his wolf pushed deep within her womb. The force of his wolf was unbelievable! And, yet, it didn't seem to hurt Kassie! As big as his wolf was, and it didn't hurt her? How was that even possible? Suddenly, his transformation stalled, and held.

Kassie bore down upon his wolf, and her walls tightened so hard, his wolf gave a final thrust shoved himself up into her womb, releasing his wolf's seed into her. That's when she felt another egg release, shocking her. Then she smiled. No. Their children. She would have twins. She knew it. How? She had no idea. She just knew. It warmed her like nothing else ever had. Holding her mate's wolf inside her body, while their children were formed was the epitome of the love she felt for him.

"I love you, Jakob. With every part of me."

"I hardly felt going through your cervix that time."

"I know. Me, too. Oh, and by the way? I felt another egg release. And, your children are growing inside of me," she whispered into his ear.

Suddenly, Kassie rolled him over, using an amazing strength that surprised him! And, she still held him tightly inside of her. This time she rode him like a pro – hard and fast, but the wolf did not extend into her womb this time. This time, it was her mate that thrust into her body.

They spent the night making love over and over, stopping to swim in the pool, only to make love in it as well.

The morning came, and the sun found two naked bodies lying together asleep next to the pool entwined in one another's arms. Satiated, and content, they woke up, and lazily stroked each other only to end in one final loving act before they had to go back. But, before they did, she had one final question.

"Now. Tell me about this blood bond."

~ 7 ~

**It's a bad thing when you do not remember the
past, because inevitably, it will be repeated.**

Tyrone rolled his eyes, and wondered why it was
that people had the worst possible timing! A call
always came during his class, while driving, while
transforming into a wolf, in the bathroom, or even
during sex! He looked at the caller, and excused
himself to answer it. He had to answer, because it was
from George Mason, and there was no way he could
miss this call. It had been almost two weeks, since he
had left Kassie's blood with him testing. He had also
kept in touch with Jakob, while he waited for
George's call, making sure Kassie was doing
OK. He'd meant to return a week ago, but got bogged
down teaching another class due to the professor who
usually taught it, came down with the flu.

Jakob also had told him that Kassie and he had sex,
and how his wolf had taken over, moving into her
womb. When he told him that she had also felt two
egg releases, Tyrone almost choked with shock and
surprise. She should never have been able to feel an
egg release. Of course, while human females could
not feel their eggs, werewolf females could. Tyrone
was concerned about this. This should never happen
with a human, let alone make a human female
pregnant! It was truly a new one for the record
books! Until he knew more, there was no answer for
any of them.

He flipped open his cell phone. He didn't need a
smart phone. They were just too damned complicated
for him!

"Hey, George. What's the word?"

Tyrone listened intently. As usual, George came
through for him, and always went beyond. He

frowned with every word he heard. George had more than one thing. The first thing only confirmed his suspicions. But, the second part had him raising himself up fast.

"Are you sure?"

"Yes. I found at least three instances of a human werewolf couplings."

"And?"

"Have they completed the blood-bond, yet?"

The last time he had spoken with Jakob, which was the night before, he had said that he planned on completing their bond as soon as possible, but Tyrone decided to veto the bond, until they heard from George, first. Jakob hadn't been happy about it, but he acquiesced.

"No. Jakob is waiting to hear from me."

"Crap! Tyrone, it's *imperative* that they complete it immediately, Tyrone. In all three cases, they each had sex, and each became pregnant. However, one couple did not complete the blood-bond, and she and her child died."

"Oh, shit! How long?"

"From what I read, it must be done within fifteen days after they first had intercourse. How long has it been, now?"

"It will be fifteen days…oh, my God! That's today! I have to call Jakob, now!"

"Call me back when it is done. I will need another blood test afterward."

He slammed his phone closed, opened it again, and dialed Jakob's phone.

Jakob had moved Kassie into his home, and his bed. Their lovemaking was almost constant, now, but his wolf did not attempt to move into her womb any more. That could only mean that Kassie was, indeed, pregnant. It was the werewolf way. Except, she was not a werewolf. But, regardless, human or were, once a female was pregnant, neither he nor his wolf could penetrate her womb. It was essentially closed to them. He and Kassie had been insatiable for each other, and sex was almost constant. Just being away from her for the shortest time caused him to have a raging hard-on! Pregnant werewolves' libidos were in total overdrive, and the men were always ready to give their mates what they wanted! He grinned wickedly at what he would do to her when she came back.

Jakob sighed as he watched out the kitchen window for her to return. Kassie and Billie had gone to pick up a pregnancy test – at Kassie's insistence. Kassie had been nervous, but, he said that she knew beyond a doubt, that she was pregnant with their children. Yet, she still wanted confirmation of it, since she was human. And, who knew…it might not really have happened. He was eager to complete their bond, but had talked to Tyrone, yesterday, who told him not to do so. He had heard nothing from George, and Tyrone had yet to call him with any information today. He placed his coffee cup onto the cabinet. He and Kassie had been insatiable for each other over the past few days. He reached down to adjust himself in his jeans as he was sporting a hard-on, again! It was already getting dark, and they were not back yet. That really didn't bother him, because his mate spread her legs for him repeatedly.

A bottle of beer in hand, he heard his phone ring. Placing the bottle on the cabinet, Jakob slid the slider to answer.

"Tyrone?"

"Jakob. How long has it been since you two had sex the first time?"

"Fifteen days ago. Why?" How could he forget his first time with Kassie? It was a fantasy come true for both of them that resulted in her becoming pregnant.

"That's what I thought! Oh, Creator!" Tyrone yelled.

"What? What is it?" Jakob demanded, suddenly terrified by the tone of Tyrone's voice.

"You MUST complete the blood-bond by tonight. If you don't, Kassie *will* die! George just told me he had found only three other instances of human and werewolf matings in the written records. For the two couples who blood-bonded within a fifteen day period, the human female mate lived, and so did their children." He heard Jakob gasp. He continued. "Jakob…with the couple who did not bond within that time period…well…the human and child died."

"Do you think that is a normal thing?" Jakob asked.

"I honestly don't know. It's possible, but we have nothing to go by. But, I wouldn't want to risk the chance."

"Thanks. I'll get back to you!"

He pressed the end button, and glanced at the clock. They weren't back yet, and he found himself shaking in real fear. He called Kassie.

"Hi, Jakob! What's up?" she answered, snickering at her own joke.

"How long before you get home?"

Kassie heard terror in his voice.

"What? Anxious to see me?" she asked hesitatingly.

"Well, yeah, but…"

"Look out the window. We're driving up to the house right now." When she didn't hear Jakob's banter, she felt a knot in her stomach, that had nothing to do with her pregnancy. "W-what's wrong, Jakob?"

Jakob saw them turn into the drive. It was dark, but he could see just as well as if it were light. Billie had to get one of their cars, since Kassie was human, so they could go into town. He breathed a small sigh of relief, then bounded out the door, and to the car yanking the door open, pulling Kassie out of it. He glanced at his watch. Damn! To do the bond right took more time than they had!

"What the hell is wrong?" she asked, her voice muffled against his shoulder.

"Jakob?" asked Billie. "What's wrong."

"Kassie. We must blood-bond, now, " he said without looking at Billie.

Billie eyes went wide. She knew her brother's face, and she had never seen him scared like he was right now.

"Blood-bond? Now? Why?" Kassie asked.

Jakob and Billie looked at each other. Billie's grew larger.

"Go home, Billie."

For a split second, Billie looked as if she would argue, but with one look from Jakob, she kissed Kassie's cheek, muttered something about "damn male wolves", and then got back into her car, speeding away.

"Let me know what's going on, Kassie?" she shouted at her, before she left.

Kassie just nodded. She knew Jakob was terrified about something. It had to do with something about her. Whatever this blood-bond thing was, it was serious.

Jakob took her into the house, got her a cup of tea, and kneeled at her feet.

"Kassie. There's no easy way for me to say this. If we do not blood-bond before midnight tonight, you and our children will die."

His tone was flat. His eyes pleading.

"I-I don't understand?"

"Tyrone just called me. I told him that we had sex, and that my wolf took over. I also told him that you are pregnant. His friend, George, who is a specialist in werewolf DNA, discovered that the only, known humans who mated with a werewolf, were three. He told me that the bond must be completed within fifteen days after their first sexual encounter. If he is right, we are the fourth."

Kassie sucked in her breath. Her hands flew to her belly, as if to protect her children.

"Tell me!" she demanded.

"Two bonded within fifteen days, and the human females and children lived; the one who did not? That female and child, died."

"So, if we don't blood-bond, we'll die?" she asked, her voice shaking.

She could feel her mate's tension and terror. He took a deep breath.

"Yes. At least that is what George told Tyrone."

"Oh, God! No!"

"Please, Kassie! I know you wanted to give us more time, but that's no longer an option! It's our form of marriage, Kassie."

Marriage? He wanted to marry her?

Kassie had already shown how strong she was, but she refused to let death take her and their children! She would gladly let him turn her to a werewolf, if it could be done, before she would let her children die! She turned to him, and he stood. He gathered her to him. He couldn't lose her. Lose their children. He would have turned her before they had mated. But, he couldn't, now. It was far too dangerous. She could not be pregnant during a turn.

She raised her head, her eyes bright with terror, and tears. She nodded.

Jakob breathed a sigh of relief. He had already told her about it, and she had been stunned. He didn't mention it, again, because of her reaction. He had no plans to do so until, and unless she brought it up later.

"Remind me? H-how does the blood-bond work?" Then, she realized something! "You said FIFTEEN DAYS AFTER? That's today!!!"

He nodded his head.

"We have to do it now, Kassie. I have to ask you first, though."

He dropped to his knees, and took her hand. Then, looked into her eyes.

"Kasseiopia, will you be my mate? Will you blood-bond with me?" he held his breath.

Kassie had no hesitation. She dropped to her knees, and took his face into her hands.

"Yes. I love you, Jakob. I want to be yours forever, whatever that means in your customs."

He pulled out a box. She gasped as he opened it. The ring was beautiful. Very, very old. Instead of a diamond, and old, fully faceted, six-carat emerald ring, and set in a beautiful basket designed gold band, had two rows of five diamonds sat on either side of it. It was the most beautiful thing she had ever seen.

"This was my great-grandmother's ring. My Mother gave it to me for my mate. Like she did, you will wear it, until you pass it to our son for his mate."

"Yes. I will, my love. Oh, Jakob! I'm so honored, and it's so beautiful!"

After he placed it on her finger, and surprisingly, it actually fit, Then, "Tell me again how it works?"

He was afraid again. Afraid it would scare her, because it involved blood letting.

"Tell me, Jakob. I will do anything to make sure that our babies stay alive! Anything! Just tell me how it works. But, before you do, I want to make sure I am pregnant."

She shook the box in front of him. He knew she wanted to use the test, but she'd rushed out too fast, before he could tell her. In the back of his mind, he did wonder why Billie hadn't said anything. Maybe she wasn't sure how much Kassie really knew. Instead, he leaned his head forward to put his ear to her belly. Jakob heard two strong heartbeats, and his eyes closed, tears running down his cheeks! She truly was carrying his children. He took the box with the pregnancy test from her.

"You don't need that, Kassie. Werewolf hearing is acute to the point of super hearing."

He looked at her.

"I hear two, healthy, and strong heartbeats."

She sucked her breath in when she heard him say that. He could hear their children's hearts beating? Her hand went to her belly, and his head rested on her hands. Tears streaked down her cheeks.

"OK. Let's get this thing done. I will not let our babies die, Jakob. Not because we were so stupid."

"It's so rare, George must have found it in some obscure werewolf library or database. I can't live without you. Without our children. I love you."

"Then, yes, Jakob. My mate. I will blood-bond with you."

He felt completely relieved over that. Now, explanations.

He sat down next to her on their sofa. Everything he had was hers, now, too.

"OK. It works like this. There is a provision for two species who want to blood-bond, but it's never really been used in current times."

Kassie just nodded.

"First, it takes place naked," he grinned, and waggled his eyebrows at her.

Kassie rolled her eyes at him. Typical of a guy! And, especially, *her* guy – uh – werewolf. How weird was that to say the word? Sometimes, she just couldn't believe the supernatural world truly existed!

"Well, that's obviously not a problem, since we spend our time together naked anyway!" she smirked.

He grinned back at her.

"Well, that's true! Next, the couple says their vows to each other. This is usually short, because by this time, the desire for each other is growing quickly. It's something peculiar to our species. But, the mate will feel it as well."

Come on! What kind of problem was that, and nope. She was always ready for him...just like she was right now! She couldn't imagine it being any stronger than the urge to get pregnant. As if Jakob read Kassie's mind, he continued.

"If you're wondering, this desire is far different than any other desire we will ever feel. It's a one-time thing, Kassie. And, the female always goes first."

She took a deep breath, but still didn't say anything.

"Next, if the mate is of another species...," he began.

"Wait just a minute! A*nother* species? Just how many 'other species' are there?" she demanded to know.

Jakob tilted his head in a very wolf-like way.

"Really? You want to waste time finding out that there are other species?" he asked her.

"Right. Never mind," she said, waving him on to speak. "We can do that later."

Jakob quirked his eyebrow upward, then continued his description.

"OK.   There is a special knife used on the werewolf's neck, so the human mate can take their blood."

He waited to see her face. She looked surprised, but not grossed out – at least, not yet.

"So, someone in the past actually made allowance for humans…I mean…other species?"

"Yes, they did. Now, shut it, mate!" he said, only to grin, his canines lengthening.

Kassie smirked back at him.

"You will take about an ounce of my blood. Third, the physical bonding of blood must take place during sex. This desire is inescapable, and will be fast, hard, furious, and you will receive semen to the point it will flood out of you, even as I continue to give it to you. Typically, this is when the mate become pregnant, but for some reason, we have seemed to bypass that particular action, and no one seems to know why. You do not have to worry about penetration to the womb. Your body has locked us out of it, because you are already pregnant. This is normal. When our climax is reached, at the moment of ejaculation, I will bite your neck. Afterward, I must drink from your pussy, until I have emptied you of all excess semen. Once that is done, the blood-bond is completed. You will feel the bond instantly, as will I. Our thoughts will become one, our bodies become one, and our souls are bonded together as one. Afterward, we cannot live without the other at this point. When one dies, the other dies. It's that strong. Far stronger than human marriage."

Kassie took everything he had said into her mind. Jakob let her think about it for a minute.

"Did you just seriously say 'pussy'?" she laughed at him. He grinned back at her.

"After everything you have learned, and just heard, all you get from that is 'pussy'?" he laughed at her.

"Well, when you throw in a sexy word here and there, how in the world do you expect me to focus?" she giggled, then turned serious. "Jakob. I love you. I want you. Only. Forever. I want to give you two healthy children. Yes. I will blood-bond with you."

He relaxed. But, then, Kassie asked the inevitable question.

"Why can't you just turn me?"

"With you pregnant, mate, it would be far too dangerous. Honestly, I don't know what would happen if you turned with our babies inside of you, but we dare not take that chance."

"After I have them, then?" she asked him.

He pulled her to him, stroking her hair.

"If you truly wish to become a part of this clan, and wish to be turned, then yes. I will turn you."

She held his face in her hands.

"I will not change my mind, Jakob. No matter what happens, I want to be like you and Billie, and the others. I want to be a part of your world."

"Then, it shall be as you wish, my love. Now, I will need to prepare our bedroom for the bonding. And, you must bathe. Not shower. Bathe. All scent must be erased from your body, because once we blood-bond, we will have our scent on each other forever. Once you are done, do not dry yourself, and there are two robes that are hanging in the bathroom. Put one of these on, and then I, too, will bathe. Put no deodorant on, or anything else. When, I am finished bathing, we will complete the blood bonding. Then, please, go downstairs. We will share a light meal."

She nodded, and he patted her butt as she went to bathe. She did exactly what he told her. They didn't have time for mistakes. She got out of the tub, and dripping wet, put on the robe, and proceeded down the stairs.

Fifteen minutes later, Jakob came to her dressed in the identical robe. He held his hand to her, and led her into the kitchen. There they shared a glass of wine, some cheese and fruit, and finally, he held her hand to lead her upstairs to their bedroom, where they would share just one of many places for many hundreds of years of bliss.

It was night, and about ten o'clock. Two hours. She didn't know how long this bonding thing would take. The bedroom was full of lit candles, casting a beautiful glow around the room. On the nightstand sat a bowl full of hot, steamy water, a mirror, and an ornate knife.

"I had to get the knife from our pastor. He is the only one allowed to hold it. You will meet him soon, since he will perform our human marriage ceremony."

He led her to the bed, and turned her toward him. His mouth gently took hers in a kiss so tender, she felt tears run down her cheeks. Then, they sat down on the bed, side by side.

Jakob took the mirror, and gave it to Kassie.

"Please hold the mirror, so I can make the incision in the correct place."

Her hand shook, holding it for him. She licked her lips as she watched him cut the skin on his neck – for her! Jakob took the knife, and made a small, half-inch slit, allowing his blood slowly drip onto the neck of his robe. He put the knife back on the stand, and stood. With that blood, he felt his cock go completely rigid and full mast in a matter of seconds.

"I claim you as my mate Kassie. I love you. You are my mate, my life, and my love. The one I choose to be with me forever. Will you accept me as your mate?"

Shivering with desire, Kassie answered him.

"Yes, Jakob I take you as my mate forever."

With those words, Kassie felt liquid flood from her sex, and onto the robe. So much, it almost had her gasping in shock at the feel of it!

He undid the tie belt of his robe, and shrugged it off. A small amount of blood remained on it, and he lay down on the fresh clean sheets. He pulled her down with him, and put her mouth to his, taking his mating kiss. Then, he turned his neck to her for her to drink.

"Drink from me, Kassie," he commanded softly.

Shaking, Kassie lowered her mouth to his neck feeling a bit nervous, but determined. Her mouth opened, and she placed it gently over the small incision to take his blood into her mouth. She was startled when she tasted not the iron taste normally found with blood, and what she had actually been expecting, but it was sweet like cinnamon and sugar. Oh, God! He was delicious! She drank about an ounce as he had told her, and swallowed. She felt an increased warmth spread throughout her body, and especially at her sex, where she suddenly flooded with more wetness than she had ever thought could happen. More flowed out of her to join her already wet robe, and she couldn't stop it. She didn't want it to stop. His manhood, already huge, shot up quickly as she had suckled his neck. Then, she knew it was her turn.

"I claim you as my mate Kassie. I love you. You are my mate, my life, and my love. The one I choose to be with me forever. Will you accept me as your mate?"

.0"Yes, Kassie. I take you as my mate forever."

His words caused her sex to flow, as if someone had turned a faucet on high. In fact, she felt as if a wave of water flowed over her body!

She undid the tie belt of her robe, as he had done, and shrugged it off. He pulled her on top of him, and gave her a kiss, that acted like a drug to her trembling body.

"You feel the desire, don't you?" he whispered. "I can smell your arousal."

"Yes? Well, I can feel yours next to me. How is this possible? I've never been so wet."

"And, you never will be, again. Just as I will never be this big, nor have this much semen within me. Are you ready to finish the blood-bond?"

He looked at the clock. It had taken thirty minutes for the small ceremony. That shocked him. It had passed so quickly.

Kassie knew, somehow, what to do from here, and she rolled off him onto her back.

"Come to me, my love. Slide between my legs, and take me as your mate."

Jakob loomed over her like a dark, guardian angel, and slowly pushed himself inside of her. He sighed with a true, werewolf groan as he entered her. That sound cut to Kassie's core, and a real desire to become what he was – as if she had always known, she should be a part of this group of people who were more than people. Kassie shook with a desire she had never felt, and thought it would devastate her for life, it was so intensely beautiful.

Jakob felt the strong, mating bond as he moved inside of Kassie. She was the epitome of everything he had ever hoped and dreamed that he would one day have. This moment, this act, was worth waiting for all of his hundreds of years! He had never felt such happiness, nor had his wolf. The two of them came together to take their mate's love and body in a dance of desire, that they would always, and forever, remember! Wetness flooded the sheets as he moved inside her fast and furious. He had never thought the experience of the blood-bond would be like this. His release was coming faster than he had expected, because his balls were full. So full, he knew it would flow out of her for quite some time. He felt it coming, and Kassie felt herself ready for the orgasm of her life.

"Are you ready for me?" he gasped.

"Yes. I am."

"Turn your neck to me."

She did as he asked, turning her head to the right, and exposing her neck to him. She quivered with ecstasy to finish their bond. And, then, she knew he was coming into her, and her orgasm released at the exact time he released his semen into her. His fangs extended, while lowering his head to her neck. The moment his ejaculation came, he sank his fangs into her neck, drinking her blood, and swallowing as he pushed into her over and over, flooding her beautiful body. When he was empty, he withdrew his fangs from her neck, and swallowed what was left in his mouth. The tiny wounds left behind, marked her as his, and would be the only marks remaining, showing all that she was his – forever.

The bed was soaked, but they didn't seem to care. They relished in their mating, and the bond that they both felt. The clock's brilliant glow showed that it was only 11:30 pm. They both looked over in surprise.

"It took THAT long?" she asked, grinning. "You think we bonded in time?"

"It's before midnight."

"Yeah, but where were the others? Does time zone matter?'

All he could do was laugh at her.

"Don't go making trouble where there is none. I'm guessing it is all relative to wherever one is!"

"Relative? Oh, that's a really good one, Jakob!" she laughed.

"Guess it is!" His lips captured hers. "I love you, Kassie. Now, I must drink from you."

They wrapped their arms around each other in a passionate kiss and embrace, before he removed himself from her body. Quickly, he raised her legs, and spread them. He watched his semen flood from her body, and lowered his head to her opening. His mouth closed over it, and Kassie heard him drinking from her. This process made her wetter than ever before, and he drank her juices, along with his as they flowed from her. Her hips arched upward, letting his mouth suck on her easier.

"Oh, Jakob! You didn't tell me what this would do to me! It's so…so…"

"Sexy?" he murmured in between swallows.

"Jakob? Share with me?"

Jakob started. It had never even occurred to him to ask her.

"You're still flooding with my semen, Kassie!"

"Let it flood onto our bed. Please? I need to drink with you!" she cried.

He abandoned her beautiful pussy, and slid upward to take her mouth with his. He opened it, and let the juices flow from his mouth into hers!

"Oh, Kassie!" he panted. "I never knew it would feel like this, either!"

"We taste so good together, Jakob!"

He nodded to her.

"Do you mind sleeping in our love, Kassie? Because, I have a sudden urge to spread it all over this bed, and fall to sleep in it!"

She sat up, and his semen flowed heavily from her.

"Yes. Jakob. If you really, really want to, we can wet the bed down with more!"

He immediately slammed into her body with his rigid, thick cock. His balls filled him immediately. Sleeping in their liquid was the sexiest thing he ever had heard!

He pounded into her hard, fast, and released a flood of semen into her, once more.

Once he flooded into her, he slipped out, and he took his hand, cupped it, gathered their juices as it flooded out of her, and spread it all over the bed, until it lessened.

He pulled her to him as they lay on the soaking wet, cool sheets.

"Now, we sleep, Kassie, wrapped in our love."

The bond was complete, and he was never so happy – sleepy, but happy.

She sighed with total contentment, and was suddenly, very sleepy.

He pulled his sleeping mate into his stomach, as they both collapsed in total exhaustion. He was so glad that his mate and children would be with him, now. He yawned, and then, he, too, slept soundly – for the first time in centuries.

A ringing kept bugging Jakob. He finally cursed, when he realized he had left his cell phone across the room. First, checking to see if Kassie was alright, and was still sound asleep. When he got out of bed, she made a very low moan with disappointment.

"What???" he answered impatiently.

It had better be a damn good reason to tear him away from his newly bonded mate!

"It's Tyrone, Jakob. Did you blood-bond?" He asked, sounding desperate.

He rubbed his head. He was still exhausted from it. "Yes. We did."

He heard a relieved sigh at the other end.

"Good. Look, I know that you are totaled out, now, but I'm on my way back. I need to see both of you in my office, so I can check her out."

"Sure. OK. But, not today," Jakob said, yawning.

Tyrone grinned.

"I understand. Tomorrow then."

Jakob hung up the phone, and crawled back into bed with his sleeping mate. Kassie groaned, and moved to push against him. She wanted Jakob badly. How could she need him again this fast? Regardless, she pressed her hips against him as he spooned next to her back. He was huge, and even though he was as tired as she, he sleepily slid into her body once more, moving gently, slowly, until he came inside his mate once again, before both of them fell asleep, immediately.

"What do you mean, You tried your best? You *tried your best*? She was supposed to die the FIRST time, when you beat her to a pulp, then pushed her off the bluff!" the man demanded of his companion.

"I know she was supposed to die! How did I know she could survive that fall? No one – no human – could survive that fall!"

"Look. I need her money! And, so do you! That's the reason for all of this shit! I will hold you to your promise, as well."

"HA! That promise has already gone by the wayside. Never going to happen as long as I draw breath!"

He grabbed her hair, pulling her neck back.

"Listen to me, bitch! You will kill her! I want proof!" he growled. Then, changed his mind. "No! Wait! I want to be there, when you kill her! The only way I can be there, means that you will do exactly what you promised, and you will do it, *now*."

His voice was quiet, now. He was never more deadly than when he was quiet, and he needed her to understand it.

"Now, bitch! You will do what I say, or *I will* kill you. You know I will, and you know that I can. I killed her parents and her grandparents. We are just lucky she hasn't remembered anything yet!

"The doctor doesn't think she will remember. That part of her brain was damaged!" she cried, her head yanked back by her hair.

"And, you want to leave that up to chance? Are you insane? We cannot take the risk! She has to die, and I *will* be there to see it. She just won't know it's me! I'll be in wolf form! I am your mate! Now, do it!"

Part of her was turned on with his bruising actions, but the other part of her hated him with a passion. She also wondered what Kassie had ever seen in him. Regardless, though, it was true. He was her mate. He jerked her hair, placing her at his neck, and her fangs struck.

~ 8 ~

Finally…memories! But, are they really real?

A hard push to her chest, and she was falling. Falling into darkness. Kassie felt burning pain on her torso, under her left arm. As she fell, she could dimly see the outlines of two people – a man and a woman. A woman with brown hair, but the man she could not see. She was pushed! Yes. Someone pushed her. Yes. A man and a woman! The ground came up to meet her fast, and then she screamed!

"Kassie! Love! Wake up!"

Startled, Kassie awoke, shaking.

"What? Huh? What? Jakob? What happened? What's wrong?"

"You were screaming something about a woman with brown hair, a guy, and you were falling."

"I remember, Jakob!   I remember falling. I remember it!" She turned her frightened eyes to him. "I didn't fall from anything. I was pushed!"

"What? Are you sure?"

Kassie nodded. She did remember it, vaguely, but she was sure of it. Jakob held her tightly, which stopped her trembling. She nestled into his arms.

"It was getting dark. I was with two people. I can't see their faces, though. I just know it was a man and woman. There was a struggle, and I remember horrible pain. I don't know why, though." She put her head in her hands. "They tried to kill me, Jakob!" she whispered.

He held her tightly. Someone had tried to kill his mate?

"Tyrone is going to be back today. He wants to check you, and our children out. There is a real chance that you will remember all of it, since you remembered that much."

Kassie could only nod. That's really what she wanted. If she could just remember everything, perhaps she might heal.

"We will tell him what you have remembered. Then, maybe he can tell if you will get all your memory back. Until then, I will remain with you constantly. If someone was trying to kill you, then there is always a possibility that they may know that they didn't. It could mean you are still in danger! If true, there was something you must have known against them! Someone who is trying to kill someone else, usually doesn't stop - especially if they discover, that you aren't dead. Come on. Let's make breakfast, and then we'll head over to the clinic."

He heard a text come through, picked up his phone, and saw it was from Tyrone that just said, "Back."

"Tyrone is back, Kassie. Ready?"

She had calmed down a bit, and would feel better, when she knew, without a doubt, from a doctor that she was pregnant, that the babies were OK, and that her memory was returning.

"Yes, I am. If Yvonne was eating for two, then I should be eating for three!" she tried to joke.

"I still can't believe you are carrying two. I never thought it could happen with humans and werewolves, but with what George dug up, I don't know what I can believe any more."

"Obviously."

After texting Tyrone that they would be there after breakfast, Jakob sat down at the bar waiting for his new, bonded mate to fix their first breakfast together after their bonding. He really didn't have a choice, since she indicated with the whisk she was wielding, for him to sit down. So, instead, he watched as Kassie made them some toast, bacon, and eggs. Once finished, they fed it to each other. Her libido was really working over time. And, finally Jakob told her that that was the way of a female with werewolves in the oven! She laughed, and told him, that she was a human, not a werewolf. Then, Kassie slapped his arm, racing him upstairs to dress. He won, of course.

Jakob opened the door to Tyrone's clinic, and stood aside, letting Kassie enter first. Billie saw her brother and his new mate, and jumped up in excitement. She ran over, and threw her arms around Jakob.

"I'm so happy for you, Jakob!"

She let him go, and threw her arms around Kassie.

"Oooooh! I hope my brother minded his P's & Q's, Sister! I'm so excited to have a sister, and a female Alpha," she squealed.

Kassie laughed at her, and then realized what she had called her.

"Gee. Thanks, Sis. I haven't been able to explain what her role is as Alpha," her brother growled at her, and rolled his eyes.

Kassie knew the hierarchy of animals, and the Alpha-Beta thing, but the last thing she had expected to hear was that she was the Alpha female! Really, Kassie! You married the Alpha male! You should have figured it out before this! You are just clueless! No. Wait. She *mated* an Alpha male! Why does that sound so much more like a sexy idea than married? She put her hands on her hips glaring at her mate. He just rolled his eyes at her.

"I'll explain later."

"Well, well! And, how are our two, favorite, new mates?" came a sarcastic voice behind them.

Kassie and Jakob both turned to glare. Venus. That woman was a real pain in her ass! And, soon enough, she would make sure that Venus knew who was top "female wolf" around here, and in no uncertain terms! A growl burst through her lips, and she found herself surprised at it. Whoa! Where did that come from, she thought.

"And, you're here…why?" Jakob asked.

"Why…I'm here to help out our wonderful doctor, of course!"

"Oh, sure she is!" Kassie muttered to her mate in her mind, not expecting an answer, of course.

He struggled not to laugh as he answered her.

"You, my dear mate, are a real piece of work!"

Kassie practically jumped out of her skin when she heard a voice inside her head. Holy shit! What the hell? And, of course, Venus saw her jump, and sneered.

"Oh! I see your new mate didn't tell you that you two could speak to each other through your minds after mating!" she snarled with a smirk. "My goodness, Jakob! What else haven't you told her about mating?"

Venus's sexy look at Jakob was deliberate, and somehow, with that look, made it seem as if there was something between her and Jakob, before Kassie ever entered the picture. That only served to make Kassie's jealousy escalate. She actually growled a second time, under her breath, but only her mate heard it. He stared at her in surprise. She sounded just like a real werewolf!

"Oh, Venus! I already knew about it!" she laughed. Kassie turned, and placed her hand on Jakob's forearm, smiling at him adoringly. "You made me jump, simply because I wasn't expecting you to continue talking. I'm still not quite used to someone interrupting our *"private"* conversations. However, I can assure you that Jakob didn't leave anything out during our mating!"

Her smile was sarcastic, and very satisfying, when she saw the surprise in Venus's eyes. She made sure that Venus did not misunderstand her meaning.

"And, I mean absolutely nothing did he leave out, Venus!"

She murmured to her mate in secret.

"Anything else you didn't tell me, mate?" Seeing him nod his head, she continued, *"You'd better tell me everything when we get back to the house. As for Venus, well, I'll give her a piece of me!"*

Jakob hardened when he heard Kassie sound so much like an Alpha female, and had a really hard time not attacking her. He sent the image of what he wanted to do to her, then, he sent her the feeling of stroking her sex, and she almost coughed.

"Well, I have to change the sheets first, you know!"

"Why?" she teased.

"Show you when we get home. Think I'll roll them up, and put them away for our kids! They'd get a big kick out of seeing the sheets where Mom and Dad blood-bonded, don't you?"

Kassie slapped his arm, while he laughed aloud.

"Ah! Isn't that sweet? The new mates are being really crude and rude, talking to each other through their thoughts. You do know it's rude, right, Kassie?"

Jakob felt Kassie tense, and he felt something else from her as well, now, but he just couldn't place it.

"Well, Venus, I'm so sorry. I mean, we didn't mean to leave you out, and we sure didn't mean to be rude! Oh, wait. Why yes…yes we did!" Kassie's grin was dripping with sarcasm.

Jakob looked over at his hearing his mate's words. Alpha, he thought. WOW! Kassie had stepped into the role, and she didn't even know it! His smile spread from ear to ear. Venus may have, and quite literally, met her match. That gave him great happiness. She had always been a pain in his ass, and he was tickled pink, finally, to turn Venus over to his mate. He felt Kassie tense again. Was that…recognition he felt coming from her? Then, just as fast, it was gone, replaced by puzzlement. Tyrone appeared to lead her back into the exam room, almost immediately. Jakob followed, but Tyrone pushed him back.

"Uh-uh. I have to examine her, and you need to wait out here." Jakob narrowed his eyes at Tyrone, who just grinned at him. "Yes, yes. I know. You've seen her naked. Blah, blah, blah. Get a grip. You're like all new mates. She'll be fine, and so will the kids!"

Seeing the look on Venus's shocked face just added to Kassie's happiness, as Tyrone shut the door on Jakob. Billie laughed.

"I remember he did the same thing with Hunter!" Billie laughed.

Then, just to rub salt into the wound for Venus, she said, "And, to think! He impregnated you before bonding with you! I mean! That's just unheard of…isn't it, *Venus*?"

"Fuck all of you!" Venus snorted, turned on her heel in a huff, and left the clinic.

Billie sighed with relief.

"That woman makes me hate my own species!" she exclaimed to her brother, then turned back to her work, looking up to clarify. "I mean female, not werewolf!"

"There, my dear sister, we agree wholeheartedly!"

Jakob just sat down in a plop, and began to contemplate what was happening with his mate. He had noticed some very strange things over the last few hours, since the two of them had awakened this morning. But, what it could be, he had no idea.

"Well, Kassie," Tyrone said after his exam was over. "Congratulations. You are most definitely pregnant with two healthy babies!"

Kassie grinned, and she felt as if she were in heaven – as if she were floating on a white, fluffy cloud! She had happy tears running down her face.

"OK. Let's see. Based on the fact that Jakob knocked you up…" he paused with a grin at Kassie's scowl. She was adorable when she did that! "Your due date is just under four months."

Kassie stopped feeling all happy and floaty at his words. Surprise all over her face, she turned to him.

"You said *how long*?"

"Four months."

"But, I'm barely pregnant! How can I deliver in four months?"

Tyrone had deliberately waited to tell her, because he wanted to see her face. He broke out in delighted laughter to her consternation.

"I'm sorry, Kassie," he said, wiping his tears of laughter away, when he had calmed down a bit. "I just had to see your face! May I remind you, that you are carrying baby *werewolves*. Well, technically, they are half and half, but the werewolf gene seems to be overriding that fact, and most female werewolves deliver within four months, not nine like humans."

"B-but…I'm human!" she argued.

"Well, that's obviously subjective. Since there hasn't been a human/werewolf mating in known, recent history, and based upon the information that we have heard, we are actually going on an "as it comes" method. And, there is no doubt that those babies are already the equivalent of two months along.

She was stunned at the information. Four months? She would hold her tiny babies in her arms in just four months? She was so shocked, she didn't notice when

Tyrone opened the door for Jakob. All she could think about was if her body would accommodate expanding that quickly. In the next minute, Tyrone answered her as Jakob walked into the room.

"I have no doubt that a human female's body will work the same no matter what species the babies are," he laughed. "Your body should expand as fast as it needs to."

"Oh, well. Ok. I guess?" she muttered.

"Well?" Jakob asked.

"She's healthy as a horse. I'm still amazed at her rapid recovery, Jakob. OK. Kassie, I want to see you back here in a week, OK?"

Kassie nodded. Jakob looked at her.

"Did you tell him you had another memory break through?"

She shook her head.

"Another memory? Kassie…did you have another memory?"

"Oh, Tyrone?" Jakob said in a snarky voice.

"Yes?"

"Kassie remembered something in a dream last night!"

Tyrone just growled at him, while Kassie laughed.

"It seems someone tried to kill her by pushing her off a cliff."

"You remembered that?" Tyrone was suddenly very serious as he addressed Kassie.

"Uh huh. But, I don't really remember anything but the pain and the push. A woman with brown hair, and a guy. I also remembered falling like a rock nothing more."

"So, does this mean she may get all her memory back?" Jakob asked.

Tyrone shrugged.

"Don't know, but the fact she remembered this is troubling, Jakob. It is possible that something triggered her memory from that dream. It is also possible that it could come at any time, and anywhere."

Kassie and Jakob followed Tyrone out of the office into the bright sunshine. As they walked, Tyrone said something that really got to Kassie. He stopped.

"You know, if you don't remember who they are, and you remembered them, without warning of any kind, you could become extremely violent. And, not being a werewolf, you are likely to attack them. Being an Alpha, human or no, still affords you far more power than an ordinary human. Superhuman, if you will. According to George, his research indicates that the human females who lived after bonding, had extraordinary strength. While not like a werewolf, of course, their abilities allowed them to fight as fiercely as a werewolf."

"Violent?" she asked in an almost whisper.

Tyrone looked at her. Did she not hear what he had just said? He looked at Jakob, who looked worried, but Tyrone realized that he didn't hear, either. He almost rolled his eyes at them. Well, he'd try to hint again.

"Yes. But, you don't fit the molds of those human females that George found. None of them were mated to an Alpha. You are. I'm going out on a limb, I know, but I'm going to bet that your full abilities will come when you become one of us and after the change."

After a few minutes, Tyrone continued when he realized that they still didn't understand what he was saying.

"If the person, or persons, who tried to kill you, even have the least little inkling that she still might be alive, they will probably come after her."

Tyrone looked at Kassie, whose face was almost a mask of real terror. He watched her put her hand to her stomach as if to protect her children.

"I know. I've already thought of that," Jakob answered. "I'll be with her all the time from now on."

"Well, now, that's a great idea, Jakob, but you can't be with her one hundred percent of the time. Kassie needs to know how to fight. And, Kassie? Whether or not you will remember, I still cannot tell you. Let's hope that this memory will lead to more. We need to know who the hell is trying to kill you, and why!"

Kassie nodded, but inside, she was a mess of nerves.

"I need to see you as soon as you have a minute. Pack politics," Tyrone said with a knowing look at Jakob.

"I'll be back in a minute, then we'll go back to the house, love," Jakob said, giving her a light kiss.

She trembled inside, and she believed she would have actually melted at his feet if he hadn't stepped away to talk to the Doc. So, while she waited, she shuffled along to a large tree that was on a relatively low bluff, overlooking a valley. This memory thing was really getting to her. Absentmindedly, she stroked her stomach while she thought about last night's dream as well as the memory that it had resurrected. She put a block on her mind, so Jakob couldn't see where her thoughts were taking her. Troubling wasn't the word. But, something was bothering her big time, but what? Kassie was positive, now, that she recognized Venus from somewhere else. Her sneering sarcasm had reminded her of someone, but she just couldn't remember where she might have seen her. And, until she did, she didn't want to tell Jakob her suspicions. Could it have been Venus who had pushed her off the top of the canyon walls? But, why? And, if so, surely she would have recognized Kassie at that point. She would have recognized her when Jakob had carried her to the clinic. Kassie scratched her head in consternation. Another mystery is if what she remembered really did happen, then she was wondering how in the world she had arrived. Sometimes, the process of deduction could really work well, but there was absolutely nothing – as if she had been asleep. She stopped right then. Unless…unless…she had been knocked out and brought here? Well, anything was possible, right? She looked up when she heard Jakob's feet walking toward her. Not realizing she was exhibiting some odd behavior that both Tyrone and Jakob had noticed, she looked up at her new mate. Gosh! He was so yummy! She opened the block in her mind to him. The minute she did, he looked very relieved. She vowed right there and then that she would never do that to him, again.

"OK, Jakob. I so want to remember who I am, before our kids get here. But, no matter how much I try, I have only remembered a small amount of things."

"Just let it be, Kassie. Don't try and push it. Don't try to remember. When you don't do those things, it seems to be when you remember. When you aren't *focusing* on remembering."

"Good advice, and you're right. I love you," she told him, as he put his arm around her waist.

"I am crazy in love with you! And, I'll show you the second we step through our door," he said, waggling his eyebrows, causing Kassie to break out into hilarious laughter.

Jakob opened the door to their house, and it had barely closed, when they were stripping each other. He pushed her against the door, put his hands under her hips, and lifted her. In seconds, she felt his huge erection thrust deep into her core! She felt a tiny flutter as her mate moved inside her. There was just something decadent about making love with him, while her children stirred inside of her. She loved knowing they were in her womb, and especially how they had gotten there.

A lone figure crept into the clinic. It was 2 AM, and he clicked the light on his desk. Sitting down, he rubbed his face hard, before he pulled out the report from his friend. He had every intention of telling both Jakob and Kassie, when they were there earlier, but chickened out at the last minute. Looking over it, he still had the same question that he had asked George earlier. He had wanted to confirm his suspicions, but the truth was, he was hoping it wasn't true. Yet, George not only confirmed it, he affirmed it with not just one test, but three. And, there it was…still in black and white! Everything confirming what he had thought, when he had first examined the almost dead girl Jakob brought into his office only two months ago.

Kassie had too easily assimilated into their world without a problem. She had guessed, according to what Jakob and Kassie had told him yesterday, who and what they were on their mating. But, for her to accept it so quickly without question, or even fear, only served to reinforce his original beliefs. And, what about her memories? Her acute hearing, and her intuition was even more proof. He regretted not having said something to them earlier, but he just couldn't bring himself to do it. He leaned back in his old-fashioned solid oak chair, that Billie and Hunter had given to him on his last birthday. He truly loved certain things from ages past, and they all knew it. He crossed his arms across his massive chest, turned his head, and stared out into the depths of the night. How and when was he going to tell them were at the top of his mind. Jakob was going to be pissed, because his own laws had been broken – their highest law – for the first time in over eight hundred years. The big problem? Tyrone was almost convinced that he knew who had broken it, whether by accident or on purpose was the question! If he was right, the shame would be astronomical, and she would be asked to leave the clan. They called it a clan in today's world, but he was old enough to remember a thousand years prior, when the families "packs". Actually, he really preferred the word, clan. But, the rules and consequences were adamant due to Jakob. Anyone violating the laws regarding humans and werewolves, would be punishable by death. Jakob had implemented the most severe punishment to stop the wanton killings by werewolves. Back then, it was so common, and so prolific, humans knew that strange looking wolves had been killing other humans on a massive basis. Jakob's Father had done everything he could short of making laws to stop the killings, but he always stopped just short of it, because he had been brought up when werewolves were given a license to do whatever they wanted with humans. His Great Grandfather had been an instigator of some of the killings and turnings. But, even though he was, he was still wary about implementing any of the set in stone laws. So, instead, he made laws based strictly on killing, but not turning. This angered the entire werewolf community around the world, and his Grandfather stepped down as Alpha, letting his son take over. At that point, there was a huge revolt. While Jakob's Dad was able to put the revolt down, there were still groups who did whatever they could to defy him – until the Alpha gave up his rule, and stepped down in favor of his son, Jakob, who had a kind and loving heart, but an arm, mind, and body of steel. He not only hated killings, he hated the idea that their society was vulnerable to discovery, and this is why he especially despised turnings of a human for no reason other than carelessness. Turning a human randomly to a werewolf was anathema to him, and he put down laws from his first days, against any werewolf killing and/or turning a human except by a mate, and the turn had to be officiated by the Alpha and Beta of the clan. It was important to keep their existence a secret. Any caught in betrayal, whether by accident or design, would be punishable by death. By implementing this new law, the werewolf world was extremely careful about turning any human, now, and some would refuse to turn a mate.

And, Tyrone, thought, Jakob had been right to do it. As man progressed through the ages, the world, literally, became smaller due to communication. Now, with the advent of cell phones, and all those cameras in them, it was even more imperative to keep their kind from human knowledge. But, it was getting harder to do so. In order for them to even get to be who they were, Jakob had finally opened his family's two hundred thousand acres of land, and established a retreat, where a couple of times a year, their clan could just be werewolves as nature had decreed. Because of his laws, pure blood werewolves were at an all time high, and this, along with the discovery that it all led to them not being slaves to the moon, were the only things that kept Jakob in power. Once his people discovered they could just be families who were purebred, their population had boomed. And, with it, the realization that they could change at will, because they were purebreds, was another reason Jakob was still Alpha. And, he wasn't just their clan Alpha, but he was Alpha of all werewolves in the world – something he was certain that he had yet to tell Kassie.

Yes, he ruled with a rod of steel, and no one dared defy their highest law, even with this one stipulation. So, Jakob had amended the law, because sometimes, werewolves might actually find a human as their mate. Humans, for whatever reason, were of the same DNA as a werewolf, which allowed them to mate with a human. That had been accorded by only a couple of different supernaturals. A werewolf, who found himself or herself mated to a human, would be allowed to change that human – should the human wish. No one dared to bring in a human to the werewolf world. But, the reason was very specific, and had to be overseen by the Alpha. Only a mate could turn their human mate, and the human mate had to agree to join the werewolves, and their secret kept.

Tyrone sighed aloud. That was until now. How was he going to tell Jakob that his mate was not human any more, because of the act of another werewolf who broke the law? And, the worst of it? The babies were in danger if, and when, she did turn, which would be very soon. And, there was nothing that he could do about it! He slammed his fist down on the arm of his chair, breaking it. Then, sighing, he stood, turned off the light, and slowly walked to his house with his steps seemingly more of those of an old man. One tear rolled down his cheek as he opened his door, and slipped silently inside. The door closed quietly behind him with a sound of finality.

~ 9 ~
Finally! A normal day…Never Mind

While Jakob and Kassie relaxed in each other's arms, on their freshly changed sheets, Jakob decided to tell her the secrets of his people, and keeping their laws. She had been so amazing to let his wolf give her his children, then the blood-bond – and all without flinching. He wasn't sure how she would take this next bit of information. The only reason that he didn't tell her earlier, and he should have, was only because he was truly afraid of losing her due to that stupid law he'd made so long ago! He vowed, right then, that he would change that part of the law, now that he had a human mate.

"Kassie?"

"Hmmm?" she answered, still in a total state of bliss.

"Are you ready for me to tell you everything else?"

Kassie's bliss ended.

"Ready to…what, Jakob? There's more?"

"Yes. It concerns the rest of the werewolf legacy, that pertains to you."

She closed her eyes. She couldn't blame him for not telling her everything. Everything was so surreal to her, even now.

"Me?? What do you mean, me?" she squealed.

"Well, first, I didn't tell you how old I was, you know?"

She just nodded, and turned her head to look at him. This was going to be one of those "OMG" moments. She just knew it.

"I really didn't ask, because it's so rude," she explained.

"Yes, well, that's OK. You have to know everything, of course."

"OK. I'm sort of ready, I guess," she told him.

Satisfied that his mate was ready, he began his story.

"I was born in Italy on December twenty-six in the year of our Lord, twelve hundred and thirty-three, and that makes me – oh, somewhere around seven hundred and eighty-four years old as of last December."

He paused as her eyes widened in real shock this time. Whatever he planned to tell her, she wasn't ready for that one.

"You're HOW OLD???" she squealed.

"I'm seven hundred and eighty-four years old," he repeated calmly. He shrugged. "Give or take."

"Give or take what? A year? Ten? A hundred?" she answered a bit sarcastically, but he answered as if he was quite serious."

"A hundred or so, I guess."

Kassie's mouth dropped.

"You're that old? And, you mated with me at the tender age of twenty-eight? Let's see…that makes you a hell of a lot older than me by at lease seven hundred and fifty years!" she sat up, and swung her legs off the bed as she answered. "Ewwww! That's just gross! You are a real, 'dirty old man'!"

Kassie's voice made it sound so nasty, and the look on his face was priceless. She grinned, then quickly pushed the sheets off them. She straddled his torso, and lowered her core, sliding her sex along his shaft, before she took him deeply inside of her body. He was always hard for her.

"Yep. I just can't imagine doing this with a 'dirty old man'!" she giggled, leaning down to drag her breasts across his face. "But, I gotta admit…it's *hot*!"

Whatever he had expected, it was not that his mate was suddenly riding him! He grasped her hips with his hands, digging them into her flesh, giving her his best "I'm a dirty old man" look, only making her laugh harder.

"Oh, Jakob! Doing this with a 'dirty old man' is such a turn on!" she laughed, deliberately brushing her nipples against his mouth. "Suck me!" she ordered.

Not to disobey his mate, he opened his mouth, and grabbed the luscious, pink nipple that was slowly sliding back and forth over his lips and eyes. She was really playing with him. And, he was loving it!

"OK. You ready for the rest of me?" he asked, as she rode him fast and hard.

"Whatever it is, I can take it! But, can YOU?" she laughed again, when she rode him even harder. She flung her head back, but still let her breasts bounce in his face. That was such an aphrodisiac to him!

"You will also live as long as I live, Kassie," he panted, meeting her thrust for thrust.

Kassie came to a sudden stop, and looked at him with her eyes wide. A little fear went a long way when you were in the middle of sex.

"What does that mean?" she asked warily.

"It means that we are long-lived, and since you already know that, I'll go with being a really 'dirty old man'." He laughed at her expression. "We can die, but it would be hard for someone to kill us. We can also live through devastating injuries, some even life threatening. We will also take each other's blood from time to time. Not for any other reason, but that we like the taste!"

He halted at her look. Kassie was speechless, even though Jakob was moving inside of her.

"Uh. And…how long might that be? I'm only good for about eighty years!"

"Well, as I said, I've been alive for almost eight hundred years. Do the math!" he laughed at her very stunned face when the truth struck her.

Kassie's eyes narrowed dangerously as she looked at her mate.

"Yes. Before you actually ask me…there are vampires, Elves, and any number of other supernaturals. Oh, and one last thing? As long as we live, we can have as many children as we want."

To make his point, he shoved his cock up in her with vigor. Her mouth dropped. She could become pregnant through hundreds of years?

"Over hundreds of years? Are you that fertile? But, am I?" she asked in surprise.

"Oh, mate," Jakob said, as he flipped her over, and began to finish what she started. "You have no idea HOW fertile werewolves are! Oh…and one last thing. You must become were."

Kassie forgot all about having him inside of her.

"What? You said what?" she demanded. "I have to become like you?"

"Yes. It's part of our law. And, I was wrong not to have told you before we mated. It's my own damn law, and I broke it!"

Kassie thought about it for a moment. She, somehow, knew she had no other relatives. What was waiting for her when she got back? Absolutely nothing! She leaned forward, and kissed him.

"Yes. I agree." She licked her lips. "Can we do it, again?"

"What?"

"Drink?"

"Any time you want, my love," he answered, and sank his fangs into her breast.

After being told that she couldn't be turned, yet, she understood why. Jakob's phone rang, and he told her that it was a business call, that would take a while, so Kassie decided to see if Billie was free. After Jakob went into his study, Kassie dressed in her skimpy clothes, and walked to Billie's house. Opening the door, Billie's face was amused when she saw Kassie. And, not to be undone, she gave her shit about it, too.

"Hey, newbie sister! What's the matter? My brother tired you out already?" she laughed.

"Did you, seriously, just ask me if Jakob had tired me out? I can assure you, sister of mine, that your brother's prowess in bed is...."

"Not another word! Too much information, so keep it to yourself!"

Both girls laughed heartily.

"I'm here, because Jakob's talking about a business matter that is going to take quite some time, so I thought I'd come to see you."

"Ah, time for the questions, right?" she guessed, stepping back, and letting Kassie come into the room. "Hunter and Jimmy are off on a little walk, so we girls can just talk. I know you have to have them, especially because you are human. And, let's face it. We girls all stick together, and I can tell you things that might really embarrass your new mate. So, let 'er rip!"

Billie led Kassie into the kitchen, motioning for her to sit on the barstool.

"Well, first. He said that I live as long as he does, and that if I wanted, we could have as many children over hundreds of years?" she ended on a squeak, her hand grasping her throat.

Billie threw her head back, and laughed. Oh, the poor girl had no idea! Jimmy was a bit older than most first children for werewolves, but it was a deliberate thing. They wanted their first round of children born about five wolf years apart. Their second round would come after they were grown, which would be in about ten years.

"Well, first, yes. You will live as long as he does. Once mated, we take on the longevity of each other. In your case, because you are human, and because of some kind of quirky cosmic rule, you will take on his. And, he wasn't yanking your chain about having children over hundreds of years – or longer. We are among the most fertile of the supers. And, Jakob is just – well, he's just *old*. I'm the baby of the family. I'm only two hundred and thirteen years old. Yep. I'm a baby with a mate, a son, and another on the way!"

"NO WAY!!!" Kassie gasped.

"Tyrone just examined me! Hunter and I have only been mated for about five years. And, I'm going to deliver right after you do! They can play together!"

Neither of the women knew what awaited Kassie, but right now, they truly had things in common. So, they opted to ignore what the future would bring, and just hugged each other. Billie was so happy she had a sister she could talk to, now! Outside, they heard Hunter, Jimmy, and apparently, Jakob's voices as they came up the stairs into the building.

"What's all the hullabaloo about, girls? Geez! You two could wake up the dead!" Hunter smirked.

Billie looked at Kassie, and grinned. Her eyes asked Kassie to tell him. Kassie laughed out loud.

"Well, really, Hunter! Is that ANY way to talk to your pregnant wife? I mean…. Seriously?"

Hunter froze stiff.

"Oh, come on, Hunter! Your wolf has been damned active lately! You're telling me you didn't even think about it?"

Jakob slapped his brother-in-law on the back.

"You STUD you!" he laughed. He grabbed Hunter, and shook his hand hard. Suddenly, Hunter smiled big.

"YES!" his wolf was wanting to prance all over the place.

"Daddy? What's going on?" Jimmy whined, his hands over his ears, because everyone was yelling. Hunter

swept up his son, telling him, "Son. We're going to have a baby!"

"Why?" Jimmy asked confused.

The adults stared at him, then broke out in delighted laughter, which just confused him more.

Jakob took his mate in his arms. He was extremely happy for his little sister. She had so wanted another child for a while.

Hunter grabbed his mate in a hold. He loved her so much. He was thrilled to pieces that there would be another pup running around. He turned, and scooped up a protesting and squirmy Jimmy!

"Group hug!" Hunter said.

"Stop it, Daddy! You're squishing me!" Jimmy growled.

The day had been wonderful. Jakob had addressed the clan at a meeting later in the day for general clan news. This is when Jakob made his announcement, about changing the law about humans and werewolf mates, which had everyone hooting and clapping in a cheer that probably scared the fur off of some of the wildlife around them. After everyone calmed down, no one really had anything else to discuss, so they adjourned early. After all, how could anyone pass that announcement?

Another memory came to Kassie in the middle of that night. She remembered the fall, and the impact of the fall. But, there was something more. When she was pushed, she felt someone scratch her under her arm. Why would she remember that one now? She shot up in bed as a sudden, violent pain hit her in the stomach.

"OH, Creator! Jakob! Help! It hurts so bad!" she cried, grabbing her stomach.

"Kassie! What's wrong?" he said, worried.

"I-I don't know!"

"Where is the pain?" he asked.

She indicated the center of her belly. Jakob was horrified. The kids! He quickly picked her up as gently as he could, and using his werewolf speed and the phone, was at the clinic, before Kassie realized she was in his arms. Luckily, the symptoms were subsiding.

He called Tyrone as he ran, who met them both. For a second time, Kassie lay on the same examining table that she had originally been on when Jakob had brought her into their midst.

"OK, Kassie. Put your feet into the stirrups," he ordered. "Jakob, you want to wait outside?"

"No."

And, that was the end of that, so Tyrone didn't argue with him.

Tyrone quickly examined her. The implications served to do nothing but confirm George's findings.

"Have you had any other symptoms?"

"No. Just that one pain. It wasn't my belly. I know the twins are fine. It was my stomach."

Tyrone turned from her closing his eyes. Knowing what was coming, he was worried. What was going to happen? No one had ever seen a human turn, let alone a human, carrying werewolf children. And, he wasn't even sure if it were possible at this point. What the hell was he going to tell Jakob? Kassie? She was going to turn, and if his calculations were correct, sooner than later – while she was still carrying her werewolf children! Now, what was he going to do? It was too late to tell Jakob. Her change would take place in days, so he decided not to say a word, because there was literally nothing he could do to stop it. Was it a stupid decision? Yes. Yes, it was.

"Tyrone?" Jakob and Kassie both said at the same time.

"What? Oh. Right. You are fine, Kassie. Sometimes, believe it or not, a baby can kick you in the wrong spot. The same thing happens when babies push on the bladder, and makes you need to pee all the time," he said, looking into Jakob's eyes with a grin.

And, how he ever grinned at the time, he was never able to figure out through the years that followed. But, the anger of Jakob? He would remember for a lifetime, because Jakob would never let him live it down!

"What part of dead do you not get?" he said, with his hands wrapped around her neck.

"You think it's THAT easy?" she gasped. She grabbed his hand, and yanked it away. Rubbing her neck, she continued. "Well, you asshole, it isn't! Oh, I plan on finishing killing her, alright. We will be killing her just like before. You understand me? But, we have to get her away from Jakob. As long as he's around, we can forget it!"

"OK. How do you plan on it?"

"Plan? Well, I know that Jakob has to go to the company within the next couple of days, and I'm sure that she will stay here. Tyrone will want to take care of her and the babies. It will be our best opportunity to grab her. I will make sure she comes out into the wilderness alone. Then, the five of us can kill her, and the spawn that she carries. Our wolves will make sure that she is torn into pieces."

"It had better work, this time, because if it doesn't, you are a dead werewolf!" He paused. :You said she was starting to remember?"

"Yes. A very little at a time, but Doc said it won't be long, before she remembers at least enough of it to put it altogether. She must be dead, before that happens."

He reached toward her, and the same hands that moments before were strangling her, now, caressed her neck, his hands sliding downward to brush her breasts. She jerked as they peaked hard immediately. Devon had never been her mate. This man was. Quickly, they stripped, and he was inside her body, before they hit the ground.

"I'll be leaving tonight," Jakob told her, holding her after taking her once more, before he left. He couldn't get enough of his mate!

"How are you going to explain me, Jakob? I mean, you can't fool everyone with a wife after only two months!" she said with confidence.

"Wanna bet?" he asked her.

"But…,"

"No. You will not accompany me to Denver. My company is yours, now. You own half of it," he told her. "You are going to help me."

"How? I don't even know what you do, nor what I can do to help!"

"I'm sure you know something."

Kassie got up from the bed, and paced. Jakob's tongue licked out as he watched his mate pace back and forth in the nude. Her breasts were distracting him from what she was saying as they swung and bounced gently with each step.

"I love you, too, but you have a great many people depending on you, don't you? People who are working for you?"

"I do."

"OK. Do I need to book your flight?" she asked.

"Nope." He kissed her nose, and smelled her scent. It was all over him, and his was all over her. They smelled wonderful together. "I'll take the corporate jet."

Kassie was surprised. "You have a corporate jet?"

"Nope. WE have a corporate jet. You own all that I own. Or, did you forget that part? But, no matter what, I will be back tonight. There is a full moon coming."

"You mean that there is something to the old werewolf and the moon bit? Is there a danger to me? To our babies?"

"No. And, the moon has nothing to do, whatsoever, with our change. However, for a new werewolf who turns, like Jimmy will do on his sixteenth werewolf birthday, and it is the full moon that triggers the first turn. We have two new ones that will turn tonight, and as Alpha, I must be there. I can help them get through the painful change. Once they complete that first turn, then they will be able to change at will. But, if you are talking about me? A mate cannot harm his mate in any way. There is no danger to you. And, because I am Alpha, no other werewolf would dare hurt you. They would fear my wrath too much. And, if they did? I'd kill them."

Kassie jerked. Kill?

"You'd kill for us?"

"If anyone at all, threatened you and our babies, then yes. I would."

"Holy crap! That's so… I don't know what that is." She shook her head pushing that to the back of her mind. "Well, then, the only thing I'm interested in owning is this!" She reached downward taking him into her hands. "One more time for good measure?"

He grinned, and flipped her over as she giggled.

"You haven't had any more of those stomach pains, have you?"

"No. Of course not."

Jakob's hand went to her belly. She was beginning to show with just a small bump, and it was just that much more real to him to watch her begin to grow with their children. He bent down, and kissed his babies goodbye.

"You two take care of you Mother!" he whispered, then felt a tiny flutter.

Kassie's heart swelled with love for this man. Her werewolf lover. The father of her children.

Billie, Hunter, and Jimmy stood with Kassie as she waved goodbye to Jakob. He tried to get her to come with him, but it had taken Kassie almost all night to convince Jakob that she needed to stay here. All it took was reminding him of the pain she had been in recently. She was really scared it could happen, again, and would need Tyrone if it did happen. Reluctantly, he had agreed, and she agreed to stay with Billie, Hunter, and Jimmy just in case. He had warned his brother-in-law that if anything happened to her, Jakob would not hesitate to kill his Beta to which Hunter gave him a single nod. Just as Jakob vanished from sight, and thankfully he had not seen, Kassie doubled over in pain. Hunter barely had time to catch her. He scooped her up, and with Billie, holding Jimmy, followed as he ran into the clinic. Tyrone looked up, and knew what was happening. No one else did.

"On the bed!" he ordered.

Hunter laid her on the bed, and Tyrone shooed them out.

Again, just like before, it stopped as fast as it started.

"What's wrong with me, Tyrone? Are my babies in danger?"

"Whatever is going on, Kassie, I can guarantee that it has no affect on the twins. Of that I can absolutely assure you. They have never been in danger."

If only he felt as confident as he sounded! But, he wasn't. Even though Kassie was better once more, He just didn't know what to actually do, or even tell anyone. It was really more of a "wait and see", since no one had ever witnessed a human to werewolf transformation in any of their lifetimes. Tyrone was always up for something brand new. In this case, though, he only knew she would change soon. Very, very soon. He allowed Kassie to get up, and go back to Billie's place. It was as if she had never had any pain at all. But, soon, the pain would be excruciating, and she would change into a werewolf. He could tell them, but what would that achieve except terror and waiting for it to happen. And, with the moon out in full tonight, the odds were quite great that tonight she would change. And, Jakob wouldn't be here to help her! Tyrone could only hope that Hunter had the

ability to help some. How it would effect her babies,
he had no idea.

~ 10 ~
When you are responsible for a child, nothing else matters!

The jet landed at DIA, and Jakob was picked up in one of the firm's many SUV's. They proceeded to his offices, which were in downtown Denver, for a meeting that had been long in coming. It was a meeting of a merger of businesses between his Father's clan and his. Or so he thought. He was sitting at his desk, when the door to his office opened, and his Mother and Father walked into the room. He was up, and ran around to hug them both.

"Hello, son!" his Mother said, and gave him a hug, and kiss on his cheek.

"How are you?" his Dad asked.

Jakob had deliberately withheld the information that his mate was human, and he didn't know what they would say when he told them.

"Great! Better than great, actually. I want to combine this into business and pleasure. And, I want you to come home to the Canyon with me this evening."

His Father stroked his goatee.

"I don't know, son. I have another business meeting tomorrow morning in Milan, and I really have to be there."

"Cancel it, please," Jakob demanded.

"Jakob! How can you talk to your Father that way! It is not your right to demand!"

Jakob put his arm around his Mother, giving her a tight, loving squeeze.

"But, Mom! I would think that you guys would like to meet my mate?"

His parents gaped at him. While his Father sputtered, and tried to speak, his Mom let out her trademark squeal when she was excited.

"You are *mated*?"

He turned to his Dad.

"What the hell is it with women and their squealing?" he asked his Dad, covering his ears.

His wife glared at both of them with her fists on her hips. Then, she rolled her eyes.

His Dad shrugged.

"Well, I'm a bit deaf from it over the years, but I just don't know why they do that. I mean, I've had scientists try to discover the squeal gene, but they have yet to find anything!"

His Mother wacked him across the shoulder.

"Shut up, Xander! You both are such babies!" she told them.

"Now, now, Mary. Temper, temper!" he warned. "Congratulations, Son!"

He grabbed his son's hand, and shook it heartily, while his Mom started with a flood of questions

"What's her name? Where did you meet? Have you met her parents? Is she part of your clan, or from another one? How old is she? Is she pretty? Nice?"

"Whoa! Slow down Mom! Give me a chance to get a word in edgewise!" laughed Jakob. "And, to answer your questions…Kassiopeia, but she's called Kassie. I left her in the Canyon, because Tyrone is keeping an eye on her. No, haven't met them. No she is not from another clan. Don't know her age, but she looks around twenty-four. She's gorgeous, and the kindest most amazing woman I have ever met!" He paused for effect, before he hit them with the piece de resistance. "Oh, and well, there is this one other thing. She's human."

You could have heard a pin drop. Both of them opened and closed their mouths. Amused, Jakob thought they looked like fish. And, then, this time, they both squealed.

"A HUMAN????? Is that even possible?"

"How in the hell did you mate a human? It just isn't possible, son!"

"A lot more than possible, Dad. But, there's even more. She's pregnant – with twins."

His Mother's legs dropped out from under her. His Dad caught her before she fell, and eased her into a chair.

"No! That's not possible, son! A human and were cannot have children!" his Mother gasped, shaking her head from side to side in total disbelief.

"Well, apparently, that's an old wives' tale, because Kassie is as pregnant as they come. She has two cubs growing inside her right now. She's just begun to show."

"Grandparents? Xander! We're going to be grandparents? Of half-human, half-werewolf babies!"

"I promise, Mom. You will love her! Dad, Mom, she's the most important thing that has ever happened to me. I love her more than you know."

His Mom was crying, but not with terror. Joy. Finally! After all these years! They would have grandbabies, even if they were half-human. She didn't really care. But, human! That was something she had a hard time wrapping her head around, and it was truly a bit strange.

"Well, that's kind of what we came to tell you, son. I can't believe all this has happened. We came to merge, but we really didn't come for business that was easily taken care of from our Rome office."

Jakob frowned. What?

"Your Mother's pregnant again!" his Father announced happily.

Jakob was thrilled! They had tried so long, and only had himself and Billie! Having a brother or sister was to be celebrated.

"Well, just before I came here, Billie told us that she is pregnant, again, too!"

"It's a sign," his Mom stated confidently. "There is a reason why the three females in our family are pregnant. I don't know why, but I'm so full of happiness right now, I could burst."

"So, will you guys come and meet her? I promised her that I'd return tonight, but I didn't tell her that I would have you guys with me."

His Father clapped him on the shoulder.

"Of course we will. Nothing is as momentous as this! Work can wait! She must be some female, and we can't wait to meet the woman who, finally, brought my son to heel!"

"Funny, Dad. Really hilarious!"

"I know. I crack myself up!" he laughed at his wife's eye roll. "So, Mary? You ready to meet our daughter-in-law?"

"Yes!" she squealed, again.

"Well, technically, she's you mate-in-law. The human marriage has not yet happened."

"What? My son? Living in sin with a woman?" his Mom joked. They really didn't need marriage, since mating was far more permanent, but it was still a joke in the clans.

The trip back to DIA was longer than they thought it would be due an accident that had happened on I70. While they waited for it to be cleared, his Father took that time to call his office, and told them he was taking this week as a vacation. Once they reached the terminal, the rushed to the jet. Once they were all situated in the luxurious seats, Jakob leaned back and explained how he had met her.

"I'm really worried about Kassie."

"Why?" his Mother asked as the jet left the ground.

"…and, she lost her memory after being attacked, and thrown from the canyon bluff," he told them.

"What? Why?"

"We don't know. Her memory is returning, but very slowly. She remembers a woman and a man, and actually being tossed from the bluff. When I found her, it was night, and she was lying in a patch of grass at the side of the river dressed in nothing but some really short shorts, a tank, and flip-flops. She was covered in blood, and she was literally at the brink of death. I was in wolf form, and she spoke to me…told me that I could eat her if I wanted, then asked me to wait until she was dead to do it."

His Mom gasped in horror.

"Son, do you have any idea who would try and hurt her?"

Jakob shook his head.

"No, Dad, I don't. But, whoever it is, I'm convinced they live somewhere in the area."

"You're sure?"

"No. Not really sure, but the deduction fits. Call it a feeling. Possibly an unknown were, or a rogue. I hope I'm wrong about that."

His Dad nodded. His Mother reached out, and took his hands. Jakob looked at her, and realized how beautiful his Mom really was. She was tall at five-foot eight inches with coal black hair and ice blue eyes, that were copied into Jakob perfectly. It was easy to see the resemblance between them. Her figure was like those women of the pin-ups in the forties, and her skin was the color of honey. His Dad, on the other hand, was blonde haired, but unusually dark brown eyes. He was a big man – at least two inches taller than Jakob – and his skin was olive in color. His Dad's Father was blonde and blue-eyed, but his Mother's Mother was olive skinned with dark brown hair, and honey colored eyes. She was from Italy, while he was an American. When someone looked at the three of them, their mouths would automatically gape at the gorgeous family, yet not one of them had an ounce of vanity within them.

"Honey…is she in danger?" his Mom asked.

"I have no doubt, and that's why it has killed me to leave her, because of this deal. I left her in Hunter and Billie's care. Whoever tried to kill her before we even met, was ruthless about it. The only thing very odd, though? According to Tyrone, she shouldn't even be alive in the first place, and certainly not after walking several miles while in that condition. She said the only thing that kept her going was rinsing her cracked skull under the icy water of the river."

"She sounds like a fighter to me," his Dad said.

"She is. A born fighter…and a survivor. And, a born Alpha, even though she is human."

"Well, let's hope you can figure it out, before the killer realizes she's still alive!" his Dad told him.

There was always a big party planned, before the full moon came up, for all the new pups. Once the celebration, food, dancing, and speeches were over, and the moon rose, the Alpha would help the new pups into their first change, and then, they would all run and feast on the wildlife in moderation. They only took what they needed to eat. But, tonight was special. Two new pups would be introduced into the clan, and everyone was excited for them.

Kassie was a bit sad to be left out, but she helped with the festivities anyway. Before it started, Billie had asked if she would watch after Jimmy, while they ran. And, she had agreed.

"I'm really glad you are here. It's kind of odd having someone who doesn't go all furry with us. Usually, we take turns staying behind, and taking care of the little ones. But, right now, there aren't little ones other than Jimmy, but next moon cycle, we will have several little children."

"Well, Jakob said he'd be back before the moon came out," Kassie told Billie. "And, he doesn't say anything he doesn't mean."

"I'm not surprised that he hasn't gotten back, yet. Those head winds can get tricky when one is in a jet, sometimes. Don't worry, Sis. He'll be back any time, now, and as his mate, you would never be hurt by anyone in the clan."

"I'm not worried, Billie. I am just hungry for Jakob to return. He called just before they left DIA."

"Yeah, he called me when they boarded. He'll be here tonight. I was supposed to keep quiet, but I just can't do it. I think you have a right to know. He's bringing Mom and Dad with him."

Kassie's heart dropped. How could they accept her as their daughter-in-law? She was human!

"It's OK. They'll love you!" Hunter said, walking into the room

"You sure?"

Laughing, Billie said, "Believe me, you'll be a breeze compared to when they met Hunter. His name isn't just his name. He is one of the foremost werewolf hunters in the world, and there are only about five of them! Hunter is number one. When Mom and Dad found that out, oh my! You should have seen them! I mean…I swear! My Dad almost lost his ever loving mind when he met Hunter!"

"Yeah," Hunter said, his arms going around his mate. "I wasn't the number one person on their list. I had a real reputation that wasn't all that good. But, when I met Billie, well, she saved me. I haven't hunted werewolves, since that day. But, Kassie…if someone is out to get you, I will become that Hunter, and I *will* bring them to justice!"

"And, if Hunter says that, Kassie, he means it," Billie confirmed.

"Thanks guys. It's just such a pain that I haven't remembered anything else, yet."

"It could be that it may not happen until you actually are confronted by whoever tried to kill you. If you ever are, it could bring all the memories back immediately," a voice said from the front door.

"You really think so, Doc?"

Her addressing him as "Doc" had been a source of amusement to him, but it was kind of endearing, too, so he smiled and nodded his head.

"Hey, Tyrone! Ready?" Hunter asked.

"Just waiting on you two!" he said, turned, and went back into the night.

"The moon will rise at midnight, but our party will happen before that. Will you stay with Jimmy?"

"Of course, I will."

"Thank you! I will feel so much better. We usually leave him alone, and he knows not to leave, but it's always a bit scary for me."

"I understand. You guys have a great run and a good time. We'll be here when you get back."

The party started at nine pm, but both Billie and Hunter had decided they didn't want her with the party, just in case the evil people would appear. And, for once, Kassie just didn't argue. Besides, her stomach was feeling very, very strange. It wasn't that excruciating pain she had been getting, but it was as if it was slowly turning inside out and upside down! So, Kassie and Jimmy hightailed it to his room, and pulled out some games to play. It was obvious that his favorite game was jacks, and just as they started playing, they heard growling. They looked at each other, then together, they stood and raced to look out the window. The backyard was full of huge werewolves!

"Whoa!" Kassie gasped.

"Aunt Kassie, that's what I'll be doing that in a few years!" Jimmy exclaimed in excitement.

Kassie turned to him, and saw his eyes glowing. He grinned at her, and she smiled back. It was really evident how very important this right of passage was for him. The two of them spent a couple of hours playing different types of games until Jimmy started yawning, and just couldn't stop. Kassie tucked him into his bed, grabbed a book she had been reading, and went downstairs. She grabbed a throw to cover herself, then settled back to read.

Kassie had lost all sense of time, she was so engrossed in reading her book. She read the last page of the chapter, shut the book, then stood to stretch. Man! Was she ever tight! Guess it was time for her to run upstairs to check on Jimmy. Just as she started for the stairs and bed, she heard a noise above her. She looked upward to the ceiling, then heard it, again. Jimmy! She dashed upstairs and threw open the door of his bedroom, only to find five werewolves, one of them holding a crying, struggling Jimmy. Not for one moment did she ask herself how she ran as fast as she did up the stairs. Skidding to a stop, Kassie screamed bloody murder. A blonde woman stood in the window opening, the moon causing the room to be like moonlight.   She turned, and met Kassie's eyes. Shocked, she confronted her.

"Venus? What are you doing? Put him down!" Kassie demanded without fear.

"You've ruined everything, Kassie! And, I mean everything! You just couldn't keep your nose out of my business, could you?"

Frowning, Kassie answered, "What the hell are you talking about?"

Venus's hands balled into a fist.

"You fucking bitch!" she yelled, then turned to the man holding Jimmy. "Toss that thing out the window!"

Before Kassie could even blink, the man, literally, leaned out the window, and let Jimmy drop. Then, one by one, in super speed, the others jumped out of the window. There would not have been a thing she could do about it. Her mouth dropped in complete disbelief, seeing such cruelty done to a little boy!

"Venus! What is wrong with you? Jimmy is just a little boy, and has done nothing to you! Are you just crazy, or do you have a death wish? Hunter will kill you – and Billie will rip your limbs from your body! What the hell are you doing, and why are you doing this? "

Venus turned, her face already beginning to change into a werewolf.

"This isn't about Jimmy. It's about you! You happened to me! You just had to get in the way over and over, didn't you? You steal everything from people, don't you? Well, I'm stealing Jimmy from Billie and Hunter, and it's all *your* fault! If you had just died, I wouldn't be in this mess! Why couldn't you just die like you were supposed to?" Venus growled at Kassie. "Jimmy is just the opening act! You will follow us, and then, I'm going to kill you – slowly, painfully by slicing your body, until every part of it is laying in the snow – and you will still be alive! And, finally, he will finish you off!"

"He? Who are you talking about?" Kassie asked. "Why?"

Venus snarled at her, and in seconds, Venus followed the others out the window. It took Kassie a moment, before her feet could even move to take her to the window. She looked down, and saw the blur of five werewolves speeding away, one of them with Jimmy in his arms! No! This can't be happening! It's a nightmare! Kassie raked her hands through her hair in shock and terror! She couldn't do anything. What could she do? What? She whirled around, and ran downstairs. She stopped in the living room, looking around frantically.

"Oh, God! What to do? What to do? What do I do?" she kept asking. She was talking to herself, trying to focus. "Kassie! Calm. down! Panicking is not going to help one bit! Calm down, and think rationally."

Rational, right! Like that's going to work! What the hell had Venus meant that Kassie had destroyed everything? Venus had said that she was supposed to die? How did she even know that in the first place? Had Venus something to do with trying to kill her? No! That wasn't possible! Telling Kassie she would die by her hand was downright horrific! But, right now, that didn't matter. What did matter was Jimmy. She had to get him back at any, and all, costs!

"OK. Think. Where would they take him?" Answer? They were running to the southeast. "OK. Southeast. What's Southeast from here?"

Kassie ran to her house, and darted into her mate's office, flipped open the computer, and brought up a map of the area. She located Billie's house, then drew a line with her finger to the southeast.

"No, no. That's the west, Kassie!"

Kassie had to stop panicking! She took a very, very deep breath, then followed the line of where the house was compared to the southeast with her finger. When she came to a clearing, she stopped. Kassie stood straight. That's where they were. It was perfect for a confrontation, as well as the best place to attack Kassie – to kill her. She was positive that would be where they were, even though she didn't know why. She had never been a strategist, but for the moment, it was as clear as glass that it was where they had taken Jimmy! She'd bet her life on it! And, she probably would! All the answers could come later, but right now, Kassie printed off the map, grabbed it, and ran into the kitchen. Jimmy would be thirsty when she found him, so she grabbed a water bottle, and turned to the front door. The fastest way out was through the front door, and that's where the remaining werewolves were still standing around. She had to somehow skirt around them so they wouldn't see her. Jimmy was her life just like her own children! There was no way she was going to let Venus hurt Jimmy! That's something she vowed right then and there. She raced out the front door in a blur, and followed the same path that Venus and the others had. While she ran, she realized that the man who had Jimmy looked familiar to her, but why, she had no idea. Oh, well. No time for that, now. She pushed herself to run faster than she had ever run in her life. She never asked herself why she could run as fast as she was. Twenty minutes into the run, the worst pain she had ever felt in her life, caused her to stumble onto the ground, gripping her stomach.

"Oh, God!" she screamed in agony, writhing on the ground. *"NO! Not now!"*

Every muscle and bone in her entire body was on fire! It felt as if her bones were breaking and bending. If she didn't know better, she would swear that her spine was contorting of its own accord. And, it hurt so bad! She wanted her mate, wanted the pain to go away, but even despite the pain, she knew that Jimmy's life might be at stake! Kassie just had to keep going, although, now, it was more like limping along until her stomach finally stopped. Finally, she could run once more, and she picked up speed after them. Oh, GOD! What would she do if they hurt Jimmy??? She couldn't let them! How was she going to find him?

Suddenly, she caught a smell in the air. Is that Jimmy? Yes! It was! How could she smell him? That just didn't make a bit of sense! Not letting that thought deter her, Kassie ran in the direction of the smell.

Jakob's jet landed. Jumping into the SUV, he, his Mother and Father started back to the retreat. They had waited just a little bit too long, and all three could feel the change coming to them. Jakob was never, ever, late to a new werewolf changing, and he was determined not to be this time, either. Parking the SUV in the parking area that Jakob bought from a man who had needed some money a few years prior, all three of them jumped out, just as they phased to wolves. Suddenly, he got a horrible feeling. He reached out to his mate, only to hear her say, "Jimmy! They have Jimmy! Oh,GOD!! It's my fault!"

Then, he heard nothing. He took off at a speed that would have made any other werewolf cringe. Without a word, and knowing something was wrong, his Mother and Father were on his heels. Whatever was wrong, they knew that it was bad. Very, very bad.

Jakob tried to get his mate back, but either she was blocking him, somehow, or something else was keeping him from hearing her. He did feel her, though. Her stomach pains were back, and they were increasing. This just increased his speed. His mate needed him, but more than that, what did she mean that Jimmy had been taken, and it was her fault? Where is she?

"Kassie! Where are you?" he sent a frantic message to Kassie, but he heard nothing at all.

~ 11 ~
Never let anyone tell you that you are human, because you might not be!

Despite the monstrous pain in her stomach that raged through her, again, Kassie ran with everything that she had inside of her. Tyrone had said her children would be fine, no matter what, but just the thought of losing one or both of them to some sort of psycho bitch, made her more than angry. She was quickly becoming furious, almost to the point of murder.

"I'm going to slice that bitch to ribbons, then drink her blood as I laugh!" she muttered aloud, as she ran.

And, she would kill her, even if she had to claw Venus's skin from her body, and gouge out her eyes. She was Alpha female, and at this moment in time, she felt it through and through. Kassie's thirst for blood was growing by the second! When her mate was away, she was responsible for their clan. She felt it, now. The power of the Alpha was surging through her body, second by second, in leaps and bounds.

"*Jakob! Can you hear me?*" she reached out through their bond, only praying that he heard her. "*Jimmy is in terrible trouble! Five weres took him from his bedroom! I can't let Venus get away with this, and I won't! I'm so sorry. It's all my fault! I promised to watch over him, and this happened! But, I'm going to kill her with my bare hands when I find her! I'm going to tear Venus to pieces with my fangs!*"

Not realizing what she had just said, tears poured down her face.

"*What? Kassie? What do you mean? What's happened to Jimmy?*" Jakob demanded, but no answer was forthcoming.

Her pains had stopped again, and now, she was pushing with everything in her to go faster and faster. She stumbled several times, before she realized that her legs had gained strength. That strength let her run much, much faster! She wasn't paying attention to anything other than Jimmy was in danger. She would not let anything happen to that little boy. Her anger replaced her fear as she ran. Her heart was beating faster her breath coming less in a pant. She found she was breathing easier which spurred her faster. And, then, Kassie howled into the night with all the anger she felt. The other wolves heard her, and Hunter and Billie, and the entire clan, ran in the direction of Kassie's scream...or was that a howl? Whatever it was stirred down deep in Jakob's soul, and pushed him even faster.

Jakob broke his own rule to contact Hunter through their pack bond. It was something that no one ever wanted to use, and was reserved strictly for a true emergency.

"Hunter! This is an emergency!"

Surprised to hear his Alpha in his head, he was really glad he did! It had been an eon, since he had heard him this way.

"Something's wrong. We just heard Kassie scream.!"

"Venus has Jimmy!"

"What?????" Hunter roared. *"What the fuck?"*

"No idea. All I can tell you is that, for some reason, she has him, and Kassie believes it is all her fault!"

"I'm going to kill Venus! She should have been destroyed a long time ago! Why would Kassie think it's her fault?"

"I do not know!"

"But, Kassie's scream carried on the air as if she was an Alpha wolf! It wasn't human!"

"She is the Alpha female, Hunter. My Alpha mate! We don't know what she can do even if she is still a human. We need to try and stop her if we can, because I'm truly afraid that she will launch herself at Venus! Venus will kill her! Can you find her?"

"Yes. Billie and I can smell her, now. She's about ten miles north of us. We're on our way, now."

"I'm about twenty away. Contacting Tyrone. Maybe he knows what the hell is going on!"

"We WILL find both Jimmy and Kassie, Jakob! We have to!"

Jakob then turned his thoughts to Tyrone.

"Tyrone? You there?"

"Yes, Alpha. What is wrong? I just heard Kassie screaming in the wilderness."

"What the hell is going on with her, Tyrone. Don't lie to me. I know that you know what's going on!"

Tyrone told him. As his revelation unfolded, it pushed Jakob faster than he had ever run in his entire life, and his Mother and Father were hard-pressed to keep up with him. They nuzzled each other, knowing something was truly wrong for Jakob to run as fast as he was. That only pushed them harder as well.

"She's what??? Get your ass here, now, and rendezvous with us! Damnit! I'm not going to lose them!"

"I'm on my way, Alpha!"

"You'd better be!" Jakob snarled.

Jakob was terrified. More so than he had ever been in his life with what Tyrone had just told him. If what he said was true, no one knew what would happen, but by the howl they had all heard, Kassie was bent on killing!

And, that's when he heard her reach out to him.

"Jakob! If you can hear me! Jimmy is in terrible trouble! Five weres took him from his bedroom! I can't let Venus get away with this, and I won't! I'm so sorry. It's all my fault! I promised to watch over him, and this happened! But, I'm going to kill her with my bare hands when I find her! I'm going to tear Venus to pieces with my fangs!"

Shit! Jimmy had been taken? By Venus? No fucking way would he leave his mate to face her! Venus's skills as a warrior were almost unparalleled, and she'd kill his mate. But, with what Tyrone just told him, the danger to everyone was unknown. His speed increased, with his parents right behind him.

Kassie could smell Jimmy closer to her. They had stopped. As scared as she was, she was not about to let anyone hurt her nephew! Nor anyone else. For the first time in her entire life, she felt she could easily murder another being – including a stronger werewolf than she was a human. She reached the clearing, that she had seen on the map. Suddenly, Kassie started stumbling forward, then she fell on her knees in severe pain. Only this time, it didn't pass completely. She gasped, and started to rise, but looked up to stare into five pairs of glowing, werewolf eyes. She was so screwed! And, she knew it. Gripping her stomach, she stood slowly, only to see Jimmy laying on his back on the cold, snowy ground, tears falling down his face in fear. And, one of them had his paw on Jimmy's neck, and she knew that *it* could break his neck in an instant. Growls met her ears. She lost her fear, and stepped forward.

"Let him go, Venus!" Kassie demanded. "I don't know what you want, but I know it's not Jimmy. Let. Jimmy. Go." Kassie repeated, not realizing she was exercising her Alpha power.

Two of the wolves standing behind Venus and another werewolf whined and backed away from her, bowing their heads in submission, and falling on their haunches. That left three of them. She knew the other two wouldn't bother her, again. They had sealed their own fate. She quietly approached the one who had his leg on Jimmy's neck.

"Let him go, and I won't hurt you," she commanded. The wolf looked to the other two, then back at his Alpha. He raised his foot from Jimmy's neck and, like the other three, backed off as he submitted to her.

"Jimmy!" she yelled. "Come to Auntie Kassie, now."

Jimmy stood up, and ran to Kassie who picked him up, and hugged him. She turned to the other two who were not submissive, but Venus started walking menacingly toward Kassie and Jimmy.

"STOP!" Kassie commanded, and the female stopped dead. "Do not take one more step toward us. Do not underestimate me, Venus."

Her ears heard crashing feet coming from every direction, and all heading straight to where they were. She was relieved. Help was coming.

A werewolf broke into the clearing, and she knew, without a doubt, that it was Hunter in wolf form. She could smell him. Smell him? Huh? Her head didn't turn as he approached her side, and quickly, she lowered Jimmy to his back. Hunter stood straight and tall at her side. Without glancing at him, she commanded him.

"These five took Jimmy to get to me, Hunter. Get him out of here," Kassie ordered. "He doesn't need to see what I'm going to do."

With a growl of protest, he obeyed her, but met Billie at the perimeter. There was no way he would allow his Alpha to be killed on his watch! He nudged Billie to take Jimmy, but she didn't. Her eyes blazed with hatred at the five wolves who had dared to take her son! She growled, and took a step forward.

Kassie turned to her.

"Back off, Billie! This is my fight."

For the first time in her life, Kassie was not going to back down to anyone! Venus was hers! Billie whined for her friend, but obeyed Kassie. Hunter handed Jimmy off to Yvonne, who was angry beyond measure that five of their own had taken Jimmy! Even though Jimmy was their only young werewolf at the moment, it could have been any of their children taken! The wolves, now, formed a perimeter around Kassie and Venus, but they did not make any attempt to advance toward them. Everyone was looking to their female Alpha, since Jakob was not here. They all were ready to back her to a fault. For her, a human, to go into battle with five werewolves was unbelievable. Billie knew that if anything happened to Kassie, Jakob would kill them. But, the laws were clear. Kassie was Alpha, and that put her at the top of the strongest female Alpha that the clan had ever had in their lives. She was willing to fight and die for one of their own, even if it meant she and her babies died in the process. No greater honor could an Alpha bestow on her clan.

"What the *hell* do you want, Venus?" Kassie demanded. "And, no! I will not *permit* you to remain in your wolf forms! All of you…phase now, or you will definitely suffer my wrath."

She was confused at how she was talking, and acting, like this. But, she couldn't stop. Weird though it was to her, she watched in complete shock, when Venus stood naked – in her human form. Venus was even more surprised than Kassie that she had no control over the command, and her face showed it. Where there were five, nude werewolves, who stood before her, now their were five in human form – one of them in shadow.

"Venus.   What is your answer to this outrage? How DARE you take Jimmy hostage!"

Venus sauntered toward her not caring about her nudity, breasts gently bobbing with each step. Kassie wasn't even looking at her. Her rage was blinding her eyes with red.

"What's the matter, Kassie? Why are you so shocked? I mean. I thought you remembered me, didn't you? You got in my way before, and you are doing so again!"

Kassie grabbed her stomach, and dropped to the ground in pain. Worse than before. But, it didn't stop her this time. Slowly, she stood, fighting the pain as she gripped her stomach.

"Let me make myself clear, Venus. You will not remain in this clan!" she gasped.

Venus laughed aloud. The surrounding wolves that were loyal to the Alpha growled at Venus. She looked around her warily.

"That's right, Venus. I'm not alone. Attack me, they attack you, and I think we have the advantage. And, the outcome will be the same. You are a dead werewolf!"

Venus stepped closer to Kassie, narrowing her eyes. Kassie stood straighter, as the pain left her.

"Are you hurting, Kassie? Well, I think you need to thank me. I've been poisoning you for the last several weeks."

That sent all the wolves into not just growls, but menacing steps toward Venus.

"Yes.   That's right, Kasseiopia Harris. I have poisoned you. Why do you think your stomach is hurting so badly?" She threw her head back laughing hard. Then, "You are in the way. You always have been in my way. You weren't there when your parents and brother were killed, were you? No. Then, you weren't there when your grandparents were sent to their maker! No. You weren't there at all! You bitch! This time, you will join them!"

Venus lunged, and Billie jumped in front of Kassie, throwing Venus back into a patch of cactus.

Kassie petted Billie, who moved in front of her Alpha.

"Thank you," Kassie whispered to her sister.

Venus stood, hissing at the spines piercing her body.

"Kassie, why the hell couldn't you have just died, when I pushed you off the cliff?"

Kassie gasped and turned her head to the figure that had been in the dark. A naked man walked out of the shadows, and into the light.

"Hello, Kassie. I see you're still alive? Well, the poison should take care of you, and your mutant spawns!"

Venus walked over to him, trying to pick out the spines as she did. "That's my line, Charles!"

The two of them faced Kassie. Looking back and forth between them, suddenly, everything came flooding back into her memory. She grasped her head, falling on her knees, her stomach pain returning.

Charles! Charles? He did this? Charles Weiss had killed her parents? The man she was supposed to marry? OH, GOD!

She finally remembered that she had been going to announce their engagement to everyone the night before, but he never showed up. She had been devastated. But, the night of the house fire, she had been on a business trip all day, when she drove up to find her parents' burning house. Both they, and her brother had been killed by someone, then the house set on fire. She was stunned, and screamed, trying to run into the house only to be held back by a fireman. The next day, Kassie was questioned ruthlessly by the police, and let go. They had nothing to hold her on, because she had the perfect alibi. She'd been meeting with a client in another city. The funeral had been horrific for her, and she had moved in with her Grandparents. A year it took, to come to grips with what had happened. Luckily, her boss had not fired her, and one morning, after kissing her Grandparents, she left for another meeting that would take three days. Kassie was exhausted when she drove back home, and shock sent her into almost a catatonic state. Again, she had arrived only to find, this time, her Grandparents had been murdered, and their house set on fire!

This time, though, the police arrested Kassie. They had nothing on her, but the prosecutor tried his best to argue that she had come home early from whatever meeting she had attended, just to kill her Grandparents. And, it was all about a huge inheritance that she would receive. No one believed her, this time. Once they could overlook, but twice spoke of deliberate. She had been put through the ringer of a trial, only to be found not guilty by the jury after several weeks. However, there was no proof whatsoever that the prosecutor's "theory" was true, so the jury could not agree with each other. And, since they really couldn't find a reason to put her in jail, or send her to the electric chair, she exonerated.

When Charles had finally showed up, he claimed that he had been in England on business, and he didn't hear about her parents a year before, or her Grandparents until five months had passed. Kassie had been so devastated, she did whatever he wanted. So, he packed her into the car, and drove her to the Lost Canyon, hopefully to help her heal. She didn't remember a lot more from that point. Just bits and pieces. Venus had beaten her up, and they had thrown her into the car. When they had arrived, Charles pulled her out of the car, her head hitting the ground as he drug her across the rocks, cutting her body into pieces. He jerked her up.

"Walk, bitch!" he had said to her.

She stumbled along, but the pain in the back of her head was killing her, but she finally snapped out of it long enough to tell him that she was done with him. Charles became livid with anger, and Kassie took his ring off, and threw it in his face. Strangely enough, he had reached out and caught it easily. That was strange, because the last guy ever to be athletic was Charles. He'd grabbed her arm at that point, throwing her forward down the path. A woman, and now she knew it was Venus, met them at a point about five hundred feet from the bottom. Venus had a crowbar, and backed Kassie into the safety railing.

"You little bitch! What is it going to take to for you to die?"

Venus brought the iron bar down on the back of her head, then pushed her over the railing. She fell to what they thought would be her death. Only, it didn't work out their way.

Kassie still didn't know why they had tried to kill her. Now, facing the two of them, she determined to find out why.

"Why? Why did you try to kill me? I didn't have anything, so why?" she asked.

Charles shrugged.

"Oil, Kassie. Oil. Oil was found on your Grandparents' land. I wanted it. I wanted the money. Your parents wouldn't cooperate, so they had to die. Then, your Grandparents refused! All I had to do was to kill all of them, marry you, and the land would be mine!"

"I doubt that would have happened," Kassie snorted.

"That's where you were wrong, bitch." Venus said.

Around her, the wolves were all stunned with this conversation!

"See? I am an expert forger, and I forged your Grandparents' will after they died. It was possible that the prosecutor used them to try to convict you of their murder. But, somehow, you continued to get out of it! As long as any of you were alive, you were in our way. Charles," she grinned at him, "Charles made sure that they all died. The final step was forging your marriage certificate! Once you were dead, he claimed the land, and the oil! And, it was going so great!"

"Yeah…until you found me alive, after all," Kassie snarled.

Charles chimed into the conversation.

"You see, Kassie…the best way to kill you was to push you over the edge of the Canyon, and that's what we did. But, I received an added perk to the equation. Immortality as a werewolf, thanks to Venus. She's my mate. Only this time, I wanted to be here when she killed you. And, now, Kassie, that's what I'm going to do. Watch her kill you."

He gloated so much, Venus jabbed him in the ribs.

"He's right. Shouldn't take that long. After all, I call challenge for Alpha! None of the clan will dare come to your aid, now. Since the poison is taking you, anyway, I figure you'll just let me kill you."

Kassie's stomach clinched, this time shoving her down to her knees. Somewhere in the pain she heard

Venus laugh, and saw her move toward her. This time, though her pain did not stop. It escalated. Poison? She was going to die after all. All three of them, and all over this bitch! NO! It wouldn't happen.

Kassie found the strength to stand to everyone's surprise. Something was changing inside of her. She could feel it deep. Above them, the moon was brighter than ever, and the stars glittered with it. Kassie could now see Venus's eyes narrow in pure, unadulterated hatred. And, then…Kassie lost it!

"Ah! So, Charles! You are nothing more than a bastard prick, who can't do his own dirty work, and has to depend upon a *'bitch'* to do it for you??" Kassie baited, watching him take a step toward her. Then she whirled back to Venus. "And, *you*, you fucking bitch! You killed my parents? My brother? My grandparents? And, for what? Oil? *Oil*! You think you will kill ME? My children? Dream on, sister! I don't think so!"

While Kassie stood Venus down, and everyone could see that it was painfully obvious that a fight was coming, Tyrone came barreling into the clearing, followed by Jakob and his parents. They heard Venus tell Kassie that she and Charles had killed her family, that she had tried to kill Kassie, but Kassie wouldn't die. Tyrone started to move toward Venus to try and stop her, but Jakob beat him to it. A strange man stepped in front of him, and quoted werewolf law.

"Venus has challenged her for female Alpha! You cannot interfere. You know the law!" He looked around him. "No one can interfere! If you do, your lives are forfeit!"

Jakob phased into his human self – naked, but that didn't matter.

"Just who the hell are you?"

He reached out, and grabbed Charles by the neck. All the wolves phased. Kassie knew there were a lot of naked people standing around her, but she did not take her eyes off her prey for one second. Yes. Venus was prey! Her prey! She began to growl deep in her chest while her mate and her ex-fiancé faced off as well.

"Why I'm your mate's fiancé! Didn't she tell you? Oh, wait. No. She couldn't remember who she was!"

"I am her mate, and your Alpha! I demand to know who you are," the Clan Alpha demanded.

"I was her fiancé – when I was human! Name's Charles! I can't imagine how I ever stomached her face, let alone her body for five long years! She was horrible in bed, but you know that."

"Patience, son!" his Father told him, placing his hand on his shoulder. "Remember what you were taught."

Jakob gathered up his strength, and nodded to his Dad. Then, his glowing blue eyes met Charles' glowing yellow eyes. He quickly lifted him into the air.

"You are not part of this Clan. To violate the laws and the territory of the local Alpha without permission is to trespass, and that penalty is execution," he warned.

"You think I care what you think, Alpha? I do not! Venus is my mate, and with her I will stand – even if it means having to fight you!" he snarled.

While Jakob and Charles butted heads, Tyrone was more interested in what was going on with Venus. She had done nothing, but cause the Clan pain and misery for all these years. He would not let her cause any more. He was about to speak, when he saw

Kassie fall to her knees grasping her stomach. Venus advanced on her with a sneer and a growl.

"Venus!" he yelled, knowing what was about to happen. "Don't! Stop! Don't go near her!"

"Shut up, old man! You're nothing to me any more. I will be Alpha, and then I will rule YOU!"

"You don't understand!" he tried again.

"Oh, yes I do. I've been poisoning her slowly over weeks. Now, she's at my mercy, and she will die at my hand!" She turned to all the Clan to address them. "Do you see how weak your Alpha is? How she writhes on the ground with the poison inside of her? She is mortal, and she will die! Jakob placed a *human* over all of you! And, you accept this? Humans have no place in our world! Follow me, and see a new era in our history! Join me, and we will destroy all humans. We will turn them, and they will join us! When it is over, all the Earth will be werewolves. The humans, finally, will be extinct!"

Tyrone's eyes swerved to Kassie. He looked up to the moon, and back down at her. It wasn't the poison that was the problem. If she turned now, Venus was a dead woman.

"Venus! You don't understand! You scratched her when you pushed her off…!"

Jakob looked into Charles' smug face, and with one twist, broke his neck without remorse. He dropped him into the dirt below their feet, and motioned for some Clan members to come and get him.

"Do not bury him. Take him into the desert, and leave him for the buzzards," Jakob ordered, then turned to Tyrone.

"She's turning, Venus! Get out of the way!" Tyrone yelled one last time.

Venus's wild eyes met his.

"Impossible! Surely you could think of a better excuse to try and stop me, old man! A human cannot become a werewolf without biting! She was not bitten! It is voluntary!"

"No it isn't, Venus! She's a human turning to a werewolf! They do not turn the way we do!" Jakob yelled at her. "And, if it comes to that, did you not *volunteer* her off a cliff?

Venus growled, but didn't take her eyes off Kassie. Tyrone tried once more to reason with Venus.

"Venus, look at her! She's in the throes of changing from a human to werewolf! Why the hell do you think she survived the fall? Why do you think she healed so fast? Why do you think she was able to become pregnant? She was TURNING!"

"Oh, shut up, old man! You are dumb. That cannot happen. Only a mate can turn a mate!"

Jakob answered her.

"That's true – if the new werewolf had a mate! But, you took that choice from her – from me! You violated our highest laws regarding humans! You turned her!"

"No! That's not possible. I did not bite her!" Venus denied, while watching Kassie scream in agony as she lay on the ground.

"How many times must I tell you that a bite is not the only way to turn a human? That's something every werewolf learns the moment they are able to understand! The scratch was very small, and was under her arm. That fact is why it has taken so long for her to turn! It was too small to let the virus fully invade her bloodstream! That's why it took so much time!"

~ 12 ~
When will some people learn that gloating comes before a fall?

He stared at Kassie who was writhing with birth pains – of becoming a werewolf. A new werewolf was dangerous. That's why when someone was turned, they made sure there was always someone with them when they turned – to help ease their transition, and keeps them from hurting others. But, this was not the same thing at all. A newly turned human has no control or cognitive powers of reasoning. Once they turn, they will kill the first thing that they see.

"No. I did this! I poisoned her! It is the poison! It will violate her body until she convulses, and dies like a rabid dog!"

"Venus…PLEASE! Your poison is not causing this! The poison was rendered null and void by the werewolf virus!"

She just flipped Tyrone the bird, and turned to her werewolf form with an evil grin. This time she leaned forward to attack Kassie.

Jakob couldn't interfere. Kassie knew it deep down. But, from what they were saying, she was already a werewolf, and the choice had been taken from her mate to change her! This was supposed to have been Jakob's right! Now that she knew what was happening to her, she felt the horrible pain as her body began to stretch and contort. Everyone watched in awe of her first turn. Jakob did everything in his power to help, but something was stopping him from doing so.

"Dad! I can't help her! Why?" Jakob desperately asked his Father.

"I have no idea, son! You should be able to help her! I should be able to help her, but I can't do it, either!" he answered his son, while watching Kassie in horror.

The pain was excruciating! Kassie had just thought she knew what pain was! When she felt her spine begin to twitch and twist, her screams escalated, as it formed into a different backbone. Next, she felt her arm and leg bones and muscles do the same thing.

"Oh, God!" Kassie cried, throwing back her head

Her feet elongated, and she was thrown forward onto all fours, followed by the bones and muscles in her hands also elongating to match the size of her back legs. Panting in pain, Kassie felt the worst happening as her face actually stretched into a muzzle, her ears moved to the top of her head, and stood to a point. Finally, she felt her teeth grow large and sharp. Kassie raised her wolf's glowing green eyes to glare at Venus. Suddenly, the transformation completed its final phase, and everyone looked on in stunned awe, as Kassie exploded from her human form. In her place, stood a shining, silver werewolf.

Jakob's mouth stood open. She was the most beautiful werewolf he had ever seen in his life. Her coat was like pure silver, which glowed as if the moon was bright above her. But, this shine was not because of the moon. He had no idea why she looked like that, but she was gorgeous! More than that, he realized, that she was absolutely and completely in control! He and Tyrone looked at each other, because no new werewolf was controlled.

"How?" Jakob mouthed, while Tyrone was completely speechless. He just shook his head, and shrugged.

The idea that a newly born werewolf would not be in control was blown to bits from Kassie's transformation, since this was something they had never seen before now. A new werewolf completely in control had never been seen before, and right now, Kassie was growling angrily at Venus. Only a fool would get in her way. Kassie had been challenged, even though she didn't know what that meant. In moments, Venus phased back into her wolf with the two facing each other, as if waiting for something.

"She's beautiful, son," his Mother said. "But, this is quite unusual. Why isn't she tearing things up?"

"Jakob, you need to keep her under control," his Father said, to which Jakob nodded.

"Dad, you are first Alpha, before me. Will you remind the clan of this law?"

"It will be my pleasure, my son." His Father stepped forward. "I am Xander, former Alpha to the Lost Canyon Clan. Heed all the words I now say. As is my right, I will explain the laws and rules of this fight." He turned to the two females who were turned toward him, their heads on their paws in honor. "The challenge for female Alpha has been issued by Venus and accepted by Kassie. It is her right to defend her status." He turned to the two female wolves. "Understand, both of you. This will be a fight to the death as law! The one left standing will be the Alpha; the other will perish either during the fight, or if she should survive, she will be banished to the four winds of the Earth, and will have no clan or family. She will, forever be alone as the punished party will be exiled from all packs forever. Do you both understand what I have outlined?" Both wolves nodded. Then, he turned to the clan. "Know this…no one may interfere in this challenge. Anyone who does will be banished forever from any clan in the world. You will be shaved bare, and one eye will be removed. You will wander the Earth, alone, without a clan or family. The challenge makes no deference between werewolf and human, if the human is mated to another Alpha or Beta. Do you each understand all that I have described?"

Growls of agreement were heard in the night air. Their Alpha female would defend her title, even though she was human up until a few moments ago.

Kassie stood face to face with the woman who dared kill her family. Venus would not live to see another morning, of that she was sure. But, honestly? She wasn't really sure about herself, either! Her lips drew back in challenge, showing her newly sharp, wolf teeth. She had accepted Venus's challenge, but unlike Venus, she had something else to fight for, and she was far more deadly, because of it.

"Begin," Xander said.

The two females slowly began to circle each other. Neither female's eyes left that of her opponent. Then…Venus lunged! Kassie almost yawned with boredom, as she casually stepped sideway, letting Venus fly past. Men had rules when fighting. Women had none, which makes girl fights so much more dangerous. Venus quickly turned and swiped her paws at Kassie's back, causing blood to ooze. But, Kassie was not attacking. Not yet.

Jakob was watching his mate carefully. While it killed him to see Venus claw her back, Kassie was biding her time.

"Good…good," he muttered. He sent her a suggestion through their link. *"Careful. Let her wear herself out before you attack, love."*

"No worries, Jakob. Trust me," she answered, not taking her eye off Venus for even a second.

"I love you!" he told her.

Venus slid forward, and turned to face Kassie once again. She growled in frustration, because Kassie hadn't attacked yet! She needed Kassie to lose her cool, so she could take her out.

Kassie yawned, and flopped her front legs down, laying her head on them. But, still, she never, once, took her eye off Venus. Venus howled in anger, and charged. Kassie held her wolf back until just the right moment. Then, she met Venus head-on, lowered her head, and bit into her left flank, letting go immediately, and sailing past Venus. Venus slid to a halt, and turned in surprise.

"What the hell?" she said in her mind. *"When did she learn that trick?"*

"What the fuck?" Jakob said to his mate. *"How did you learn to do that?"*

"Not now, Jakob!" Kassie growled.

The anger built quickly. Venus's mate was dead, and her stomach coiled ready for the next attack. Venus charged, and this time, she sidestepped Kassie, and bit hard into the back flank, causing her to growl in anger. Kassie turned on a dime, and sped back to Venus where they met, claws flying as they each dug into the other.

Finally, Kassie managed to get her mouth around Venus' neck. Blood, fur, and flesh flew from her mouth as she gouged it out of her neck. Venus growled at her, obviously in terrible pain, but she turned and lunged, yet, again. The two females were savage, biting and clawing each other, and the fight continued.

The Clan members were all looking on with excitement and terror. Jakob wasn't going to lie to himself. His mate had no experience in fighting in wolf form, but she fought as if she had always been a werewolf! He was in awe of her battle tactics. It didn't keep her from getting mauled, but she never let Venus see her anger. That, in itself, was amazing.

When he saw a couple of Venus's wolves begin to move toward them, he leaped in front of them both, and Hunter joined him, and both growled, causing the two wolves to back down and bow. Both of them kept one eye on the two wolves, and one on the incredible fight unfolding before them.

The females were definitely tiring. This fight had gone on long enough. Kassie decided it was time for it to end. She was done with this bitch, and decided to show her just why Kassie was Alpha female! Each female was bleeding badly from their wounds, and both were obviously growing weaker. They faced each other. Kassie knew that this was it. This was where she needed to end this. She was Alpha, and this woman had not only challenged her for Alpha female, but she had literally tried to end her short life! If she lived, she might very well come after Kassie again, but she also knew her babies would be highly vulnerable to this shitty female. That is what spurred Kassie to get rid of Venus – now.

Jakob was watching Venus carefully. There was nothing he could do, but if Venus tried to pull something, he could warn Kassie through their bond. That's when he noticed something. No doubt the fight was in the last moments, and that's when Jakob's eyes widened as he realized that his mate was holding her wolf in check, creating a false exhaustion for Venus to see. But, she was far from exhausted, and that is when what Kassie was doing dawned on him. Kassie was toying with Venus! For the first time, he felt confident, and he stood taller as he watched the fight end. It could only end one way. One of them would die.

Finally, Venus made her last, huge, and fatal mistake lunging over Kassie's head, intending to grab her throat and snap it. She missed, but Kassie did not. Kassie opened her mouth, and snapped off Venus' right, rear leg. With the leg in her mouth, and she spit it out as if it was foul! She spit it out of her mouth.

"Yuck!" she told her mate, who chuckled into her mind.

Venus was hobbling on three legs, the stump of her right rear leg running red with blood, she still tried one more time to grab Kassie's throat. Kassie sidestepped her, and bit down on Venus's neck instead. Then, she closed her mouth hard, snapping Venus's neck.

It was over. Venus lay dead at her feet, and a feeling of satisfaction spread over her. Around her, there was silence. Total and complete silence. Charles was dead thanks to Jakob. Venus was dead because of the female Alpha of their clan, and their newest werewolf member. Kassie stood over her kill with her head held high. She met each wolf's eyes, daring anyone else to challenge her. No one else wanted to challenge her, and even the two who were on Venus and Charles' side, bowed their heads to her. They all fell down on their front paws in honor and acceptance of their female Alpha. All except Jakob's parents and Jakob. Jakob's Father watched his son for the acknowledgement of Kassie's kill.

Jakob phased back into his wolf form, and approached his mate. He saw tears forming in her beautiful green eyes. The first fight to the death is very hard. He had his own share of fights, and he knew what she was feeling. He came to her, and put his arms around her neck in comfort. Her bloody muzzle was trembling, and a large tear ran down her cheek. Then, something that only a skilled warrior is given within the werewolf community, and in honor of his mate, he backed away from her, phased, and fell on his front paws, lowering his head to her. This was the greatest honor any wolf could ever give his mate. He acknowledged that she was his equal.

All Kassie could do was stare at Venus. What she had done! She had killed someone! The ones who had killed her parents, brother, and grandparents. And, for what? Oil…money. She phased to human, then turned to shuffle into the woods. The pain of her wounds nothing compared to the pain in her hears. Angry tears rolled down her cheeks, as she slammed her fists into the nearest tree over and over, breaking her knuckles, and cutting her hands to pieces. Finally, the little tree broke under her strength, and even though blood poured from her hands, she heard screaming, only to realize it was her.

"NO!" she cried. Why the hell did she remember? Why? Jakob had come to stand just beyond her, and he knew that cry. It was the same cry as he screamed, when his little brother had been killed in a freak snow skiing accident a hundred years earlier. His mate was suffering from what she had just discovered. That she was a werewolf, and that she had killed someone. Even more, that the urge to kill one who had wronged her had surfaced. Her Alpha persona had surfaced, and she would need to learn how to curb that urge. But, remembering her calculating stance as she fought Venus, he knew that she had full control. Why, he didn't know, but perhaps Tyrone could help all of them understand what really happened to a human who was turned.

Jakob reached for his mate to fold her into his strong, steel arms, holding her steady until she stopped struggling and just collapsed in them.

"It's OK, my love. I know how you feel. Killing someone is horrible."

Frowning, she looked up at him with tears.

"No. You don't understand, Jakob! This isn't about me killing her. She and Charles deserved that judgment. It's about what they took from me! From our children! My parents, brother, and grandparents were killed by that bastard Charles and Venus! They murdered them! Our children will never know their family on my side! But, do you know what the worst part of all of this was?"

Jakob just let her tell him in her time. He knew.

"Money."

"I know, sweetheart. But, you will tell our children about them. Who they were, and what they did with their lives. They won't be forgotten as long as you tell them stories about them. Charles and Venus didn't win. No one will ever mention them again anywhere on Earth in the clans. But, what they will remember? You, and your amazing turn, control, and fair judgment. They will remember our children, and those that are still yet to be born. We don't really understand why these things happen, but if there is a fairness and correct judgment, then that is all we can hope for in this world – human or supernatural."

She sniffed, and nodded her head, knowing that he was right.

"Come on. Let's go."

"Wait! Won't they think I am weak for crying?" she asked.

"No. They will think you are strong that you could acknowledge the part of us that we cling to every day – humanity."

Phasing to their wolves once more, they trotted back to the clan. His Mother and Father looked at each other with pride. They both remembered when it had been their time of fighting. They both stood tall and strong. The senior Alphas stepped forward on either side of their son. All were still kneeling.

Kassie just stared at them in surprise, and yet, she knew what it meant. She was humbled, now. Once they all rose, the howls were deafening. Kassie looked at them all, and then, she howled her first warrior howl, letting her wolf do the honors. That's when she felt movement inside her. She hadn't forgotten them, but at least she knew they were alright! She stared down at Venus, and shook her head in sadness. They would never really know what had caused her to lose her mind. It was the only way that Kassie could effectively forgive her.

Tyrone's eyes watered, but he had no animosity to Kassie for killing his nurse. He did not mourn for Venus. She had betrayed her clan, murdered several people, and tried to kill their Alpha female. No. He had not remorse or love left for her. Jakob and Kassie watched him walk away. Hunter jerked his head to their third and fourth, to remove the bodies. They wouldn't be missed. The bodies were always burned at daybreak to avoid being seen from any satellite photos.

Jakob motioned everyone to go about their business, and he waited until they had all gone. He nodded to his mate to phase back. He smiled a little, when she was a bit clumsy about it, but she did it. He reached for her, and held her tightly while she cried. He knew she had not wanted to show that weakness in front of their clan.

"I killed a person, Jakob!"

"No. You killed a monster, Kassie." He pushed her away so she could see him. "It is our way. She challenged your authority. Her big mistake was not realizing you were turning."

"How did you know?"

"Tyrone told me on my way back."

"But, how?"

"Well, I have a permanent rule unless there is real trouble. The Alpha can speak, and hear, any were's thoughts from anywhere. I couldn't hear you, because you were turning. That's what Tyrone says. When a new wolf turns for the first time, their minds are in chaos, and it is impossible to connect with them. That's one of the reasons why we need to be around them to help. I'm sorry you were turned, Kassie. I wish I had been here. Maybe it would have been easier?"

Kassie shook her head.

"No. It wouldn't have been. I was enraged at what Charles and Venus had done to my family. It's been over a year, and it still hurts. But, when I changed, my wolf was more enraged than I was. I let her take over. I had to, because I didn't know what to do."

He nodded.

"You did good. Now, let me look at your wounds."

He turned her around, and except for one that was still healing, her others were gone. He breathed a huge sigh of relief.

"Run with me, Kassie. It will help you. I guarantee it."

He phased back to his wolf form, and Kassie followed him, but this time, there was no pain from the turn. Side by side ran a coal black wolf, with glowing blue eyes, and a beautiful shining, silver wolf with green eyes, whose coat glittered in the moonlight.

Kassie never forgot her first turn, her first fight, and her first run with her mate as the years passed.

WOLF CANYON MEMORY

There is never an end to any story…only more of the story!

Kassie wiped her hands on a towel, tossing it onto the kitchen counter, that was made from a solid piece of black granite with gold specks. She looked at the meal that both Jakob and she had made, then walked to lean against the door jam. With a huge grin, she surveyed the huge family room of the five-thousand square foot penthouse that she and Jakob had bought in downtown Denver, Colorado four years prior, after their human wedding.

Even today, she still was in awe of how many had come that day. Until that moment, Kassie had never fully understood Jakob's real influence and place in the world's clans. But, when clans from all over the world descended to the retreat, she figured it out very fast – followed by her almost hyperventilating! They were not there to see Jakob, but her. Billie had to get Jakob to come, and calm her down. Luckily, he had not seen her in her gown. Billie would never have let him in if she had been in it. They had all brought tents, campers, trucks, and other items to stay for a whole week of celebration, even though Jakob was taking Kassie somewhere secret on their honeymoon. The canyon had been covered with them, quite literally, as far as the eye could see. And, she had been able to see a very long way, thanks to her newly acquired werewolf eyes. She was the first human to be changed into a werewolf in hundreds of years, and no one was going to miss this wedding! It was the wedding of the centuries – yes, I said centuries – and everyone wanted to meet her. If they couldn't meet her, they just wanted to say that they were there to see this monumental step in the werewolf world. The introduction of the mate of the number one Alpha in the world, and she was a newly turned human, just made everything so much more special.

Jakob wasn't just *an Alpha*...he was *The Alpha*...elected by the world's werewolf leaders, long ago, to lead all of them into a new, and hopefully better world. And, from the respect they all gave to him, he had succeeded. But, what she didn't know was that she was the leader of all the females. Like Jakob, Kassie wasn't just *a female Alpha*...she was *The Female Alpha*. It was on her wedding day when Jakob, Billie, Hunter, and his parents finally got through to her just how important her place was in the Clan, she almost passed out on the floor! Luckily, Jakob had caught her before she hit it. She'd turned her head to him. He was laughing at her? Really?

"Hey! Like who wouldn't faint after hearing that?" she muttered to no one.

"OK, big brother! Out! You shouldn't see the bride before the wedding!" Billie said with a most innocent face.

"You have to be joking!" Jakob said, but with a smart-aleck smirk, he obeyed. As he left the room, he called back, "That's so 'human' of you, Billie!" To which Billie just made a juvenile move by sticking out her tongue.

The venue was held outside at the full moon, as per werewolf tradition. Their werewolf and small, but human family, friends, and Clans, all gathered together for the festivities of a lifetime. Many of their human friends knew who and what they were, because this was something that both Kassie and Jakob had wanted. Kassie's best friend, Janie, had been let into their secret, and now, stood as her maid of honor, while Jakob's Father was his. The colors were beautiful and subtle. The bridesmaids wore ice-blue silver strapless gowns that were long in the back, and rose in the front almost to their knees. They each had a pair with silver ribbons, which laced around the legs in a very Grecian style, and three-inch heels. Their hair was piled on their head, ringlets straddling the sides of their faces. Hunter and Billie were their seconds, and finally, it was time for Kassie to walk down the makeshift aisle. Earlier that day, she had stood in awe of the beauty brought to this desert land of red rocks. Rows upon rows of snow-white chairs had been placed on either side of the aisle, which was lined with green cedar swags draped between solar-celled post lights, each with three globes. These were loaded with dusty pink peonies in groups of three – a favorite flower of her Father's. For her Mother, twinkling lights were woven through the cedar swags, and looked just like fireflies. Her Mom had loved those tiny little glow bugs! A white runner ran down the center of the aisle, and was covered with peony petals. The makeshift altar was a huge white wrought iron arch, covered from top to bottom with the same cedar and peonies, sparkling with the same, tiny white lights.

The only thing missing were her parents and Grandparents. She was wondering if she was to walk down the aisle alone. However, just before the ceremony, Xander walked through the door, kissed his mate, and then turned to Kassie.

"You know, I know that your Dad would have been honored to walk you down the aisle, Kassie. And, I know I'm not him, but I consider you my daughter, and I would consider it a true privilege if you would consent to allow me to lead you down that aisle in memory of your parents and Grandparents?"

Kassie felt tears form at such a kind and sweet gesture, and all she could do was nod. He kissed her on the cheek, and the women all left the room. Then, he held out his arm to her, and she took it, and walked down the aisle to her forever after fairytale life.

Kassie still got tears when she thought of that honor, and she would never forget it, because at the end of that aisle was her mate and true love, and within her was the proof of that love. She wasn't showing at all, yet, and that was alright with her. Sighing, Cassie watched her beautiful family sit in front of the Christmas tree that they had all chosen together. The children were, now, twelve, and their Father was on the floor showing them both how to work the new computers that they had gotten for Christmas. That just reminded her of when they were born, and she actually giggled. OK. It wasn't funny to her at the time, but it sure was, now!

Four months after their wedding, Kassie was panting with labor pains. Jakob's parents had flown in for the births. Billie was holding her hand, and bathing her face with cool water, while Jakob was delivering his own children, because Tyrone had to leave for a long-standing conference, and couldn't get back in time to deliver them. His Mother stood next to her son to take the babies. Werewolf babies were born as humans. But, right now, that didn't matter one bit to her, because her pains were coming fast and hard.

"It's time, Kassie! Push!" Jakob commanded.

"I am pushing, you jackass!" and she continued to cuss up a blue streak!

Billie was grinning. She'd said the same thing to Hunter when Jimmy was born, and a great deal more! And, his Mother was grinning as well. All women who have had babies have said all kinds of things to their husbands including things like "I hate you!" and "You will never touch me again!"

"The head is crowning! Another push!"

Kassie yelled with the pain as she pushed her first child into the world and into his Father's hands. He stared at his first-born son. The next Alpha in his line.

Hunter and Jakob's Dad were pacing out in the office. Hunter remembered when Jimmy was born. He heard Kassie scream, and then, a nice loud howl from a baby. He was an UNCLE! Yes! Xander just looked at him, and shook his head even though his smile was almost as large as his face!

Kassie was in between contractions, and his Mother took her grandson to clean.

Billie held Kassie's hand a second time, as the next pains came, and she strained to push her second child into the world.

"I see the head! Come on! Just one more push, baby!"

"If you don't stop telling me to push, I'm going to eat you alive!" she yelled at him.

With that last push, all pain was gone, as she felt her second child slide from her body. Her mate held their daughter in his hands. He couldn't take his eyes of her. She was beautiful just like her mother. Oh, SHIT!

"I'm so going to have to deck the guys!" Jakob muttered.

Billie and his Mother laughed out loud, while a very tired Kassie smiled tenderly at her mate.

Jakob stood up carrying his daughter to her Mother. As he placed her in Kassie's arms, Kassie whispered, "She's beautiful," kissing her daughter's little blonde head. Then, she looked up at

Jakob. "Thank you for our children," she whispered to her mate, who leaned down to kissed the woman who had taken his heart.

Billie and her Mother finally shooed Jakob out, so they could clean Kassie, as well as get the babies washed and prepared. Once Kassie was clean, they both kissed her forehead, and left the room. When that was done, their Father had taken both of their children, and disappeared out the door to show them to their Grandfather and Uncle.

When the door opened, Kassie gasped at the most beautiful sight she had ever seen, knowing she would have this memory until the day she died. Her mate walked into the room with their daughter in one arm and their son in the other. The door shut silently behind him. Jakob walked to Kassie, and placed their son in her arms. Kassie's eyes softened when she saw him. He was the miniature replica of her mate except for one distinction. He yawned, and opened his beautiful green eyes, that were just like hers. They blinked at her, and a tiny ghost of a smile touched his lips, before he closed his eyes to sleep.

"She has my eyes, Kassie," he told her, as he laid their daughter into her other arm. She, like her Mother was blonde, but her little fist was in her mouth, and her tiny glowing blue eyes were open looking around her. She looked up at her Mother, and grinned a toothless grin. Her eyes closed with a tiny sigh, and Kassie watched her sucking on her fist gently as she slept.

She looked up at Jakob.

"I think someone might be a bit hungry."

He smiled, and took his sleeping son from her arm.

Kassie pulled her gown down, and placed her daughter at her breast. She latched on sleepily, and started to drink. Kassie leaned her head back, and sighed in contentment. Jakob just stood and watched his two beautiful girls. He had seen women nursing many times in his life, but it was nothing compared to watching his own mate feeding their daughter at her breast. Something deep stirred in Jakob at that moment, and he knew he would never forget this most beautiful sight. Was this how his Father felt when Jakob nursed at his Mother's breast? How Hunter felt when he saw the same thing with Jimmy? The need to protect his family was even stronger than to protect himself. Kassie knocked him out of his thoughts.

"She's asleep, Jakob. Take her, and give me our son."

He took their daughter, and handed her their son, who was also making the sucking noises with his mouth. Jakob watched as Kassie placed their son at her other breast. Like their daughter, he latched on and began to eat. Jakob leaned over, and kissed his son's head, while he was feeding. Then, he looked up at his mate. How could his groin harden for her at a time like this? Kassie seemed to read his mind.

"It's normal for the Daddy to want his mate, while he watches her nurse their child, Jakob."

"Normal? How can it be normal when I want you so much right now?"

"I don't understand it myself, but your Mother told me that you would feel this way. She remembered your Father after you were born, and his reaction to her."

"Ok, no! I did not need that picture in my head, Kassie!" he laughed.

"Well, she also told me something else kind of neat if you want to know?"

Jakob's eyes were wary, but "OK. Give."

"She also told me that nothing made her happier when both you and your Father suckled at her breasts at the same time." She looked up under her eyelashes with amusement at the sight of his face in shock. "What? Did you never think of that?" she giggled.

Him? Suckling her at the same time one of his children did? Oh, man! He hardened even more at that thought.

Kassie patted his hand, and whispered.

"I really can't wait until I am able to feel you feeding with your children. And, when I heal from giving birth, the possibilities can be endless! I've been told that I will have far more milk than I need even with two babies nursing. So, either I have to have a breast pump, or I guess you will need to help me get rid of the excess milk, so my breasts won't hurt. So. Do you want to buy that breast pump for me?" she asked coyly.

"We'll go ahead and get one, but I'm willing to do my duty to keep my mate from being in pain! I mean…it's a tough job, but, if I need to, I need to."

They both laughed.

"Names?" he asked.

"Well, I was thinking. Could we name them after my parents and yours?"

He nodded approval.

"Great idea. So, for our daughter?"

"My Mother's name was Iris, and my Dad's name was Michael."

"And, my Mother's name, of course, is Mary, and Dad's is Xander. So, how about Michael Xander Lane, and Mary Iris Lane?"

Kassie loved them, and agreed immediately! He kissed her forehead, and then added, "Our next son will be named after your brother, Kassie."

Kassie was overwhelmed with the idea of having another little boy someday.

"Oh. I did forget a little info," Jakob said.

Kassie rolled her eyes as her son finished nursing, and she pulled her top back up.

"OK. What this time?"

"Werewolves grow fast. It takes about six years for them to reach adulthood."

Kassie sucked in her breath. "But, I thought Jimmy was three?"

"He is…in human years. Technically, a werewolf child is three years to a human's one. So, in six years, he will be eighteen."

"I have a lot to learn!" Kassie shook her head. "I'll never figure all of this out!"

"Well, one thing I still haven't been able to understand how you knew how to fight in the first place? I mean, it was amazing to watch!"

She grinned and handed him Michael.

"Put them in the crib, and I'll try to explain," she told him.

After they were both in the makeshift crib, he walked back, and sat on the bed where she patted.

"OK. So. Give."

"I would never have known how to fight, but you see, when I left school, long before any of this happened, I kind of got into kick boxing, because of my best friend, Janie. She loved it, and suggested I learn a bit of it. I tried it, and had such a great time, I signed up for classes. After a few years, I actually won an amateur kick boxing contest. It wasn't my thing, really, but my instructor decided it would be good to test me out. So, I did. It was my first, and only fight, but I won it! Janie was the best when I got in the ring, and I credit her for the whole thing. And, I credit her for the reason I was able to fight Venus."

"So, you really did know how to fight? Amazing!" he said. He brushed her hair out of her eyes. "It will be time to leave next week, and go to the city for a few months. It's already December 5th, and..."

"OMG! It's almost Christmas?" she squealed, only causing her children to whimper, but they quieted down after a minute, when Kassie slapped her hands over her mouth.

Kassie's memory of that would forever warm her. Especially now, since the twins were so much older. Hard to believe that they were only three in werewolf years, but that's just the way these amazing beings were. She still found it hard to believe she was one of them, too. But, it got easier every single day! Changing was a breeze, now, and mating in wolf form was really incredible! Sometimes, she had admitted to her mate, she almost liked it better than human form! He was always willing to accommodate his mate with that at any time!

Well, dinner was ready, and his Mom and Dad, Billie and Hunter would be there in a minute, so she shuffled the children off to get dressed, and followed them with Jakob on her feet. He slipped his arms around her waist when they got to their room.

"Have I told you, lately, how beautiful you are?" he asked, nuzzling her neck where his mark was.

Pretending to think about it, she answered, "Weeelllll. Not for at least, oh, fifteen minutes!"

He laughed, as he scooped her up into his arms, and dumped her on the bed. With his wolfish grin, he joined her.

WOLF CANYON MEMORY

From Author LK Kelley to you:

Thank you so much for taking the time to read my newest book! After 7 years of being in my mind, I am thrilled to be able to offer it to you as my first stand-alone book! I had a blast writing this story of Jakob and Kassie. I wanted to present a book that had drama, mystery, and I hope it ended the way you would want it to end! Endings are always so difficult to decide upon and to write, but I'm still a firm believer that a book needs a slam-dunk ending or an ending that makes you say "Ewwww". I hope that you will try my other books @ many different bookstores, and see why my books are award winning and 5 Star books! See the entire list on the next page along with links to my author pages as well!

Thank you, again, for reading my books! I hope you enjoy them!

Please join me on my website:

https://firebird4554.wixsite.com/white-wolf-prophecy

5 Star Book List:

The White Wolf Prophecy Trilogy:

Book 1: The White Wolf Prophecy – Mating
Book 2: The White Wolf Prophecy – Hall of Records
Book 3: The White Wolf Prophecy – Scroll of Time

The Anaerris Code:

Book 1: The Anaerris Code – Gem
Book 2: The Anaerris Code – Jaxx (coming in 2018)

Wolf Canyon Memory

LINKS:

Twitter:

https://twitter.com/LKKelley1

Facebook author page & fan page

https://www.facebook.com/lk.kelley.5

https://www.facebook.com/whitewolfprophecytrilogybook/

You can find all my books at my author pages on the following links, and all fine bookstores anywhere.

https://www.amazon.com/-/e/B00HFX3ZBQ

https://www.barnesandnoble.com/s/%22Lk%20Kelley%22?Ntk=P_key_Contributor_List&Ns=P_Sales_Rank&Ntx=mode+matchall
https://itunes.apple.com/us/author/lk-kelley/id1111749220?mt=11
https://www.kobo.com/us/en/search?query=LK%20Kelley&fcsearchfield=Author

<u>OTHER SITES TO EXPLORE</u>:

https://www.walmart.com/ip/The-White-Wolf-Prophecy-Scroll-of-Time-Book-3/53274703#about-item

https://www.goodreads.com/author/show/7477009.L_K_Kelley

<u>READ THE FIRST 2 CHAPTERS OF</u>
<u>The Anaerris Code ~ Gem</u>

**the
ANAERRIS CODE
LK Kelley
a Gemma Sinclaris Series
Part 1
Gemma
By LK Kelley**

WOLF CANYON MEMORY

...PROLOGUE...

Above me, two, ancient moons shine – one of brilliant lavender, purple, and white, and one of blood red, yellow, and black. Both obscure one-fourth of the night sky, casting an eerie light on the world of my birth, which is charred and blackened by hell-fire and blood. I stand upon an enormous bluff, and stare down into the great, blackened valley, while the final war rages. A massive river of red races toward the brilliant lavender moon...the blood of my people and his. Tears of blood stain my cheeks and clothing while I watch the end of two races of beings. My race will be gone – including me, if I refuse to agree to be turned. A sound behind me. I know it is he. I can feel him as I have always done, since we met. Our kind should never be together, but it is as inevitable as time itself. I turn to see my attacker's body, which no longer has its head attached. Blood gushes forth from it. I meet his frightened eyes, and follow his horrified gaze down to the fatal wound in my chest where blood runs freely. I will bleed out in seconds.

"NO!" he yells, as I begin to collapse.

He catches me long before I hit the blackened earth below me. I stare at the man I love, knowing I should not love him. We are enemies. He has no tears to shed, but he gently cradles me in his arms, his tortured red eyes begging me with the same question he has asked many times. I can barely move my head, but I nod once, knowing the precious cargo I carry for my race and his. I want to be with him forever. And, if I'm still alive, my own race will also continue. I must change, no matter what, into whatever form. His mouth lowers to my neck kissing the pulse that is rapidly quieting as my heart silences. I feel a momentary sting as his fangs bite into my neck. To be with him forever is all I ever want, and I must complete the task that I was given by the ancients. Warmth trickles down the back of my neck as I feel the liquid of life slipping from me, echoing the death of my planet. I hope we have not waited too long. He lifts his head, his mouth dripping with my blood. I see in his sad eyes that he is hoping the same. I slide gratefully into the unknowing.

Time and space stand still. For how long, I know not. I awake, naked, on a soft bed covered in crimson silk. He sits with his back to the headboard, still cradling my lifeless body in his arms, patiently awaiting my awakening, and then, I will always be with him. I lift my eyes to stare at the man I will be with forever. I am ready as his lips lower to mine while my new, strong arms pull his nude body over mine. He is not gentle with his kiss, and I would never want him to be. I kiss him back frantically, feeling wetness between my legs as he spreads mine with his. He plunges into my heat, sheathing himself as deep as possible, and thrusts hard and fast into my body. My hips meet him with the same desperation and desire. I need him like I do not need air to breathe. As our orgasms reach their climax, I feel his hot seed jet into me. I can feel it enter my womb! He has so much! He stills, and I open my eyes that I know are still ripe with inhuman desire. I stare at the couple that is reflected in the mirror above our bed. My bright red eyes look back at me. I am whole again, and in the arms of my great lover for all time to come.

It is time. He shows me the crystal that I had entrusted to him, and I breathe a sigh of relief. It is safe, and ready for the one who must receive it. One who knows not of his part in the great scheme of the Creator. I must make sure that the Codex is written, and both it and the crystal must be kept apart. Both are dangerous alone, but together would cause unimaginable chaos. Our race has always been banned from writing about our history. I have been charged with finding a way to write what I was given in an indestructible method. But, I will use not only my own powers, but those given to me by my mate. I will make sure that we do not lose our heritage. If we must sacrifice our own lives, then so be it. At all costs, the one safeguard I carry must be kept safe until a time when the "gem" is needed.

Time ceases to exist in the realm we chose for its magic, where an ancient friend of mine offered to help. An ally who believes, as do we, that nothing can be left to chance. It is time to travel to the one place the Council would never expect us to hide the book. As for the crystal? My love has given it to one we know we can trust to protect it, sending him to a primitive planet known as Earth. And, we will hide the flesh-blackened codex – sealed with the most terrifying of magic that cannot be opened by any living soul, or they will die. My magical friend sees the future, and tells us that a time will come when both crystal and book will join together. Because of this, she sends an envoy with the "gem". And, now, we are leaving behind the only one who has the power to open and to read... the codex. And, then, it passes into legend and myth.

And, this book will forever be known as...

the
ANAERRIS CODE
By LK Kelley

The Beginning

"DADDY!" screamed eleven year-old Gemma Elwood, as she ran toward the house, and down the driveway with a tiny little dog at her feet. "DADDY! DADDY! HELP! HELP! MOMMY!"

William Tyler Elwood flung open the door the moment that he heard his daughter scream over the thunder and lightening that scraped the sky. Gem flung herself into his arms. Gemma and his love had just left the house minutes before he heard Gem's voice.

"DADDY! MOMMY! HELP MOMMY!" she screamed, finally getting her words right.

Tyler felt his stomach draw up in knots as he heard the terror in her voice. Without a word, he threw Gem into the new, red truck that he had just purchased, and drove like a maniac to where Gem pointed. Tears ran down her cheeks as she sobbed. Tyler stepped out of the truck.

"Gem. Stay here," he told her, then turned to see smoke and flames coming from below him on the mountain.

Terror gripped him as he flung himself over the edge, and started slipping and sliding his way down the embankment to get to the black Honda SUV that lay at the bottom of the mountain side. As he got closer, he saw his wife, Corina, laying on the ground in an unnatural position. He slid his way down, using his hands to keep him upright, rocks and grit scraping them to almost bloody pulps until he reached her. She had been flung almost thirty feet from the vehicle, and she hung from a low branch, where she had been impaled. He gulped as sobs racked his body. He had no option but to pull her down. She was dead. There was no life left in her beautiful green eyes. Crying uncontrollably, he slid her off the eight inch limb, and gently laid her down on the ground pushing her blonde hair back from her face. Looking into the face that had held his love for so long, he found himself in an almost catatonic state as he held the love of his life.

"Oh, Corina! My beautiful love! How did this happen?" he asked as reality set into his mind.

His clothing was blood soaked with her precious life, and he buried his face into her neck. The storm crackled around them, and rain poured from the sky mixing with his own tears and her blood from the massive hole in the middle of her body. And, then, he heard crying above him. Who was crying? Then, he remembered. Gem. Gem was crying. He turned his head upward, and saw her peering over the cliff. Corina would want him to watch after her, now. All he wanted was to join her in death! But, he couldn't. Not with his precious little girl needing him. He took one last look at his wife, laid her body down, then began the long climb back to the top. Once he was there, he fell on his knees, and pulled his crying daughter into his arms.

"It's OK, Gem. It'll be OK."

"No! It will never be OK again, Daddy!" she cried.

"I know, Gem. I know."

~ 1 ~

"Alone is never where I wanted to be, but then, I do have Lola!"

Lola, the pug, dodged a pillow that her pet just threw. Lola had been very worried about her over the last few weeks. She hadn't been able to write one, damn word on her laptop. She must have writer's block. The next words confirmed it.

"I'm so sorry, Lola!" Gem apologized, whipping her up into her arms, and giving her a kiss on her tiny head. "I didn't mean it! Really, sweetie, I didn't. Oh, Lola! What am I going to do? I don't have an idea for my next novel series!"

Lola loved her little pet, so she did the only thing that was really in her power. She turned her head, and licked her pet in the mouth. She and her pet had much in common, since both of them were adopted. Gemma Marie Elwood adopted Lola from a Pug Rescue organization in Denver, Colorado, and she had been with Gem for a very unusually long time. In fact, Gem really didn't know when Lola came to live with them, and truthfully, Lola was a bit anxious that Gem might discover that very soon. Strangely enough, though, all Lola knew was that she had never been happier. She had only complaint with her pet, and that was that Gem should be feeding Lola much more food than was placed into her bowl twice a day! Gem claimed it was to keep her trim and healthy. Lola didn't believe that for one minute! Nevertheless, no matter how many times Lola pulled the "I'm really starving" face, Gem never bought it, and would never give her any more, or less. However, sometimes, Gem would give in and cook her an egg, or maybe put some peanut butter in a Kong Ball, which kept Lola busy for hours trying to eat it all, with a bone treat, sometimes. In consequence, Lola grudgingly admitted to herself that she was healthy, trim, and had tons of energy! She could run rings around other pugs her age, since most were kind of fat! In addition, her Vet was very pleased with her health, and it always made Lola a smug pug! Pugs had a problem with weight, causing them to become sedentary with little energy. Another condition specific to pugs was with impaired breathing due to their flat little noses. And, being overweight just made it worse. At least Lola just didn't have that problem, so she forgave Gem for not feeding her as much as Lola really wanted. OK. So. If she could, she'd eat all the time! Lola loved everything – well, except for lettuce. She hated it! Ick!

Gem carried Lola over to the sofa flopping down, and leaned her head on the back of it.

"Lola, I'm stumped! I don't have an idea in my head!" Gem told her. "My publisher is about to have a cow! I have to come up with something really soon!"

Since she was little, Gemma Marie Elwood kept spiral notebooks that she called her "Dreams Diary". Spiral notebooks weren't the most elegant diary, but then, they never had much money. In them was written every dream she ever had that she remembered. It was those dreams, which gave her great ideas for her books. After her Mom had died, she became plagued by new and horrible dreams that were terribly disturbing. She would awake, screaming, and every time, her Dad would come to her rescue, holding her until her shaking and terror calmed.

Questions followed those dreams about her Mom's death – and, one particular question she repeatedly asked, yet was never supposed to ask, she did anyway.

"Why? Why? Why?" she would ask, but that question was never answered, of course.

There were things that never added up in her Mom's death, and her Dad had not been forthcoming with any information. Whatever the mystery surrounding her Mom's death was, her Dad took it to his grave. He had always told her that her Mom had hydroplaned during a horrendous storm, sending her SUV flying over the cliff. Gem could remember running and running back to her house after she found the wreck, but, she could remember nothing more, and her Father would never answer her questions. Most importantly, though, she always had the queasy feeling that she was in the SUV with her Mom. If so, though, she had no memory of it. But, another question plagued her. If she was, why wasn't she hurt or killed? She had not had a scratch on her!

Her therapy doctors had told her Dad that she had deliberately blocked out what she had seen that night. However, despite all her therapy sessions, the dreams continued to escalate. The night her Mom died was also the first night she dreamed of a frightening place of blood, death, and war. Pick something! During the nights, Gem would awake in a cold sweat that drenched her sheets. Of course that meant that she had to change them in the middle of the night, before she could go back to sleep. And, then, the dreams repeated. During the days, though, she tried to reason it all out, but when she thought of it too much, her head would feel as if it were about to explode. That one particular dream, though, had always remained the same. But lately, it had begun to change. Now, *she* had become *a participant* in it! Because of this, she could see from both the objective and subjective points of view. However, trying to figure out which was which, was becoming increasingly harder, especially since she kept hopping back and forth between someone else's eyes and her own. Confusing was not the word for it! She needed to do something about them!

Putting that aside for the time being, she walked to her desk where she kept a drawer under lock and key. Gem inserted her key, unlocked, and opened it, pulling out one of her older diaries. Because she actually believed that sometimes it was beneficial to hand-write, Gem grabbed a pencil, and curled up on her sofa, while Lola plopped her tiny body on the arm of it, falling asleep almost instantly. Gem began to write out her dream, trying to remember the omniscient point of view, and the first person point of view. And, in this case, it was really hard since the scenes kept switching constantly.

"Let's see," she said aloud, and while biting the top of her pencil, she began to write.

"OK. I'm standing on a bluff. Everything around me is blackened as if burned to a crisp. Nothing is alive here. There are no trees, no grass, no water, no signs of habitation any longer. And, it is certainly not Earth, but another planet somewhere. Two moons – or were they planets – take up half of the sky above me – one in lavender and white, and the other black and red! Below me is an unbelievably deep valley – so deep, that those fighting below resembled ants scurrying to and fro. And, even though everything seems so dark, I can still see everything."

"How weird is that?" she asked herself, nibbling on the eraser. Then, Gem continued to write and mutter to herself. She smirked, and said, "And, that is the fate of an author!"

"Massive armies fighting beside a red river spanning the ground below her, as if it were a vein within a giant being in the cosmos."

Gem's mind escalated, and her hand began to write as if possessed!

wanted to read. She wanted something unique like her last Trilogy. Despite the fact that she was one of the more popular writers, and her books were making a small amount of money on Kindle, it was just not enough. She wanted to be able to live as a writer. Since Gem couldn't do that, yet, she was forced to supplement it by working as a cashier at the only grocery store in town owned by Macklin Simmons of Simmons Grocery. In addition, she also held a part-time job at the library. Since she was majoring in writing, it was the best possible world for her! After all, not only did she have to live and eat, she also was paying off her Father's hospital bills that had incurred after he spent two months there just before he died. She figured she would be paying those off even after she was dead at this rate!

Pacing more, she muttered, "I just need a new angle on the supernatural, Lola. But what?"

Lola flew under her feet, and nudged Gem, again. She only did that when…wait. Gem's eyes grew wide. She just realized that Lola only did that when Gem went to her hole-in-the-wall town's library. Her eyes narrowed with suspicion looking into Lola's eyes with shock. Was Lola communicating with her? How the hell could that be? She was a dog. No. That would be the most ridiculous thing she had ever heard!

"Are you talking to me, Lola?" Gem just had to ask, anyway. Lola cocked her head to the other side, and nudged her nose against Gem again. Frowning, she squinted her eyes at her. "No, you can't be, right? I mean, animals can't talk," she said, and laughed as she deliberately slapped her forehead with her hand, causing a loud cracking sound. "Gem, you're losing it! You really are! You've been living alone for far too long, and writing way too many fantasy novels! Now, you're starting to believe what you write?"

Looking at Lola, she said, "Well, I guess going to the library will get me out of the house!"

To which Lola just nodded, receiving another surprised look from her pet. Well, she did love to look at the ancient books that were in the climate-controlled room. She was so good with books that she had been put in charge of the ancient books and documents. She stood up, and slapped her legs.

"You're right, Lola! I do need to go to the library. I'll be back before dinner. You want to go out, or stay in today?" she asked her not expecting an answer.

Nevertheless, Lola cocked her head at her well-trained pet. It sure did take her long enough to get through to Gem. While Lola usually loved inside, today she just wanted to run and play. After her brief potty break earlier, she had seen that it was already a perfectly beautiful fall day. And, she figured the shit was going to hit the fan soon enough, so she had better take her breaks, now, before she couldn't any longer. Lola darted to the back door, and looked back at Gem wagging her tiny, little curled tail. With the fenced yard, Gem didn't have to worry about Lola getting in too much trouble, and she had a huge place to run. She had meant to put a doggy door in, but kept forgetting to do it. On the patio, Lola had a little doghouse just in case Gem didn't get back in time if it rained, or was later than usual. In the winter, Lola would always stay inside! She hated the cold, especially when it snowed outside, and her butt was always so cold! But, it was still nice even though Thanksgiving was just a few weeks way. Right now, all Gem needed to do was to leave a few snacks, and Lola would be all set for the day.

"You know, Lola? If I didn't know any better, I would swear you could understand every word I say!" she muttered.

Lola heard her, stopped, and barked, bringing another shocked look from Gem!

"Nope! Not going there, Lola! I already have enough of an active imagination!" she laughed.

Gem set a large bowl of water for Lola on the deck, a small snack, then closed and locked the door. As if she had anything valuable in the house. She grabbed her purse, phone, and laptop, then jumped into her rattletrap of an old, rusted-out Ford truck. People laughed at it, but she loved it. It was all she had left of her Father, except for the house. While she drove, she reflected, yet again, on how her Mother had been killed in a car accident eleven years ago. Gem had been running on the road, but she still had no memory of why! Her Mom had been driving to Simmon's Grocery, simply because she was out of sugar, eggs, and milk. No matter how hard she tried, she had never been able to remember. Since her Dad had died, his truck was more important to her than ever.

Anyway, she had to drive, and she certainly couldn't afford to buy one, used or new. She was barely making ends meet as it was. Jobs were scarce since the 2008 mortgage debacle, and the only real job she could find was at Simmon's Grocery Store. At least, both the house and truck were paid for, and just recently, her book trilogy had begun to sell in spurts all over the world. Even so, it would be quite some time before she saw any money from it. She had several rejections at large publishing houses, so she had found an Independent Publisher who accepted it immediately. She really didn't know why the sudden sales were happening, and neither did her publisher, but hell! She wasn't complaining. Maybe, just maybe, she could finally become a best-selling author. But, still, it was hard work to get her name and books into the outside world. If only she had the money to go to book signings, and other appearances. But, where she lived, there was only the Sinclair Library owned by the tiny college, where she worked from four to ten every other day, and a couple of very tiny bookstores which never had booksignings. Even sadder? They wouldn't even carry her books! So, her only alternative was to rely on social media – especially Twitter. At least this way, Gem could get her name out faster all over the world!

When Curt and Jerry Elwood adopted her as a baby, they legally changed her middle and last name to Gemma Allen Elwood, her middle name taken from her Mom's maiden name, and her Dad's last name, of course. Her publisher wanted to change her name, and she balked at it. Together, they decided that she should write under the alias of her real name, G.A. Elwood. At least they never changed her first name, because, as her Dad always said, she was the brightest "gem" in their lives. Her Dad had toyed with the idea of calling her "Rusty", because Gem's hair was the exact color of rust. Gem was one of the few girls whose red hair did not run riotously around her face. She kept it a long length down to the middle of her back, and it was loaded with soft waves that only emphasized her pale skin, and of course, the freckles on her face. OK. The freckles she didn't like, but that just wasn't something that could be changed, and she had accepted that fact long ago.

Sighing, Gem had to finish her research, before she would head to work as a cashier at Simmons from 9 to 11 pm. It was really lucky, because the grocery store was right next door to the library. She wanted, and needed, a full-time job, but the economy was very bad in their neck of the woods, and at least her part-time job gave her money for food.

The Sinclair Library had assigned Gem her very own parking place, because she was the well-known celebrity in town thanks to her books. And, that meant that she didn't have to waste gas! So, Gem turned into the library's parking lot, putting the truck into park – just as a huge bolt of lightning flared, making her jump.

"That's just great!" she whined to no one as she stepped out of her truck, and into the random hard drops that always comes with a bad storm. What the hell?

She totally ignored the black lettering above the door that declared the name "Sinclair Library of Fate" in her desperation to get inside. The name had too much of a conotation to it, so it had been shortened by the public to just the Sinclair Library, and finally, just the library. Hoping she could get into the building before the next lightning strike shot from the sky, Gem quickly ran up the three short steps into said building. The second she stepped inside, high winds began to whip about in almost hurricane force. The trees bent halfway, and then, a deluge broke loose. Gem paused in the foyer to look out the door's windows. Watching the wind blow, she was truly thankful to the fates that she was allowed to get her toe inside, before she was caught in it!

"Whoa!" she whispered, drawing back in surprise when she saw a metal something fly by the door. Not good to stand here with that happening!

Turning she ran up the ten stairs leading into the main room of the library. As usual, no one was present at two o'clock in the afternoon. Ordinarily, the only other person inside it was Taylor Tamson, who was Gem's best friend. Taylor was about nine years older than Gem, but their friendship was immediate the day that they had met six years prior. She was about five-foot seven inches tall, and had an absolutely gorgeous figure! She was extremely well-proportioned, despite giving birth to her two children – Shirley who was six and seven year-old Marcus. Taylor had two very unusual features. First, her snow white hair flowed down her back to her waist, which she deliberately kept in either a tight bun or a long ponytail. Her second feature were eyes of lavender, so pale, they were almost white. And, her eyes drew men to her like flies, even though she had been married to Richard, or Rick, Tamson for the last ten years. None of them even had a prayer of getting anywhere with her, and she generally ignored them. Not that it deterred them in anyway, but her skin was fair, her lips pink and plump, and it looked as if her legs never ended they were so long. And, that kept the men – and boys – trying to gain her favor!

Both little Shirley and Marcus loved Lola to distraction, and Lola returned that love when Gem let them pug-sit for her. There was no doubt whatsoever that Lola would protect them with her life if need be. Recently, Taylor and Rick had been thinking about adopting a pug from Colorado's Pug Rescue just as Gem's family had done. And, Gem was encouraging them to do so. She wasn't thinking of herself, but if they did, then, Lola would have a friend to play with when she would stay with the children.

Gem headed for the librarian's desk that was situated within the middle of the library to put her things into the file cabinet, and then looked up into Taylor's face.

"Hey, tall and lanky!" Gem laughed. Between the two of them, Gem was short, and maybe had a few extra pounds, which didn't show even though she thought they did, while Taylor was just tall and skinny.

"Hey, yourself, Ms. vertically challenged!" Taylor laughed back at her. "So, back for more torture? And, why are you here so early today, anyway?"

Gem plopped herself on the stool that sat behind the desk, ignoring Taylor's question for the moment.

"Man! Did you notice the storm outside? I mean, I've never heard or seen the wind blow this hard!" As if on cue, a huge gust of wind hit the side of the building, and shook the narrow windows above that circled the building. Both girls jumped.

"Wow!" Taylor gasped. The girls had dropped to the floor when they heard all the rattling.

"Yeah! What you said," Gem agreed. "Oh. To answer your question? I needed to do some research to find something new and different for my next book."

Both stood back up, and Taylor signed onto the computer.

"OH! Well, I get that. Besides, I really don't think we're going to have that many customers today!"

While Gem agreed by nodding her head, Taylor grabbed two dusters, and tossed one at Gem. Following Taylor, the two women started dusting the shelves. For the next two hours, they circled the room talking as they dusted. No one entered during the entire time, but then, the storm had not abated at all.

"Anyway, to answer your question of earlier, before I was so *rudely interrupted by that big blowhard,*" she grinned, "when am I not here for torture! I so miss not having an internet connection, Tay! But, I'm stumped. Writer's block," she poked herself in the temple. "I need a demon idea, before my publisher is put into the hospital with a coronary!"

"So, that publisher of yours is giving you a hard time?" Taylor asked as she ran the feather duster across the shelves and the top of the books as if there was dust when they both knew there was none.

"Yeah. He wants me to write...wait for it.... A Demon series!"

Taylor stopped dusting, and turned around with wide eyes.

"Seriously? Why would he want that? Most all of them are alike! Why would he want you to write one of those?"

Gem stopped dusting. She tilted her head as something came to her.

"Taylor, will you explain to me why we are always dusting dust-free shelves and books?" Watching Taylor shake her head, Gem continued. "Oh...he thinks it's going to be good for his publishing company, and wants to get in on the bandwagon, I guess. At least that's what he told me. I think it's really silly. I wrote my fantasy books without the normal paranormals on purpose! I didn't want to be like everyone else," Gem giggled. "Seriously, though? I almost wanted to tell him to vamp-off!"

Taylor, who was standing on the third rung of the ladder, dropped her duster, fell off the ladder, and onto the floor erupting in boisterous laughter.

"V-vamp-off?" she roared. "Did you really just say that? That's just s-so h-hilarious!" she gulped between breaths. "W-whoa, girlie! You are sure full of *something*! Gem, you should be writing comedy!" Taylor laughed even harder.

"Hey! You mean bullshit? Taurus, remember?" Gem pointed to herself. "And, let's face it! I have always had that talent!" Gem joined Taylor on the floor laughing so hard, they had their arms holding their stomachs.

Their laughter almost drowned out the hurricane force winds and rain outside. It was really lucky that no one was in the library at the moment, because the girls were laughing just far too loud. After about ten minutes, their giggle boxes landed right side up, but stopped immediately, when a man came through the door with a disappoving frown. They picked themselves up off the floor, and strolled back to the desk with huge smiles on their faces. Both women knew he came every other day at exactly four thirty pm every Monday, Wednesday, and Friday...and he was never late. The last two hours had flown by, Gem grinned at the pun, and she had gotten nothing at all done with her research!

The two women quickly went about doing their job. While Gem perched herself onto the stool that was behind the desk, Taylor opened the locked, desk drawer, automatically pulling out the key to the climate controlled room. Turning, she frowned in dismay as she walked toward him, noticing that he had already removed his coat, and was shaking it out, drops of water being flung everywhere!

"What a jackass hypocrite!" Taylor told herself. *"I bet you'd never do that in your own really fancy home!"*

Professor Hawkins sat in an overstuffed chair with a table and reading lamp that sat to the right of the chair. Gem had deemed this chair "Professor Hawkin's chair", and they kept it vacant at all times. Gem had told Taylor over and over that she thought he was a dick, andTaylor agreed with her every time.

Taylor asked which books he wanted to see today, and after he "ordered" them, she turned to go back to her desk when to her surprise, he actually addressed her! That was a new one!

"My dear Mrs. Tamson," he began, condescendingly, "Must I remind you both, that it is highly inappropriate to find our Librarian and her assistant, laughing loudly – and on the floor – inside the Sinclair Library?" he admonished her, then glared at Gem who pretended she hadn't seen it.

Professor Jaxxon Philip Hawkins was his name...and...he was the bane of her existence! Always complaining about something, he was a true enigma. He always sat in the same chair, always had the same, black leather, duster on with a hoodie underneath, and the hood flung over his head! No one could see his face that well, since it hid most of it, but, when one did get a glimpse of his eyes, they were indescribably gorgeous, deep brown eyes with flecks of blue glitter. And, from what she could see of it, his face was tan, as if he spent a lot of time in the sun. He would come and go from the Sinclair Library like clockwork, always asking for ancient manuscripts and books, but never the same ones, which was a bit peculiar to her. But, he also did one other thing that made Gem grit her teeth over and over to keep from smarting off in a retort. He always butted into other people's conversations without remorse, interjecting complaints into those conversations. He thought he was right and smarter than everyone else! And, even though he rarely addressed either Gem or Taylor directly, when he did, it was to criticize them for some stupid infraction. She narrowed her eyes at him when her "inner imp" invaded her body, which gave her the courage to do what she did on the spur of the moment, to finally say something to him. Of course, that led her to slap her hand over her mouth after the words spewed forth! Without thinking, Gem stood and walked over to him. Taylor saw her, and recognized that look! She quickly started shaking her head at Gem, who paid no attention to her.

"Oh, shit!" Taylor murmured under her breath, seeing Gem's eyes turning bright green as she approached Professor Hawkins. There would be no stopping her, now. As for Hawkins? Anyone on the receiving end of Gem's sharp tongue when she got started, well, Taylor cringed when Gem spoke.

"Oh? And, just why the hell do you object to laughter, Professor?" she demanded with hands on her hips.

His piercing, brown eyes glared with disapproval at her, raising his eyebrows in surprise that anyone would actually talk back to him! He smirked at her audacity.

"I do not object to laughter, young woman. Only where it happens and when. And, it is most obvious that a library is not that place!" he answered with sarcasm in his voice.

Gem started toward him, when a hand touched her shoulder. It was the only thing that made it through her angry haze. She turned to look at Taylor.

"Don't, Gem. It's OK. He was correct to point our inappropriate behavior out to us. I apologize, Professor Hawkins," she told him.

He darted the same piercing eyes at Taylor, and sharply nodded once in approval. Gem glared at the Professor, then turned to glare at Taylor. She took a deep breath. Professor Hawkins was clearly waiting for her apology.

"Tough shit! He'll be waiting for an apology until hell freezes over!" she thought, looking into his eyes. He was clearly not going to back down. *"Nope. Never gonna happen!"*

Aloud, Gem told Taylor, "I'm going to the CCR, now."

Gem turned on her heels, and stalked off in a huff toward the CCR room. Taylor turned, and walked back to the desk, when several things happened simultaneously. A huge bolt of lightning crashed, causing a fireball to appear inside the library, and just missing Gem. She was stunned into silence as she watched the ball of fire travel leisurely across the library, before it dissipated, knocking out all electricity to the building. Anyone who has ever seen one knows that it is a scary sight to behold. Then, immediately, a massive gust of straight-line winds blew out the windows on one side of building, hitting books and bookshelves as waves of various sized glass flew toward Gem.

Watching as if in slow motion, Gem knew she would never make it, even if she ran! She knew, without a doubt, that she was going to be struck by millions of shards of glass, and would be cut to pieces! There was no way that she would be able to move out of the way in time. Dropping to her knees, she tried to cover as much of her body and head as possible, and slumped forward waiting for the shards to slice her. That's when she heard Taylor scream, as if from a distance, followed by another scream, "NO"! Then, suddenly, Gem was slammed by something that felt like a tank, knocking her out of the way of the oncoming glass.

"Umpf!" was the sound Gem made as she felt her body fly sideways, and out of the path of the glass. One of the tables stopped her from going any further, as she smashed into it. Her head hit the corner of the table, and she uttered an oath.

"*Fuck*!" she said yelled.

More lightning and thunder followed, and rain began to blow into the library onto the shelves showering down water onto the precious books.

"Taylor! Do you have something to cover these books?" Professor Hawkins yelled, as he knelt next to Gem to make sure she was alright.

"Yes!" Taylor told him loudly, then turned and ran to the storage closet grabbing a couple of tarps that were only there, because of the manager's convertible, antique T-Bird.

"Are you alright?" Professor Hawkins asked her in a tender voice.

"Y-yes, I-I guess," Gem answered, rubbing the bump that she had on her head. Her hand came down, and she saw that it was bloody. She stared at the blood dripping from her hand, but tried to stand, anyway. That was a futile move, since she fell back down on her ass, as a wave of dizziness hit her.

Hawkins obviously tried to help her, but she waved him away.

"I'm fine! Go! Help Taylor get those books covered!"

"But, you're bleeding," he stated the obvious.

"Yeah, yeah! I know! Don't care! Please, Professor! Help her cover those books! It's just a little bump on my noggin'!" she whined, closing her eyes.

Nodding, the Professor darted to help Taylor. Gem opened her eyes. Wait! Noggin'? Who the hell says that type of word? One word came to her...concussed! Yep. That's what was wrong, because the minutes that followed had her questioning her sanity.

"Jaxx!" yelled Taylor. "Take your time, but hurry the hell up!"

Hawkins left her, while Gem shook her head, trying to clear her vision, and decided to lean against one of the table legs closing her eyes. That's when her blurry vision saw Professor Hawkins and Taylor fly up to the top of the shelves to cover the books. She frowned. Flying? Gem closed her eyes, and when she opened them seconds later, she saw Taylor on the ladder with Professor Hawkins, helping her cover the lower books with one of the tarps. Gem groaned, and rubbed her head, again. Where the hell was the tank that had pushed her out of the way? It had saved her body from being scarred for life, if not saved her very life. But, what was it that hit her in the first place? Gem tried to stand to her feet, but they collapsed from under her, and she fell back onto her ass.

"Damn! That's twice!" she murmured in anger.

She tried, again. This time, she managed to pull herself up by holding onto the table edge. Her legs were really wobbly – probably from a bit of shock. Her body was bruised, but at least the bruises would be temporary. No such luck if she'd been hit by the flying glass! She'd just be in a lot of pain until the bruises healed. That was alright for her! Bruises were good!

Professor Hawkins dashed to her side when he saw Gem trying to walk unsteadily toward them.

"Are you alright?" he asked her, grabbing her arm as she stumbled, almost falling, again.

Nodding, "Yeah. I think so. I'm sore as hell from that tanke that hit me, and knocked me against the table," she said, "But, at least I'm still alive."

"Good. Stay here," he ordered, earning a "no one tells me what to do" look, which he ignored, of course.

After he finished helping to cover the windows, Taylor asked him a question.

"Professor Hawkins?" Taylor said. "I wish we had some wine, or other booze in here, but we'll just have to make do without it. Could you get some coffee for Gem while I finish hanging the tarps?"

Without question, Professor Hawkins, first, helped Gem to the chair where he usually sat, pushing her gently down into it. His heart, if he had one, would have still been pounding in fear! He could have lost her! Instead, he turned to Gem.

"Ms. Elwood? How do you take your coffee?"

"Oh…uh…two sugars, please?" I think.

He put the sugar into the cup, and brought it to Gem as well as one for himself, and Taylor.

"Damn! It knocked out everything even the phones!" Taylor complained, taking a sip of her coffee. She tried her cell, and threw it down on the desk. "Even the cell towers must be down!"

"More coffee?" Professor Hawkins asked Gem as he poured a cup of coffee for himself.

"Sure. I suppose. Thank you, Professor Hawkins," Gem told him.

"My pleasure, Ms. Elwood," he answered in such a soft voice, Gem's head shot up in surprise. But, he had already gone back to the drink station provided by the library.

Finally, Taylor finished, and rushed over to Gem's side.

"You OK?" she asked, kneeling next to the chair. "I am so very, very sorry I couldn't get to you, sweetie!"

"Hey, no worries! But, yeah. I guess I'm OK. My head hurts, though," she complained. "By the way...did someone get the license plate of the tank that hit me? Anyone know what it was? What knocked me out of the way, anyhow?" she asked.

Taylor looked at Professor Hawkins as if for an answer. With a sarcastic grin, she asked him.

"Well, Professor Hawkins? Did you get the "tank's" license number?" she asked sweetly, earning a glare from him.

"There," he pointed to one of the library tables that was lying on its side – right where Gem had been before she was knocked out of the way.

Gem looked at the table in surprise, then turned to look where the Professor was pointing. How had she missed it? She didn't remember seeing it there earlier. But, then, again, her head was still woozy. She shuddered when she thought that if the table hadn't hit her, she might have been cut to pieces! But, how on Earth did it get thrown there? She looked back at him, and he shrugged.

"Must've blown sideways, and caught you in its path."

Really? Gem wasn't sure she bought that, but then, with her head hurting so badly, she decided to let it go – for now, that was.

"You want me to call Simmons and tell him that you won't be in tonight?" Taylor asked.

"No. That's OK. I'm all right. I'm only going to be there for a couple of hours, anyway."

"You're sure? Head injuries are not to be taken lightly, you know."

"Yeah."

"OK." Taylor looked at the clock. "It's only six thirty, so I want you to stay right where you are until you need to go next door, OK?"

Gem nodded without an argument.

"Wow! No argument? Who are you, and what did you with my best friend?" Taylor smirked.

"Very funny. Ha ha," Gem answered, leaning her head back on the chair, and closing her eyes.

Taylor walked toward Professor Hawkins who was standing at the inside glass doors looking out on the still-raging storm. Gem raised her head, and looked on in puzzlement when she noticed that their heads twere ogether, and whispering – almost as if they were great friends who like to argue, that is! Gem leaned her head back. She decided the worst thing she could do was to think, and began to doze.

A shake on the shoulder woke her, and her eyes opened to lights once again.

"It's five till seven, Gem. Are you sure I don't need to call Simmons?"

"Oh, goodness! No, no, Tay. Really, I'm fine. I see the lights are back on," Gem remarked. Standing up, she tested her legs, and equilibrium. Actually, she felt quite a bit better! "Seems, everything is in place! I'm OK. I'll get my purse, and walk next door. Has it let up at all, yet?"

"Seems so," Professor Hawkins told her picking up his belongings and walking to the door. "Well, I'd better leave while it has let up. Besides, my night has officially gone the way of the dinosaurs, so I guess I'll come back in a couple days."

"Strange man," Gem murmured in consternation, when he left.

"You have no idea," Taylor agreed under her breath, and watched as Gem left the library.

"Hey, Simmons," Gem called as she walked to her register, and logged on.

"That was some storm," Simmons said casually.

"Yeah, it was."

"Anything interesting happen when the lights went out?" he asked her with narrowed eyes.

Gem cocked her head. He couldn't know what had almost happened to her. So, ignoring his narrowed eyes, which was weird in itself, her intuition told her not say a word about her almost being sliced to pieces.

"Well, as a matter of fact, yes!" she rambled while putting on the purple vest that all employees had to wear. He waited. "The lights, the phones, and even the cells were knocked out, too! I mean, I thought that Taylor was going to have a coronary! You know how she is about her iPhone! It's like an extension of her arm and her fingers! And, a couple of windows blew out, and we had to cover the shelves underneath the windows – you know how high they are – and the books from getting ruined by the rain."

Simmons just looked at her.

"That's all?"

"Well, yeah. That's about it."

"Where did you get the bruise on your forehead?" he asked.

"Oh, that?" Thinking fast, she made up a lie on the fly! "Lola. She was rambunctious to a fault this morning! She leaped out of the bed while I was on the floor, looking under the bed for one of my socks, and jumped onto my back, using me like a step stool, and landed on my head, which pushed my head into the bed's steel leg!"

Narrowing his eyes again, she could swear that he didn't believe her, and even more than that, he seemed as if he was irritated at her. But, she shrugged, and her first customer appeared who had braved the storm's aftermath to shop.

Ignoring him, "Hi, Mrs. Wayne! Storm didn't keep you away, did it?"

Two hours later, when her shift was over, she grabbed her purse, and hung up her vest.

"Night, Simmons! See you in a couple of days!"

All he did was nod. He was just acting so damned strange tonight. And, she hadn't been the only one who noticed it, either. The rest of the employees were gossiping about it as they left.

"What was wrong with the boss, tonight? Anyone have a clue?" asked Timothy.

"Dunno, but one thing is for damn sure…he looks as if he's a man who was angry at something not going his way!" Jane remarked.

"Well, maybe. Night everyone!" Gem said.

Gem walked next door to her rusted bucket of bolts. Just as she opened the door to the truck, she got a really, really strange feeling. Nothing ever happened in this little out of the way town of about six hundred people. Well, not counting the excitement of the library. Starting the truck, Gem pulled out of the parking lot. Musing as she drove, about seven years ago, some really old woman on the opposite side of the world, had left all her books, oddly, her entire collection of first editions of books as well as money to establish a building with enough to keep the library self-sufficient for a hundred, or more, years – if it lasted that long! The money also included the funds to build a climate controlled room inside the building to keep them safe. The collection was so old, many were written in the forms of Tomes, scrolls, and even the oldest known type of books, codices. No one in the town knew who she was, and as far as anyone could determine, no one was related to her either. Even now, people were puzzled about it, and very curious as to who the woman was who left it to them. But, it was such a curiosity, people from all over the area came to it. And, it also drew the academic world as well such as Professor Hawkins.

The collection was amazing, and extremely expensive. Only a few people were allowed into the CCR, because of their value. If anyone, including the academics, needed anything, only the manager, Marshall Adams, Taylor, and Gem were actually allowed into the room. It would be very difficult for someone to escape with any book. It was rigidly controlled as were the few who were chosen to sit down with them to study. Clean, white, and disposable cotton gloves were always provided for those who touched the books, and they had to have experience with ancient documents to be allowed to handle them.

That was just about the only thing exciting to have ever happened around here. But, Gem's gut instincts were rarely, if ever, wrong, and it was coming through so strong, now, it caused her to be nervous. She'd never felt this way. But, there was definitely something wrong! Shadows were everywhere there was no light. In fact, she could almost swear one of them was moving! Lately, she had a fanciful, and over-active imagination.

Just as she reached home, and got out of the truck, it clicked, and she totally forgot about her terror and pain! She had it! Her story-line and plot for her Demon series! Gem threw up her hands, and wiggled around like Rocky while humming the tune.

"YES!!!!" she cried joyfully.

Unseen by her, a moving shadow disappeared into the night.

~ **2** ~
"What is it with the Storms?" ~ Gem

Gem stretched in her bed like the Cheshire Cat from Alice in Wonderland. The sun was a dancing glow on the horizon, quickly heading below it as dusk hit. Brilliant, orange and pink fluffy clouds caused patterns in her room as she lay there for a while just looking out the window. Last night seemed a long time ago! She turned to look at the clock on the table beside her bed, and that's when she felt the bruising all over her body. She had slept the day almost completely away! And, still, her body ached!

"Ouch!" she whined, and a tiny little body jumped on top of her stomach, causing more pain!

Licking her face, Lola had decided her pet had stayed in bed long enough! She really had to go outside, like, now! Using her teeth, Lola pulled the covers away trying to force Gem out of bed.

"Why, what's the matter, Lola?" she grinned.

Lola looked at her.

"Want to eat?" she laughed.

Lola jumped off the bed, heading to the kitchen door.

"Ah! Potty time?" Gem laughed harder when Lola just stopped, sat down, and glared at her pet. Seriously? Her pet was laughing about it?

Finally, Lola couldn't hold it any more, and barked loud. Gem laughed, got up, and padded to the kitchen to open the back door. Lola practically flew off the deck with Gem's laughter following her. Gem just stood at the door waiting, and…opened the door again to allow the much relieved pug back into the house. Now, Lola had more energy as she ran in circles between her pet's legs. Food! She was soooo hungry!

Gem scooped one-third of a cup of Lola's weight controlled food, and waited for her opportunity to put the food into her tiny metal food dish. Seeing no opening, she bent down, and before she could empty it all into the bowl, Lola jumped, and knocked a lot of food from the cup. Gem wasn't bothered, though. She knew that Lola would wolf down what did make it into the bowl, then she'd make sure she had every piece that fell on the floor.

While Lola swallowed her food, which took about a half a second, since she was more like a vacuum cleaner, Gem made a cup of coffee with the Keurig Taylor and Rick had given to her last Christmas. It was her favorite gift – ever! While her coffee was making, she placed her Fruit Loops in a bowl, then realized she had no milk! Damn! Oh, well. She reached for a snack for Lola, and tossed both of them out the back door so Lola could finish her regimen.

Gem traipsed to her computer, and began writing. She'd send her publisher an e-mail when she went into town later. She had a great idea, and that should pacify him for a few days. She hoped.

A noise at the door brought her out of her "in the zone" area. Realizing it was Lola, she opened the door, and let her into the house. Lola started bouncing around like she did for her food. It wasn't time to be fed! Or…was it? She turned and looked at the clock, feeling her mouth drop. It was already nine o'clock? It sure didn't seem like it could possibly be that time, but it was! It *was* way past time to feed Lola – an herself as well!

Gem realized her own stomach was growling, as she placed Lola's food into her dish making sure she still had plenty of water.

"Well, there's a shocker, Lola! Why do you think I'd be hungry? I had a couple of cups of dry Fruit

Loops and coffee. I only missed lunch...and, snacking...and, dinner!" she muttered while raiding her refrigerator only to slam the door. "Fuck! There's nothing in this place to eat!"

That meant a drive to town to get some groceries. She hated to shop at the place she worked, but she didn't have any choice in a small town. Or, she could just run down to the convenience store to pick up something, and buy her groceries tomorrow either before or after work. Yes. That would do.

"Hey, Lola? Wanna go with Mommy to the store?"

She sure didn't have to ask Lola twice, because she started leap-frogging all over the place as Gem tried to put her harness around her! Lola always enjoyed it when she got to ride in the truck. Her pet was just so slow!

Gem looked down at her clothes. Oh, well. She had on her lounge pants and a black tank top, so she pulled on her flip flops and grabbed her purse picking Lola up in her arms.

"OK. Let's run down to the Sip 'N' Stop, and I'll pick up a treat for you, too. Shouldn't take more than ten minutes," Gem said to Lola.

It only took her about five minutes to drive to the Sip 'N' Stop, and she pulled into a parking space in front of it. Getting out of the truck, she heard a rumbling in the sky, and looked up into the sky. A small bolt of lightning crossed its way across. She looked into the truck at Lola.

"Lola. Looks like we have a storm brewing, so you wait here. Mommy won't be long at all."

Lola didn't mind. She just loved to get away from the house sometimes. She put her paws upon the door pulling herself up to look out the window. A flash of lightning startled her for a moment, and she narrowed her eyes. That was never good. She was charged with taking care of her pet, and she couldn't get to her. Now what? Something was odd about the lightning. She'd seen it before, but she sure hoped she was wrong!

Gem charged into the store quickly.

"Hey, Gem."

Newton was the store manager, but was all by himself in the store.

"Hey, Newton. By yourself this evening?" she answered.

"Yeah. Tina couldn't make it. So…whatcha doing?" he asked.

"Out of food. Well, except for Lola's, that is. I'm out of *human* food. Just grabbing a couple of things."

"How's the pug?" he said.

"She's in the truck. She really wanted to come with me."

"Well, better hurry. Looks like it's blowing up a storm."

"Yeah. Just like last night," she murmured with her head stuck inside the refrigerator, dragging out some soft drinks and milk.

"Last night?" Newton asked with a frown.

"Yep." She shut the door, and went down the canned aisle first, then the snack aisle.

"What storm, Gem? Last night? There wasn't a storm last night!" he told her.

Gem slapped her purchase down on the desk, and proceeded to swipe her debit card in the reader. It beeped at her reminding her that she had to use the chip in the card. It was a recent change by the government.

"What do you mean there wasn't a storm? It was awful! Blew out the windows in the library, and I almost got sliced into beef tips by the glass!"

"No. There was no storm, Gem. We are not that far from the library. We would have heard it if there had been one."

"Well, Taylor was there, and so was Profess...."

Wind whipped across the glass windows accompanied by massive rain. Lightning flashed without stopping, and thunder was so hard the entire building vibrated. Things flew off the shelves on the store, and a loud screech was heard outside. In horror, Gem watched as her old rust bucket of a truck was picked up, and thrown sideways. It disappeared somewhere outside, and they both heard it hit – hard. Gem was already to the door. Newton tackled her to keep her from going outside just before she reached for the handle on the door.

"LOLA!!!!!!!!!!!!!!!" Gem cried in the middle of her screaming. "LET ME GO! I HAVE TO GET TO HER. FUCK YOU! LET ME GO, Damnit!"

"You can't go out there, Gem! It would be suicide!" Newton yelled, trying to hold her back.

Another huge wind gust hit the windows, and broke one side of the glass throwing tiny glass pieces into the store. Both Gem and Newton hit the floor. Then, suddenly, it was just as quiet.

"*Fuck!*" Newton cried, while standing. "Is that what you meant by a storm last night?"

Gem shook Newton off of her when he tried to help her up, and sprinted toward the door. Tears were cascading down her cheeks as she thought about Lola in the truck. Why had she brought her? Why? Now, she could be hurt, or worse, dead. As she jerked open the door, she ran flat into Professor Hawkins, and fell on her ass. She didn't stay, but jumped up to run past him. He caught her arm.

"Ms. Elwood. You can't go out there. It's a mess."

That just made her angrier than she had been.

"Get the fuck out of my way, Professor! Lola is out there!" she screamed, and tried to push by him.

Suddenly, she heard something breathing hard. Something that sounded like Lola. Gem turned, and saw Professor Hawkins was holding Lola in his arms, and she looked just fine! Gem darted toward him, scooping Lola out of his arms, and hugging her tightly burying her face into her soft fur. After a few minutes, she looked up into the Professor's dark brown eyes, and stared into gorgeous...red eyes? She blinked. No. Must have been her imagination. They were as brown with those blue flecks of glitter as ever.

"How? Where?" Gem stuttered.

"She was crawling out of a rusted truck, and ran toward me. It's obvious she was trying to get to the store and to you," he explained.

"The truck?" she asked while kissing Lola and holding her tightly in her arms.

"Well, what was left of a truck, anyway."

Tears flowed down her face. Both men found her extremely attractive in her PJ bottoms and tank top. Holding Lola to her as if she would never let her go, Jaxx's eyes narrowed at her. This could be a problem.

"Look, Ms. Elwood, let me take you home. "You and...what's her name?"

"L-lola," she cried silently.

"Right. Lola. Let me take you both home. I'm assuming that rust bucket of bolts was yours?"

She nodded. Her truck was gone, and of course, it wasn't insured, because it was not worth insuring. She turned her head up to him.

"I don't want you to go out of your way, Professor. I can walk it. It's only a mile up the mountain."

Gem had never been one to be so emotional, but this was far too real. Lola could have been killed, and it was all her fault!

"Thank you so much for saving her, Professor! I will never forget it," she told him, and moved to leave when Hawkins grabbed her arm. Electricity, or something that sure as hell felt like it, shot into her in mere seconds, and covered her body right down to her toes! Her eyes jerked upward seeing his eyes staring at her with…what was it? She shook her head. No she hadn't seen anything on second thought. That would be way too weird! He was an older man!

"I don't think so, Ms. Elwood. You've had a trauma, and you don't need to walk in the dark alone. That would be extremely foolish."

Even though his tone was usually rough, it wasn't, now. The electric pulse that flowed from his body into her was completely unexpected. That was unusual, and he'd never felt it before. Not in his entire, long life! The pulse not only flowed from him into her, but he felt a pulse from her flood into him! What the hell was wrong with him? He felt…what? Sorry for her? Anger? No. Not anger. Irritation? No, that's not it, either. He focused his eyes on her terrified ones. She had believed she had lost Lola, and the tears marking her beauty only made him want to hold her forever. To take her pain away. So, what is that called? He never stopped to consider humans before. At least not until now. She knew him only by his designation as Professor, and that's the way it was. Shaking his head, Jaxx was here for one purpose, and one purpose only. Whatever this feeling was, he had to get rid of it. If he didn't find what he was looking for, his entire mission would be a failure. Everything would be gone. And, so, frankly, would the human world. What he couldn't figure out was why Lola was here. Listening to her soft words as Gem cuddled Lola was anathema to him. And, he wondered what Lola thought of it.

Jaxx's eyes held hers for what seemed like hours on end, when in truth, it had to be a few seconds if that long. But, it felt like an eternity. Then, he dropped his hand from her arm as if he had been shocked. Still they stood staring at each other.

Finally, Gem shook her head slightly as if to free cobwebs from her brain. For some reason, she didn't want to be in a confined space with the Professor. This situation was way too weird.

"T-thank you, sir, but it's OK. Really. I've walked from town, before when the weather was nice," she said by way of an explanation.

He narrowed his eyes at her, then he said, "No. You will not. You will allow me to escort you to your destination. I will brook no argument on this."

Surprise gripped her. She had never heard him say more than a short sentence here and there over the last six years. And, usually, he did not address her, but when he did, his statements were always blunt, and really mean! In fact, she had been certain that he didn't talk much at all! Well, this incident sure blew that out of the water! And, did he really say he would "brook no argument"? What the hell kind of talk was that? Who actually said stuff like that any more. Well, he was an older man, so she'd give that to him. He had to be at least sixty-five. She really couldn't tell. Give or take an inch, he had to be six-feet two inches. He always had that infernal hoodie on, just like now, and never took it off even in the library, so she couldn't see the color of his hair. His eyes, though, were always mesmerizing. The reason she hadn't been able to look away. But, those eyes pierced her as if he was trying to see through to her soul. She couldn't move her eyes from his, and it appeared that he was having the very same problem. Oh! That's just sooooo gross.

Never gonna happen! Somehow, she found the strength to rip her eyes from his.

"Thank you, Professor, but..." she started to decline his offer again.

"Do not argue," he ordered, and she found herself obeying him.

Jaxx turned to Newton.

"Insurance?" he asked.

"Yeah, man. I have it."

"Good. If you need anything else, let me know," and with a nod, he grabbed her elbow to lead her to his car, which amazingly, was still intact.

Opening the door, she remembered why she came in the first place.

"Oh! My food!"

Jaxx cocked his head, nodded once, and went back inside to retrieve her purchase.

It was a very short trip to her house, but as they rounded the corner, they saw a brilliant orange glow. Gem's heart almost stopped. It was fire! As they drove closer, Gem gasped in horror as she realized her house was almost burned to the ground. It had obviously been struck by lightning. Despite the rain was falling hard, she stepped out of the car leaving Lola inside of it. All she could do was stand and stare as the rain erased the tears that were streaming down her face.

"Why?" she whispered almost to herself.

Jaxx turned to watch her. He had never felt the need to be attached to a person, place, pet, or thing, so he was having a difficult time processing why she was crying. She dropped to the mud on her knees. Her tank top was thin, and he could easily see through it. She wore no bra, but then, she'd probably been going to bed before she realized she was out of food. Her pants were muddied, and sagged enough to creep lower than her butt crack, so he got a good look at it! He felt a sudden rush of desire enter into him. Sex was fun, yes. He never felt desire, no. But, her nipples were easily seen through her top, and the sight of her crack made his cock swell with blood anticipating thrusting into her body. He had never felt physical desire for any woman – his kind or not. He also had a sudden burst of jealousy, knowing that Newton had seen her breasts as well! Shit! What the fuck was wrong with him? This woman was vulnerable. His entire existence was to protect the innocent. But, how would he protect her from him when he felt this way? Well, he couldn't leave her kneeling in the mud, and there was no way she was going to move, so he picked her up in his arms, and putting her in the front seat of his car, got behind the wheel.

Again, the soft whisper, "Why?" came from her. Her soft, sexy voice just increased the size of his cock. He had to take her somewhere, but where would she be safe?

"Gem?" he asked softly. No reaction. He asked louder, "Gem?" Still nothing. Finally, he raised his voice even louder.

"Gem!' he yelled, and her head jerked toward him.

"I'm sorry, but you're in shock. Is there someone I can leave you with?" he asked her, but his body was demanding that he take her home, and bury his body inside of hers. Fighting it was almost too hard.

"I-I guess you can take me to Taylor's house, Professor," she said quietly. Then, "What am I going to do?"

Everything was in that house. Everything she had in the world – including her job! She had no idea why everything had been taken from her. What had she done? And, she almost lost her best friend! She turned to see Lola was alive, and sound asleep in the backseat. At least she still had her.

"What did I do to deserve this?" she muttered so quietly that a normal person would never have heard it.

But, Jaxx did.

"Nothing, Gem. You did nothing wrong. There is always a reason behind everything. The fates will allow it to be seen when it is time," he told her.

"Really?" she cried louder. "I don't believe that! The 'fates' my ass! They can all go to hell!"

Cursing the fates? Did she just actually curse the fates? What was wrong with her?

"Cursing the fates is never a good idea, Gem," he told her.

Without turning her head, she sneered.

"I don't care! First of all, they aren't real. Second of all, I don't care, and I'll curse them all I like, MR. Hawkins!"

Damn the man! Acting as if the Fates were real! Idiot!

"I'm a college graduate, and believe me…no one I know would ever treat them as 'real'…because they are not real! Surely, you, a Professor, know that?"

"Here," he said ignoring her, and giving her his cell. "Call Taylor. I have her number stored."

"Thanks," she muttered, wondering why he would have Taylor's number in his phone.

Desperately punching the buttons on his iPhone, she kept missing, and had to dial at least three times. Taylor answered on the first ring.

"Yes, sir. Your orders?" Taylor's voice said.

Orders? Sir? Why would Taylor be saying something like that?

"Hey, Taylor?"

"J – uh – Gem? Is that you? Why are you using Professor Hawkin's phone?" Gem could hear the surprise in her voice.

"Another massive storm hit, Taylor. I was out of food, and ran down to the convenience store. It hit, and Lola was in the truck, which was picked up and thrown sideways."

"Oh, no! Is Lola…?"

"No. She's fine. Professor Hawkins showed up, and brought her to me."

"I was wondering why you were talking on the Professor's phone? He's there?" she sounded surprised.

"Uh, yeah. He tried to take me home, only…" Gem gulped.

"What, Gem? What happened?"

"Lightning strike. My house is gone," Gem gulped tears back, again.

"Oh, sweetie! I'm so sorry! Tell me that you're coming here with Lola. You are, right?" Taylor asked.

"H-he's bringing us, yes," Gem's voice broke, and she couldn't speak any more.

Jaxx grabbed his phone out of her hand.

"Taylor, she's about to have a nervous breakdown…not that I blame her at all, of course. She's been cursing the fates." He heard a gasp of horror from Taylor. "Yes. No. Yes. We're on our way."

He shut the phone down, and put it in his pocket. He hated using the damned things! They were just too ridiculous for words considering he was able to contact anyone he wanted at any time without them. But, to function in this world, he had to appear to be like humans. Taylor could easily have blown their cover. He sighed, and turned to look at Gem. He never had a heart. He wasn't built that way. But, her sadness was piercing him where a heart would be, and that was so not good. No. Not good at all. He'd never have feelings for a woman. Ever. Oh, he used them for sex and fun, but that's it. This girl, though. She could turn out to be a real problem for him, and he couldn't let that happen.

Jaxx turned down Taylor's street, and stopped in front of her house. He still couldn't believe she had not only married a human, but had children with him! How could she be happy? But, she sure seemed to be. Nope. Jaxx just couldn't understand it at all.

Beside him, Gem sniffed as she exited the SUV, and opened the back door to pick up her tiny little dog who was sound asleep. Lola didn't even move, but snored adorably as they walked to the front door with Professor Hawkins, who seemed to think that she needed him to hold onto her arm to keep her from falling, or whatever. When he had reached for her elbow, a bolt of electricity shot through her entire body, again! It had startled her so much, she had flinched. Her eyes shot up to the Professor who looked at her with the same dumbfounded look that said, "What the fuck?"

The tense moment was interrupted when Taylor threw open the door, and ran out to grab Gem in a huge bear hug! Richard and their two children followed after her. Over Gem's head, Taylor glared at Jaxx. What the hell was he up to this time?

Letting her go, Lola, who had just woken up, almost suffocating when Taylor hugged them, started to wiggle to be let down. Gem sniffed, and handed her over to the two kids who hugged her tightly, much to Lola's happiness. She had awakened when Taylor had almost suffocated her in the bear hug she had given Gem. Lola admitted it. She was truly worried about her pet, but it was also nice to be loved by so many after that harrowing close call when the wind blew the truck sideways, and into the tree with her little love pug inside it! Lola excelled at being loved! Her very size and face made everyone love her instantly. While she wagged her tiny, curly tail, Gem was caught in a wooly mammoth hug by Richard, who was, quite literally, a giant of a man at 6 feet nine inches.

"I'm so sorry, Gem. I truly am. I know how much the house and especially the truck meant to you," he told her quietly.

Richard always had the ability to calm her down just by his voice, and Gem felt calmer than she had over the last couple of hours. He pulled away from her.

"We'll help you, Gem. You know that, right?" he asked her.

Gem couldn't trust her voice at the moment, so she just nodded. Then, her legs buckled. Jaxx was behind her, and caught her while Richard grabbed her from the front. Jaxx couldn't believe the surge of jealousy he felt when he saw Richard touching Gem, and he growled at Richard, whose eyebrows rose at the sound in surprise! Richard carefully released his hold on Gem, giving Jaxx a knowing grin. Jaxx's surprise at the grin made him wonder why he felt that way? He'd never felt jealousy – ever. In fact, his emotions were non-existent. At least, that was what he had always been told. It was his lack of emotion for anything, or anyone, that made him so dangerous.

Gem turned around.

"Thank you, Professor, for bringing me here. I'm so sorry, because I just know you wanted to have a hysterical woman on your hands," she managed a tight grin at him. "And, thank you for saving Lola for me! I'm just so glad that she was o-okay."

Gem broke down into tears once again, and Richard guided her into the house with Shirley and Marcus following him, holding tightly to Lola who wanted her pet, and tried to wiggle down to get to her.

"I'll be right in, honey!" she called after Richard, then whirled on Jaxx.

"What in the fuck is wrong with you?" she demanded.

"Nothing! If she wasn't your best friend, I would have left her alone!"

"Gem Elwood is *not* your responsibility. You know it!"

"Oh. So, what? Had you rather me stand aside, and leave her to her own devices after her entire world hit the fucking fan?"

Taylor narrowed her eyes at him. Something wasn't right.

"Since when do you care about humans?" she asked warily.

"I don't, so don't get any ideas, Taylor. I have my orders just as you have yours. Gem is not your responsibility, either!" His voice was low, but held a note of authority.

"So, why didn't you just leave her?" she asked.

"Taylor, hon?" Richard called.

"This isn't over, Jaxx. I'm considering telling the council about this!"

Jaxx snorted.

"Go ahead. You know I don't give a fuck what that group of blowhards says or does. I have never bowed to anyone. I will *never* bow to them, and you know it."

"Fine. Go away!" Taylor hissed, and turned to walk into the house. She stopped when she heard Jaxx's voice.

"I will leave for the moment, Taryln, but I will not stay away," he growled at her.

Taylor turned on her heel, and shot him an angry glare.

"You *will* stay away from Gem!" Taylor answered with her own growl, then slammed the door behind her with finality.

Finding himself standing, staring at a shut door, surprised the hell out of him! No one had ever shut a door in his face! He was livid, and stomped back to his SUV. Just before he stepped into it, he looked into the distance where the rumble of thunder, and the lightning was slowly dissipating. He got behind the wheel, then put his arms on it staring. Something was not right about this. The thunder and lightning last night, the heavy deluge, and the shards of glass heading straight for Gem – as if they were guided. And, then, tonight. He'd been on his way out of town, and drove upon the devastation that wrecked Gem's life with her dog and her truck. Also, caused by a storm. But, what he didn't tell anyone was that hers was the only vehicle that had been thrown into the tree. If she had been inside it, she would be dead. If he didn't know any better, he could have sworn that the two storms were after her – or someone was causing the storm to target her! No! That was just plain crazy! In his entire life, never had he seen a force of nature target one particular human. Besides, who would do this in the first place? He slid his arms off the wheel, and turned the key. Fuck these stupid vehicles! He didn't need one at all, but he had to continue to play this charade until he found what he had been sent to find. He drove off, and straight to his house.

"Gem, I'm so very sorry!" Taylor kept telling her.

"It's okay, Tay. I-I'll have to figure out what I'm going to do, now, though. I have no car, or house. Hell! My computer was burned to a crisp, my clothing, and everything I owned! The house wasn't worth a dime, and neither was my truck, but they were free, and I didn't have to pay rent. My books are just beginning to give me a little bit of money every third month, but now, I have to find a place to live, pay rent, figure out how to get from point A to point B, and to do my writing." Gem's voice sounded defeated, and Taylor had tears in her eyes.

"Don't worry, Gem," Richard said. "You can stay with us as long as you need until you can figure out what to do. Besides, we have three cars. You can have one of them."

Taylor smiled at her husband. Who said that humans weren't awesome! To hell with the council who thought they were nothing but animals beneath them! They believed that they were made to serve them, but through a glitch in the system, had been given total freedom! The idiots on the council were fucking bastards! And, if she didn't know better, she would bet a month's salary that Jaxx hated them, and a second bet that the Council was terrified of him! Why, she had no idea, but she would swear it was true!

"I can't take your car, Richard," Gem gasped.

"Yes, you can, sweetie," Taylor backed her husband up. "Look. We can't drive three cars at a time, and one just sits in the garage, anyway. We drive it, what, Richard?"

"Maybe, if it's lucky, a couple of times every three months?" he surmised.

"Close enough!"

"And, cars are not made to just sit," Richard added. "You'll be doing us a favor."

Gem looked from one sweet face to the other while she considered their offer. It would help her out for the time being. And, if they would let her stay until she could find something really, really cheap, then that would help.

"Okay. I will. But, just until I get back on my feet. I'll pay you back."

"The hell you will!" Taylor growled. "We are as close to family as any blood bonded family. Come on, you can take the basement room."

"I thought you had been using that as your workout room, Taylor."

"Uh, well, yeah, but we had it renovated into an apartment for Richard's, uh…," Taylor stumbled over the words as she tried to think up something.

"My great aunt. She came to stay with us a while back for a couple of days," Richard finished.

"Right," Taylor agreed. "She wasn't here that long, though, and we just didn't want to change the room back, so we just kept it like it is."

"Yep. And, I moved all our exercise equipment to the building out back, and fixed it up into a full gym," Richard finished.

Great aunt? Gem was a bit confused.

"You never mentioned it, Tay," she stated.

"Oh, right. Well, you see, the woman is a menace. She's a bit of a jackass, and I just don't like to talk about her."

Gem frowned, then yawned, and Taylor laughed throwing her arm around Gem.

"Look. When Jaxx told me he was bringing you here…I mean Professor Hawkins…I rooted around in my closet for some clothes that should fit you. Tomorrow, you and I will go shopping for some new clothes, OK?"

Gem just nodded.

"Well, let's all eat. What does everyone want tonight?" Richard called to the kids.

"Pizza!" was the unanimous answer, and even Lola was wagging her little tail at the word.

Gem laughed a little at that one.

"Well, I could have made book on that answer!" she joked.

"Then, pizza it is!" And, Taylor pulled out her cell.

<u>**And, now…a sneak peek of**
The Anaerris Code ~ Jaxx</u>
LK Kelley

the
ANAERRIS CODE

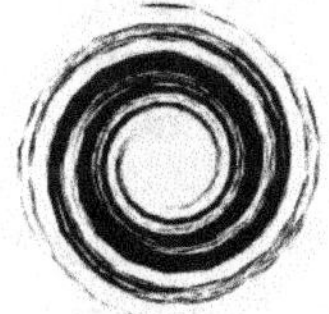

a Gemma Sinclaris Series

Jaxx
Part 2

By LK Kelley

WOLF CANYON MEMORY

~ Monologue ~

Gem: "Thank you, everyone! Thank you for being here! I want to welcome you all here, and I'm so happy you will be front and center for my strange life!
So, are you ready?"

(Cue: Lots of applause and cheering)
"Alright, then! So, to bring you all up to date so far, you will remember that my life was boring, basically. I was a writer, and my publisher wanted me to write a supernatural book that had to do with vampires.

Next, these really strange storms happened, and I was drawn into a situation with Professor Jaxxon Hawkins, who, strangely enough, turns out to be one of the Fallen angels, who comes from a place called Onaerris. It's a moon somewhere in the cosmos out there."
(Cue Gem: Points to the heavens)
"Yep. That's right! Outer space, no less! From there, I discover that I am some sort of universal super being with massive powers (still waiting for all those), who is supposed to save my Mom's home moon, Anaerris, my Dad's home moon, Onaerris, another moon called Domaerra, Earth…and, oh! By the way! I'm supposed to save the whole damn universe, too! No pressure! Anyway, I also find out my bestie, Taylor, is also one of the fallen, and Stan, the local car restorer. Both are married to Richard and Stacy, and together the six of us are trying to figure out what we are supposed to do.

To date, I have been chased by storms caused by the bad guy and girl, Eloran and Delinear, been put in a volcanic prison, somewhere in the cosmos, broken out of it, and jumped off an 8000 foot cliff only to find out my first power was the ability to create a Vorc'ara – or, I guess the best way to describe it is a stable wormhole of sorts. I also discovered a book in the library where I work that has the secrets that I will need, along with my mate, to save everyone, as well as my little pug, Lola, who turns out to be a Fae in disguise who has whisked Taylor and Rick's kids to safety in another realm, while Jaxx and I used the book, and the last thing I remember is a brilliant white light after it took me over, then blew up the cabin we were staying in. At least my friends are all OK! Well, I hope they are, anyway. And, why is it the cosmos keeps wanting to dump me in worlds with volcanoes? My mate is missing, and I am missing him terribly!"

(Cue: Commercial)

"What? Oh! Right! Well, gang, I'm being told that it's time for a commercial…have you ever wanted to eat when you are not hungry? Well, you have to try the most delicious nut bar I have ever tasted. And, you all know the name of my favorite life bar, right? So, what's it called?"

(Cue: Audience yelling followed by cheering)

"Nuttier than a Fruitcake by the Great Cosmos Nut Company!"

(Cue: Gem. She stands, grabs a bar from above her in the midst of the nighttime stars, and chomps down!)

Gem: That's right!

(Cue: The crowd of Lolas barked in a standing ovation!)

◎

Gem: Could this get any more ridiculous? No. I really don't think so!

~ 1 ~
Waking up is Hard to Do! ~ Jaxx

Jaxxon Hawkins felt lethargic and extremely tired as he woke. But, he was sure that was only temporary. Well, until a terrible cold invaded his body. Somewhere, he wondered why being cold could happen to him? He never felt the elements like this! His mind began to wonder as he fell in and out of consciousness. Why? And, were those voices he was hearing? He slowly drifted as if his soul drifted on the wind.

"What do you think, Doctor?" a man asked. His voice was strangely familiar, and Jaxx struggled to figure out where he had heard it.

"I.Caaanot.Sssay.Myyy.Looord." a strange voice answered. It was guttural, raspy, and the sentences short and clipped with a voice hissed much like a snake.

"But, he will get better, right?" asked a soft voice, and while not as familiar, Jaxx thought he recognized it somewhere in the back of his mind.

"Yooour.Booodies.Arrre.Nooot.Suuuited.Tooo.Thi sss.Cliiima..."

A strangled yelp ensued. It reminded him of a stuck pig!

"I am not interested in your opinions, Doctor! Only facts! Now...I ask you one more time. Will Jaxx make it?"

"Heee.Isss.Onaeeeris. Heee.Wiiil.Myyy.Looord!" the voice squeaked.

"Good!" the familiar voice said. Jaxx heard a thud, and then, the voice ordered, "Now, get out!"

Jaxx heard a door slam shut, and that soft voice spoke once again. Obviously female, he thought.

"Please, my love! It's not his fault that Jaxx is this way! Weren't you just a bit too aggressive?"

"Too aggressive? Hell! I wasn't aggressive enough with that sleazy son of a bitch! He would just as soon as killed Jaxx as look at him! I'm Onaerris, but I am not some fucking moron!"

"Well, perhaps you were right, when you put it that way. His kind has always made me shudder with disgust! I mean…a serpent? Really?"

"It's too bad we had to bring that son-of-a-sleaze bag to a place of such gentle creatures!"

"I agree. But the sweeties don't know the first thing about humanoid bodies, and unfortunately, that left Doctor Hsss! He's been imprisoned here for eons, and this is part of his sentence for trying to kill them. You and I both know that the gentle creatures are not always all that gentle!"

"Yeah. I know it; you know it," he snickered. "And, luckily Hsss does, too! He's absolutely terrified of them!"

Where the fuck had he heard that voice before, Jaxx wondered? He struggled to think about it. Ah, hell! He needed to open his eyes – now! They flew open, and immediately beheld his – brother? And, next to him was … Analyse! He tried to speak.

"J-Jolinaer?" he could barely get the name out of his mouth. His mouth was dry, and miserable.

"Jaxxon!" Jolinaer exclaimed. The bed shifted under the weight of Jolin as he sat.

He clasped Jaxx's arm, while Jaxx did as well, but his arm was weak.

"Jaxxon. It is good to see you, again, my brother!"

All Jaxx could do at the moment was to nod in acceptance. Then, Analyse stepped forward.

"How did you get here? We saw a bright light, and chased it down. We found you completely knocked unconscious!"

That brought Jaxx out of his momentary stupor of surprise, and he sprang up from the bed onto his feet in one, fluid movement. He grabbed Jolin's tight, black t-shirt to keep from falling, while Jaxx grabbed his brother's shoulder to keep him from falling.

"Where is she?" he demanded.

Jolin looked at Analyse with a very puzzled expression. She looked back at him, just as puzzled. Jolin looked at Jaxx, again.

"Who, Jaxx? There was no one with you," he said quietly, tolerantly. Maybe Jaxx had hit his head? He was certain that he didn't know what he was saying.

Jaxx huffed, and pushed Jolin so hard, he stumbled, but didn't fall. He stared at Jaxx in shock. It was as if he was fixated on something – or someone.

Analyse stepped forward, and placed her hand on his shoulder. He jerked around, and caught himself just before he grabbed her by the neck. He was angry. He had to find Gem! He wouldn't stop until he did.

"What do you mean, who? Gem! Who do you think I'm talking about?" As their faces continued to frown in puzzlement, he continued. "GEMMA! You know? Your DAUGHTER?"

Jaxx was yelling, and he knew he sounded like a maniac, but Gem was his life! His mate! He wouldn't rest until he found her. Analyse's eyes opened wide with horror, and she started to collapse. Jolinaer stopped her from falling. She looked up at him, pink tears in her eyes.

"Oh, Jolinaer!"

Jolinaer turned to look at the stricken face of his brother. The shock of finding him on Domaerra was almost too much for him, but Jaxx hadn't even questioned where they had been all these years! But, even that seemed pale by comparison. If his daughter was missing, then why was she missing. But, Jaxx was losing it, and he didn't know why. And, he needed answers.

"Jaxxon! Stop it! Calm down, brother!" Jolin ordered, raising his voice.

Jaxx frowned, and looked at Jolin. Was he kidding? His mate was nowhere to be found, and Jolin had the audacity to tell him to calm down? Over his immortal dead body, he'd calm down! But, before he could speak, Jolin had him in a headlock. He couldn't move. Damn! Jolin had always managed to immobilize him with this trick! He could never break out of it! A loud growl escaped from his throat.

"That is enough, Jaxxon!" Jolin looked at Analyse who had slipped to the floor anyway. She was sobbing silently. Watching her broken almost killed his heart! They had left to keep her safe, and now, it would seem, she was missing. He stopped a moment. "Hold it, Jaxx. Exactly how did you meet Gem, Jaxx?"

Jaxx looked up in surprise. The question shook him out of his fixation.

"Jolin? What the fucking hell, Jolin! Why are you on Domaerra? Why is she on Domaerra? Where the fuck have you two been all this time?" Without breaking his stream of questions, he continued in one breath. "I can't believe that you are showing up, now, of all times! How did you get here? Why did you leave Gem in the Fae realm until she was taken to Earth as a baby? Why did you let them give her human DNA? Eloran and Delinear are after all of us. Imaerra kidnapped her, too her to some volcanic realm in an alternate dimension, and luckily, she was able to open a Vorc'ara, and she didn't even know she did! Why are you here? What is the matter with both of you? Why won't you answer me! Did you hear what I said? *She is MISSING!*"

Jolin and Analyse dropped their mouths at his flood of questions. A thought came to Analyse.

"Jaxx. Answer us! How did you meet Gemma?"

Jaxx was breathing hard. Oh, sure, he didn't need to, but right now, it almost felt good. At least it kept him from making the mistake of his life – that being killing someone! He looked back and forth between them, breathed deeply, and finally calmed down a little bit.

"Holy shit! It really is you!" he gasped in surprise. "Where am I?"

Jolin finally was able to approach Jaxx.

"Yes. It really is me, Brother!" he said, and the two brothers embraced each other.

"You are on Domaerra. How did you get here?" Analyse asked him.

Jaxx backed up from Jolin to stare at Analyse. She looked just the same as she did when he saw her thousands of years ago! And she was still beautiful, but not quite as beautiful as her daughter. Gem was the most beautiful woman he had ever seen in all of his existence!

"Is it true? You really know our daughter?" Analyse asked, grabbing Jolin's hand.

Sighing, he replied.

"Oh, I know her, alright. She has a lot of protection – at least she had it until that damn book of yours got in our way! Not only do I know her, but...," he paused for effect. He wasn't really sure how they would act when he told them the truth. OK. So. He was actually feeling like a coward!

"Yes?" she asked him. "Please, Jaxx! Tell us how you met her?"

'...she is mated!"

Both Jolin and Analyse gasped aloud.

"M-mated? To w-who, Jaxx? I can't believe it!" she asked.

"Yes. Jaxx. We never expected to find out she was already mated at such a young age!"

Jaxx looked at them as if they were from another universe!

"Young age? Gem is twenty-two years old!" he answered.

"Well, technically, she would be about ten thousand and twenty-two years old," Jolin said calmly, looking off into space as if he was thinking about it.

Analyse turned around, and stared at him as if she had never seen him before. He turned, and saw her stare. Grinning, he laughed.

"What? OK, my love," he said, drawing her to him. "You know it's true!"

"I don't care if it's true! She's our little girl, and I want to know who the hell she is mated to, and when it happened!"

Analyse whirled on Jaxx, and grabbed him by the throat, lifting him into the air.

"I'm not going to ask you, again, Jaxx! Tell me who is she mated to?"

Looking down at her, she wasn't really hurting him. He looked at Jolin, then Analyse, then Jolin, and last, Analyse, again. His mouth turned up in an extremely evil, and slow grin.

"I thought you two understood?"

"What? What should we understand?" Jolin asked.

"OK. So, who, Jaxx! I'll snap your neck like a twig if you don't answer me right now!" Analyse demanded.

Grinning even wider, as Jaxx suddenly heard what he needed to hear so desperately, and answered with one word.

"Me!"

○

Meanwhile, Gemma was in real trouble…

○

Gemma screamed when she saw the dark figures approaching her. One of them grabbed her, and slapped his hand over her mouth, dragging her behind a large rock. She growled behind the hand, until he growled back at her.

"Shhh! Are you trying to get us all killed?" the man said to her.

That answer silenced her faster than anything else could have. Killed? How could she get them killed? She had no idea where the hell she was! All she knew was she groaned, because, once again, she was standing in the middle of a volcanic world! Why the hell was she constantly getting put into this kind of situation?

She saw him motion to some others to get down behind some other rocks close by them, and they scattered fast. When she got out of this – for the alternative was not acceptable – she was going to kill something … or someone!

"Are you going to be quiet?" the man asked her without moving his hand from her mouth.

She looked up, but the steam and clouds were so heavy, he was just a figure in the mist. She could see him in a general outline, but that was about it. She took a deep breath, and decided she could trust him –

at least for the moment, and she nodded. Gem knew she couldn't see him, but she could see his head nod up and down, and his dirty hand released her. She took a deep breath, but kept it silent. Then, Gem heard voices.

"O-over there! That's w-where I s-saw that l-light, m-my Lord!" a voice stuttered.

"You're sure about that, Navoer? You had better not be lying to me!"

She heard a sound as if someone was being slapped. For a moment, she almost felt sorry for the guy, then she realized that they had to be looking for her! Gem threw her own hands over her mouth to keep her from screaming.

"I-I p-promise I am n-not, m-my L-lord!" he answered with a sniff.

Was he bleeding? Shaking her head, why should she even care in the first place? She needed to keep quiet, and pressed her hands tighter to her mouth.

"I also saw the light, my Lord," another stronger voice told him.

"What was it?" the leader asked.

"I have no idea, but I do know that the light was brighter than a supernova! I have never seen anything like it before! Whatever it was, I also saw someone being thrown out of it! Because of the mist, I couldn't tell you who or what it was, but I do know that fact for sure!"

"Look around, and miss nothing! I am returning to the Citadel to report to the Mistress," he said. "But, be warned! Do NOT come back empty handed, because if you do, you will be thrown into the Lake of Fire! Do you understand me?"

Gem didn't hear an answer, but she was quite sure that they were nodding in fear. Who was the Mistress, she wondered. And, where the fuck was she? Maybe she needed to find that out, first!

"We cannot let anyone know that Onaerra is still occupied! It would ruin our plans to take Earth! And, the Mistress would kill me – and anyone else! So, remember that, because it means you!"

Gem's head popped up! Mistress? Onaerra? Take over Earth? She was on Onaerra! Why did the book send her here, and where the hell was Jaxx? Silent tears began to slowly stream down her face. Shit! Jaxx … where are you? The sound of many footsteps started moving. The sound of them lessened, and she realized that some of them were moving away from them. She almost sighed aloud, when she heard more voice.

"OK! Look everywhere, and don't leave one stone unturned! Our lives depend on us finding the being that was thrown out of that light! Do you hear me! Find it!"

Gem's stomach became tighter in terror when he heard many footsteps moving quickly. She knew that they were looking for her! But, being terrified would get her nowhere! She had to calm down! It would do her no good, and she knew it!

She heard a slight noise, and turned to see the person who had dragged her behind this stupid rock, saving her life, move his hand in a military style. A couple of figures a few feet away, moved quickly away from the rest of them. They took off at a run, and most of the other figures took off running after them. The figure behind her moved, and she heard an almost sickening sound of bones crunching. Knowing it would only incapacitate for only a few minutes, she started to stand, and the figure grabbed her arm, leading her in the opposite direction of where the others had run. She followed him without hesitating.

The air was stifling! Breathing hard, she could feel the heat bearing down on her with the extra exertion, when the figure admonished her.

"Stop breathing! You don't need to, and it will help you in the heat!"

Stunned, she realized that he was quite correct. She had forgotten that she did not need to breathe! The moment she did, she realized that it did help with the heat! Seconds of running turned into minutes, minutes turned into hours as they ran. Yet, surprisingly, she never felt tired! Whatever was happening to her, she knew she was evolving into something. But, what? And, all that paled, because she wanted Jaxx!

Finally, the silent runners stopped at a mountain – that wasn't running with lava! He placed his hand on the rock, and it turned to living lava, followed by his entire body! The area began to shimmer. In seconds, it was gone, and an opening appeared. She was pushed toward it. The moment she stepped into the opening, she was hit with a massive blast of icy cold air! She stopped suddenly, enjoying it, but it didn't last! She was pushed from behind.

"Go!" he ordered. "Don't stop!"

She ran, until she came to a huge room, and came to a halt, surprise on her face. It was massive! It kind of reminded her of the entrance to the Ministry in Harry Potter, but even a bit darker with torches scattered here and there.

"Over here," the man told her.

She followed.

"Is this really Onaerra, or did I just imagine I heard that?" she finally had the voice to demand.

"Please sit down, before you fall down, Gem," the man told her.

Surprise gripped her as tightly as his hand gripped her wrist, when the man said her name!

"How do you know who I … ?" she began, when the man turned around, and she gasped as he turned, and smiled at her. Then, "Mr. Simmons? I-is that you? B-but, h-how … ?"

How could Simmons be here? He was Onaerris? How in the hell was everyone around her fallen angels, and she never knew it?

"Shhh!" he shushed her. "The men here are the only ones I can trust! And, I do not need you giving us away!"

He looked nervously around. Satisfied, he took a deep breath, and using gestures that she guessed came from something like black ops, they scattered into the shadows of the room. He turned back to her.

"We don't have much time, Gem. The one who was looking for you has gone back to the Citadel, but he could still send his minions back here.

"Now, what?" she asked. "And, how in the hell did you get here, anyway?"

"That's not important right now. What is important is that we need to hide you. Where is Jaxxon?" he asked her.

"Jaxx?" she repeated, as if she was stupid.

"Yes. You know? Your mate?" His voice sounded contemptuous.

"Uh…" she started.

"Is he here, Gem? You have to tell me! These bastards don't fool around. This is a totally different world than he left! And, ruled by something that is just … indescribable. He needs to get you out of here! I don't know how you arrived on Onaerra, but you have to leave!"

"I can't leave," she gritted through clenched teeth.

He looked at her as if she had horns growing from her head.

"Vorc'ara?" he reminded her.

"Ooooh! Right! I wonder why I didn't think of it?" she said in a small voice. Of course, she didn't think of it. She just wasn't used to being able to open a vortex to the Creator knows where!

"Get the fuck out of he...," Simmons began, but hearing a squish coming down the hallway. "Oh, hell! How am I going to hide you?"

Simmons turned, and his head darted everywhere. Where was she? Gem was nowhere to be seen. Maybe she had already left by the Vorc'ara? She had to have done so. Good. Less problems with her there! He turned to see the ruler of Onaerra come slithering down the hallway. He grimaced. Every time he saw the "thing" that had taken over Onaerra, he cringed. He was glad that Gem would not be seeing it!

Gem opened her mouth to tell Simmons that she was right next to him, when she watched him look everywhere around him. He even looked straight at her, so why did he not see her? If she was confused before, she was even more so, now. The squishy sound coming from the hallway became louder and louder as it got closer to them. She stood by Simmons' side, and watched him grimace and cringe. As she wondered why, the squishy sound started into the torch light. It was beautiful! The face of the ethereal creature coming toward her made her feel almost lethargic. But, in an instant, she shook that feeling off as she stared at it. Everyone always imagines the big bad guy as a worm or reptile or some other creepy crawly thing! They are wrong. Evil could also come in the form of beauty, too. Especially at the moment. And, that was what slithered into the great room. She had no idea what it was, but one thing she did see, and it almost made her toss her cookies! It's front was a beautiful woman. She was stately, tall, glided instead of walked with the blackest hair she had ever seen on anyone that flowed down her back almost as long as she was tall – twenty feet tall, that is. Her eyes were the darkest black, but almost blue. Her complexion was a dark olive, her lips plump and red, and her boobs were at least a triple, what? X? They were massive! Her gown of pastel pink, gathered at the waist, which pushed her breasts upward, but just barely being held up, let alone her nipples covered! They bounced with each slither. Her gown drug the ground as she glided along. She watched Simmons bend over in a very deep bow as she passed by him. And, then, she saw the back of the "thing". Behind her, giant streams of fluorescent, blue slime was expelled behind her with each step, and left a trail on the floor. And, then, the second it touched the stone floor, it turned a dark, brownish green! OK. That was so disgusting! She caught herself, before she lost everything in her stomach as the rancid scent of decay and death hit her nose! From behind, it moved more like a serpent, and nothing even remotely resembling a humanoid being. She held her breath, because if she didn't, she would give away the fact that she was there. Gem still didn't get why no one could see her, but at the moment, she *really* didn't care. It was a good thing. She wasn't too sure why Simmons was here, but honestly … had she really been surrounded all these years by other fallen angels? The answer came to her in her mind, and almost made her gasp aloud.

"*Yes, my love.*"

She closed her eyes in relief.

"*Jaxx!*" she exclaimed through their bond, catching herself just before she gave herself away with a gasp.

"I am with you, Gem. Where are you?"

"I don't believe this, but that damn book spit me out on Onaerra! How did that happen? Where the hell are you?"

"On Domaerra ... with your Mother and Father!"

"What!" Gem yelled.

She was suddenly very afraid that she had given them all away, and quickly looked around her. She sighed when she realized the pink thing, which put out shit, was no longer in her vision.

Mr. Simmons looked in her direction.

"I thought you were gone!" Shaking her head, he continued. "Talking to your mate, my dear?" he asked with a sneer.

"Oh, hell, Jaxx! Simmons is here, and he is not smiling very nicely!"

"Simmons? What is he doing there?" Jaxx asked her.

"Don't you know?"

"No."

As if she had paid no attention to him, she continued.

"And, by the way, Jaxx. What is that filthy, twenty foot high stinky pink thing that looks just like a woman on the front, but from the back, looks and smells like a garbage dump?"

"Huh?" Jaxx asked. *"What twenty foot high pink thing?"*

"Wait! You don't know? But ..." her voice cut off in mid-sentence as Simmons raised his hand, and hit her in the face. She fell to the floor unconscious.

"Gem!" Jaxx cried, as he felt his mate leave his consciousness.

"Gem?" Nothing. Louder, *"GEM!"*

His face must have shown how distressed he was, because Analyse addressed him.

"Jaxx? Jaxx, what's wrong?" she demanded, her voice shaking.

"Jaxx," Jolin said. He knew that demanding wasn't going to get Analyse anywhere with him. Only a calm reasonable voice would do it.

Jaxx looked over at Jolin, and he saw Analyse's face. His face must have shown how distressed she was, because a tear streaked down her face.

"I don't know. I was talking to her, and she had just told me that Simmons was with her, and then … nothing."

"Who the hell is Simmons?" Jolin asked him.

"The local grocery store owner. I don't get it. Who…?" he started, when he heard a gasp from Analyse.

"Simmons? *Simmons*? That just isn't possible! It can't be him!" she cried.

Both Jolin and Jaxx looked at her in puzzlement. They looked at each other. How could she know Simmons?

"Analyse? You know him?" Jaxx asked her. "How?"

Silence met his question. He waited patiently for her to answer. It was obviously difficult.

Several minutes passed, and she answered him.

"I can't believe it! How is he still alive?" she spoke to herself.

"Who is he?" Jolin wrapped his arms around his mate. "Please, my love. Explain."

"Huh?" she asked turning her head, looking at him with blank eyes, before she realized that Jolin was waiting for her to answer him. "Oh. Simmons is not Simmons, but Simoche!"

Jolin stepped back in shock. Jaxx looked at him, and suddenly understood!

"No! He's dead! I killed him myself!" Jolin yelled.

"I know! He killed me! How, Jolin? How could he still be alive? You beheaded him!"

"I have no idea!" Jolin admitted.

"Hold it!" Jaxx said. "IF he is dead, then how is he alive?" he turned to Jolin. "How did I not recognize him?"

Jaxx shook his head in shock. Then, a horrible thought came to him. Simoche. How had he not recognized him? And, now, he had his mate! What would he do to her?

"I have to get to Onaerra! Now!" he demanded of Analyse.

She nodded silently.

"Wait," Jolin said. "We can't just appear on Onaerra! We are both wanted!"

"I can't worry about that right now! I have to go …. NOW!" Jaxx said, and Analyse nodded in agreement.

"Calm down. You both know what can happen if we try to go there without some type of plan!"

Jaxx just glared at him. His mate was in danger, and Jolin was telling him to wait?

"You both know it's not feasible for us to go running into danger without some type of plan!" Jolin's voice was the sound of reason.

"But…" Analyse started, then shut up when she saw her mate shake his head.

"No. I want to get him as much as you do, Jaxx, but if we get ourselves killed, then he will still have her in his clutches! We don't go into this with our eyes closed. We have to make sure that if we get there, we can rescue our daughter! We need some surveillance. My contact will tell me where we can enter Onaerra through your Vorc'ara safely!"

"Contact?   You have a contact?" Analyse expressed surprise combined with suspicion at this revelation. "Why have you never told me that?"

"Because, my love, we have had no reason to contact my contact. Now, we do."

"But is he trustworthy?" Jaxx asked.

"Absolutely," he told them without a doubt. "But, it's not a him."

"What did you say?" she asked with suspicion in her voice.

He turned to Analyse, and grinned sheepishly.

"It's a her!"

WOLF CANYON MEMORY